FIT FOR PURPOSE

Acceptance - Book One

Briony Beattie

A Dedication

*Every word written is in respect, pride and honour to all
who serve their country, have been affected, or injured.*

CONTENTS

INTRODUCTION

I am challenged daily with a physical disability. Taking that plunge in organising a fundraising event has, at times, seemed almost an impossible task. So, why not use the skills that are available to me, like writing a series of books dedicated to showing my support and giving back to veterans?

On the 11th November 2019, the Fit For Purpose Mission was launched. Now officially in operation, we are delighted to be working alongside other veterans and Game Rangers International in providing individual veterans the opportunity to use their skills in sponsored projects and local communities.

50% of all sales will go back into supporting individual veterans and sponsored projects.

Fit For Purpose Mission

Mission Statement

Helping individual wounded veterans who are experiencing the psychological and physical scars of war, by empowering them to be involved with sponsored projects that use their unique skill sets, as well as enabling them to learn new ones.

Motto

Soldier on, no matter what...

Vision

Supporting individual veterans to realise greater self-worth, by empowering them to participate in projects aimed at helping communities in need.

x

Values

To help

•To help individual veterans in need.

•To offer individual veterans the opportunity to use their skills in helping others.

•To help individual veterans accept, live with and change their lives for the better.

To act with integrity

•We are professional and fully committed to the FFP Mission.

•We treat every individual veteran and sponsored project with utmost respect and dignity.

•We treat everyone as we would wish to be treated ourselves, at all times.

Give back independence

•Give individual veterans a greater sense of self-worth again.

•Give individual veterans a greater sense of belonging and comradeship.

•Give individual veterans a good reason to soldier on.

High level summary (Why do we exist?)

The Fit For Purpose (FFP) Mission exists to support individual veterans realise greater self-worth by empowering them to participate in carefully selected projects, which are aimed at helping communities in need.

The individual veterans that we will support are experiencing the psychological and/or physical scars of war. Our great hope is that through their participation in the FFP Mission, these individual veterans will move closer toward finding their own inner peace and self-acceptance. Ultimately, this will change their lives for the better.

How are we trying to achieve this?

We aim to do this by supporting bona fide projects that can provide individual veterans, who are going through the psychological and/or physical struggles of everyday life, with the opportunity to use their unique skills and experiences to help communities in need.

For example: Mission Njovu (Zambia 2021) - an individual veteran will be selected to work alongside Game Rangers International, to utilise their skills in training Rangers and helping local communities in need.

A PERSONAL MESSAGE

For me it is just as important to remember veterans and serving personnel who are still living and fighting a constant battle of the physical and emotional scars of war.

Every year, across the world at the eleventh hour, on the eleventh day of the eleventh month, we remember.

We remember those who made the ultimate sacrifice in keeping ordinary individuals like ourselves safe.

We honour and remember them.

And we must also honour and remember those who survived and are left behind.

They are living!

Briony Beattie

ACKNOWLEDGEMENTS

I grew up during a time when Rhodesia was heading toward independence and there was an ongoing civil war. My father served in the army's PATU - Police Anti-Terrorist Unit.

I would like to take this opportunity to thank my father for his service and pay respect to all those Rhodesians who made the ultimate sacrifice for their country. You are remembered.

We are inclined to forget the unsung heroes of those colonies and the soldiers who played a huge part in the world's wars. They should be commemorated for their service and never forgotten. Thank you for your service.

I put my folks through hell. My rapid mood shifts and inner frustrations have caused heated arguments between my family, but they have supported and helped me through the difficult times. My parents have never given up on me.

Through thick and thin, the struggles and hardships, my folks have been a testament of strength for me and my siblings. They have taught us the morals of being a good person and appreciating the small things in life. They have scraped the barrel to pay for medical treatment and equipment that I have needed growing up. My folks have gone without, to give me a chance in life.

We have shared laughter and tears and memories that can never be broken. No amount of money will ever come between the love and happiness that we share as a family. Thank you to Mom and Dad for the love they have for me.

Having the right cover design for your book is just as important as writing and feeling the story within. I searched long and hard to find someone with that same passion and commitment, but from one unforeseen tragic circumstance to another disappointment after disappointment, my hopes were slowly fading. I eventually built up enough courage to reach out to my mom's youngest sister. Aunty Patti is a talented artist who has mainly painted for the purposes of a hobby, painting for family and friends and having her beautiful creations displayed on their walls. Despite being oceans apart, Aunty Patti worked with me through each stage of the creation and visualised what I could see in my mind's eye. Aunty Patti's love and passion for painting has given my book cover true meaning and sense of purpose. I feel extremely blessed in having Aunty Patti go through this journey with me and working together on future creations for the Fit For Purpose trilogy.

Hope, my oldest sister, has supported me throughout this journey. With her whirlwind of energy, she has been there, encouraging and lifting my spirits.

My little brother, Stuart, is my rock. His level-headed approach has helped cement the strong bond we share as a family. He is my calmness and strength through torrential storms of doubts and insecurities. His unconditional love and support have encouraged me through each stage of this process and nothing is ever too much to ask of him.

I owe a heartfelt gratitude to my oldest brother, Sport. He has always taken the time and effort to introduce or mention me to everyone he meets. He is there supporting and encouraging me through every project I undertake. He has worked through some of the technicalities in this book and has spoken to many of his military friends about me. It was through Sport's persistence that two veterans reached out to me.

Out of respect and privacy for the following acknowledgments, I will use first names only. James and Jordan contacted me in 2019. Taking me by total surprise, their messages brought a sense of upbeat and hope in moving forward with my book.

A Platoon Commander with the 2nd Battalion The Rifles, James was seriously injured after standing on a Taliban mine in 2009. Through life-saving treatment, they were able to save James's limbs, although he lost sight in his left eye. With extensive rehabilitation, James fought his way through the challenges with sheer determination and inner strength.

James has been an immense help in working through my questions and Angus Brown's character. He has given me an insight into Jimmy Ferguson's injuries and ways of moving forward in the books to follow.

James is a true gentleman. He has put his trust and shared his experiences with a stranger. I will honour his trust and forever be grateful to him.

Serving in the Royal Air Force, Jordan completed a tour in

2012, initially providing reconnaissance for the battle group within his Regimental Unit.

Jordan has not only provided me with a source of information into military life, but has also worked through each of the chapters, offering humorous stories and phrases.

He has been a great support, not only for my book, but for me personally. Sharing many of the same interests, I have been able to shift my focus and share a laugh.

Jordan has put his trust in me and shared his experiences. Again, to a stranger. I will honour his trust and forever be grateful to him.

Due to the pandemic, I have been unable to meet either James or Jordan in person. I have had the great pleasure of speaking to James in virtual reality. However, I look forward to the day when I can meet James and Jordan, and finally give them the sincere gratitude they deserve. They are awesome guys and I am honoured to have them on board and going through this journey with me.

An ex-marine, Alan, I met through my folks. When Alan walked through the door, I had this moment of spookiness. Alan is the reincarnation of my main character. From his appearance to his mannerisms, he represents who Jimmy Ferguson was before his injuries. Unbelievable!

I had a fantastic evening talking to Alan and hearing his stories. He offered some great input and I am profoundly grateful. I also know that should I ever need help; he is only a phone call away.

I must also offer my thanks to Police Scotland and my local station for giving me the opportunity to have a chat and be shown around.

INTRODUCTION TO
THE AUTHOR

If you can imagine a brain transplant from one normal func-
tioning body to a physical impaired one, the short circuit between brain and body are unable to find that connection to
function as one.

This is me.

I am a disabled woman with cerebral palsy. This has affected
three of my limbs; my right arm and both my legs.

I started writing as part of a healing process, in the hope of
putting some ghosts to rest with finding and accepting that
inner peace. However, I ask myself daily, "Will I ever accept
and understand why I cannot do something that in everyday
life for most is the norm?"

I was eight years old when I was due to have my first extensive
operation in South Africa. The consultant told me I would
walk normal, unaided, within six months.

I did not! That's a huge responsibility to carry on your small shoulders when you trust and believe everything they say.

The expectations were high and it influenced how I saw myself in the years that followed, up to now.

I blame myself.

I live a life where I am either too disabled, or not disabled enough. And, not being accepted in both the disabled and abled community is difficult to comprehend.

I suffer daily with the mental and physical frustrations. I struggle to accept that I cannot do something and blame myself for not trying harder. These conflicting emotions have sent me to a point of destruction. I physically and verbally abuse my body; thumping my legs and fist smacking my head. I have bruised and pulled muscles, or deliberately almost broken a finger.

My body and mind do not connect.

I maintain a daily routine and present myself well. To the naked eye, I look fine. But inside, I am sad. I am angry. I feel hopeless and lonely.

The stigma towards mental health is being highlighted more than ever, but what if you live this life of isolation and confinement? What if you have no friends? What if your mental and physical state has sent you into a downward spiral of anger and confusion? The eerie silence creeps deeper into your everyday existence and picking up the phone to ask for help is not a considered option.

This assumption that only old people who live alone are lonely, is a far cry from the reality of life. I am lucky if I get one visitor a week. A bonus if I get two.

The world can be an extremely cruel and lonely place to live in.

By using my own life experiences throughout the book, I have been able to express myself more freely and use my frustrations through my characters. However, I have also discovered other emotions and writing this book has turned into an autobiography of sorts; The life I always wanted and the life I have had to live.

I too wanted to join the army. I genuinely believed I would walk and live a normal life.

This has been a challenging realisation just on its own. Emotions, I have come to realise that I was able to suppress through my anger for the lack of inability to do everyday simple tasks.

Now, I am fighting another battle.

I have struggled with a disability my entire life. I have adapted to those struggles. But now, those same mental and physical struggles are getting that much harder.

TIMELINE

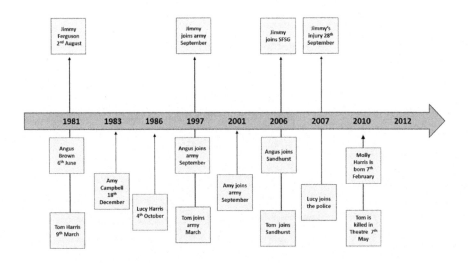

Jimmy Ferguson 2nd August
Jimmy joins army September
Jimmy joins SFSG
Jimmy's injury 28th September

1981   1983   1986   1997   2001   2006   2007   2010   2012

Angus Brown 6th June
Amy Campbell 18th December
Lucy Harris 4th October
Angus joins army September
Amy joins army September
Angus joins Sandhurst
Lucy joins the police
Molly Harris is born 7th February

Tom Harris 9th March
Tom joins army March
Tom joins Sandhurst
Tom is killed in Theatre 7th May

28th September 2007

"BOOM!"

There was a loud thundering explosion -

CHAPTER ONE

*Five years later – Saturday, 31st December
2011 New Year's Eve*

C oming around, Jimmy felt disorientated and confused by his surroundings as he tried to sit up. But, his left hand slipped and he fell once more, cutting himself further on the broken glass that lay shattered around him.

On realising he had fallen out of his wheelchair and wasted an entire opened bottle of whiskey, the anger and bitterness boiled over inside him. "Fuck you, Jimmy!" he screamed, fist smacking his head. Thump! Thump! Thump! he thumped his legs, or what was left of them.

Exhausted and frustrated, he dragged himself towards the couch and pulled himself up. Not bothering to pull up his boxers that had already slipped down slightly from the effort, he reached for the new bottle of Jack Daniels that had been waiting for him on the left side table.

Taking a long deep swig, his shoulders slumped while he listened to party revellers enjoying the celebrations of the coming New Year. He shuddered as fireworks exploded, haunted by his memories.

"Fuck you, Jimmy and the whole fucking world!"

Jimmy was a drunkard now, plain and simple. He never had a sober day if he could help it. He spent his days drinking a combination of cheap beer and whiskey, anything he could get his hands on.

He slurred his words by lunchtime and passed out by the afternoon. And what little food Jimmy ate, was in the form of frozen meals. He never left his flat, but got his weekly shopping delivered.

"Why doesn't everyone piss off?"

When Jimmy was discharged from the British Army because of his injuries and Post-Traumatic Stress Disorder, he refused to continue his rehabilitation therapy. He did not see what good it would do; it certainly would not bring back his legs or his career. Being around him was like waiting for a bomb to explode and his family, his army family, the only family he ever knew, slowly gave up on him.

That is when he turned to the drink more heavily than he had before. Now there was no one to tell him to lay off, to say that he had had enough. Now the bottle was his only best friend and it did not improve his temper.

Darkness had filled his life a long time ago, a bearing weight of despair carried on his shoulders. The pain deep within grew stronger as life was slowly being sucked out of him. And so, the days went on, hour after hour, flying by without recognition.

Grey Scottish skies and low clouds clung to Jimmy's body and soul. He could not remember the last time he had had a shower or brushed his teeth.

Sat on the couch, Jimmy looked out the grimy window, watching the dark wintry weather rushing past, dark clouds feeding his sense of misery and hate for the world.

Looking around the room, he saw the thick layer of dust that had built up on all shelves and surfaces. A generation of cobwebs had accumulated in all corners and the once clean oak effect flooring was now sticky and shabby. Every facet of Jimmy's life, from his finances to his well-being, to his day to day routine, was in a deep soulless and sorrow driven rut.

He stared at the broken picture hanging off the wall that was dusty and dirty and had not been cleaned for months, more likely years.

> *"Shit," he thought, "A bit like my life, hanging off a thread. What is there left for me? What is my purpose? Why can't the world just leave me alone? Fuck this. I will show this world how to end a life properly!"*

Jimmy was going to go out with a bang!

He threw his head back, tossing the handful after a handful of paracetamols into his mouth like a bag of deathly candy and brought the bottle of whiskey to his lips. Minutes became like hours and seconds were like days and what seemed like an eternity was only, in reality, an hour.

"Whit the fuck!" Jimmy spluttered whiskey and half-digested tablets, faintly distinguishing the dark figure standing in the doorway. Struggling to focus and with no vigour in his upper limbs he fell to the ground, forgetting that he had no legs, his whacked-out and contractured body determined to fight on.

"Fookin get oot!" Jimmy screamed, using his adrenaline-fuelled surge of anger. But with the upper hand, the intruder lunged forward and kicked Jimmy in the gut.

"You fucking cripple," the contemptuous intruder said as Jimmy choked, a taste of dirt and blood filling his mouth and he retched up a thin stream of vomit. With the intruder lunging forward again, Jimmy's head hit the ground and he blanked out.

CHAPTER TWO

Arriving back at the station for what was turning out to be a lively night with party revellers starting their New Year celebrations early, Constable Lucy Harris was two hours into her night shift. Starting her shift at 22:00 hours and hoping to finish with no further incidents at 07:00 hours, her radio crackled once more and she and her male colleague responded to the call.

Approaching the ajar door, the property situated on Rosetta Road and a short distance from the Peebles police station, was in darkness. With caution and trepidation, the male officer pushed the door. Swinging open with ease, they were hit with a strong stench of body odour and alcohol. "Police!" both officers called out. But with no sound of disturbance following, they stepped in and searched for a light switch, finding themselves confronted by mayhem.

A drunkard stupor gone overboard. An overturned wheelchair, army memorabilia, pills, smashed glass, empty bottles, drawers pulled out and emptied, all lay amongst the bloodied, bruised, disabled man.

As Lucy took a pair of gloves from her pocket and tread carefully towards the beaten man so as not to destroy any evidence, she radioed for an ambulance.

Looking around, she made a mental overview of the room –

He pulled drawers out in anger, looking for something. Ex-Army? Is he on drugs? He tried to kill himself. He drinks himself into oblivion. Place is in a mess...!

Feeling for a pulse, Jimmy was thin and pale, his face sunken and battered. His unkempt shoulder-length hair caked to his sweaty bloodied face with the ink coloured shoulder sleeve tattoo peeping out his t-shirt clearly showing more colour than his sickly body.

She glanced over at the cracked, framed portrait photo and saw a tall, strong and proud young man standing to attention in his neatly pressed uniform. Corporal Jimmy Ferguson, 25130571 of the 2nd Battalion The Royal Regiment of Scotland, Royal Highland Fusilliers was inscribed at the bottom. The man lying on the floor was not the same man in the photo and suddenly a moment of sheer sadness filled her heart to breaking point, her brother never far from her mind. But she could not allow her sorrow to cloud her judgment as she coughed, breathing in the vile fumes. She cleared some of the broken glass surrounding his body and gently pulled at his boxers to preserve his dignity, when Jimmy stirred and groaned with pain.

"The ambulance is coming do not move," she said.

Through his blurred vision, Jimmy blinked against the bright light as a taste of blood and iron filled his mouth and with a sudden retch, he vomited the remains of the pills all over the officer's shoes.

"Oh great! Some night this is turning out to be!" Lucy said, jumping backward.

"You certainly know how to choose em," the male officer said, returning from inspecting the front door. "There are no signs of a break-in, but there are spots of blood," he said just as Jimmy grabbed Lucy's leg and tried to pull her to the ground, ready to fight the intruder once more, but Lucy pulled away.

"Calm down! You are hurt!" she said as Jimmy lashed out with his left arm and both officers tried to hold him down.

"Someone wis fookin' here!" Jimmy growled in a heavy Scottish accent.

"I found you on the floor. You are hurt," Lucy said.

"Fookin hell, ye stupid bitch, aren't ye feckin listenin tae me?" Jimmy spat, not wanting to be someone who was weakened by his vulnerability. His voice was the only means of power he had left in him.

"I heard you the first time! Now calm down, so we can establish what is missing!" Lucy said.

"Calm down, otherwise you will be arrested!" the male officer said, his glaring appearance seeming to have some effect on Jimmy. He calmed down and allowed the ambulance crew that had now arrived, to examine him.

While Lucy and her colleague assessed the situation, the

ambulance crew examined Jimmy. Cleaning the dry blood, dirt and debris around his wounds, they found fragments of broken glass in the palm of his damaged right hand. "You are going to need stitches and a more thorough examination," the male ambulance technician said.

"Just feck off!" Jimmy said with rage.

"Jimmy, we are here to help you," Lucy said, crouching down and getting his attention at hearing his name.

"Was something in this presentation box?" she asked, seeing it lying on the floor amongst other army photos, together with his green and maroon berets and his Dagger and Jump Wings patches.

"My fuckin Queen's Gallantry medal!" Jimmy screamed, fist smacking his head and taking in the chaos scattered around him. He tipped over the edge, acting in a crazed manner and Lucy requested another officer.

* * *

The three officers restrained Jimmy and five minutes later, his adrenaline-fuelled rage had eased and Lucy continued to speak calmly and directly as they transferred him onto the stretcher board.

"Right, Jimmy. Can I call you Jimmy?" Lucy asked.

"Fuckin call me whit ye like!" he said.

"Do not speak to me like that! We cannot help you unless you help us! I am Constable Lucy Harris. Jimmy, it is then...!" she said annoyingly.

"There are no signs of forced entry. Was your door locked tonight?" Constable Harris asked, the three officers standing and giving Jimmy a feel of claustrophobia.

"I don't know and don't care!" Jimmy said bluntly.

"Have you taken something tonight, like drugs?" Lucy asked.

"A' don't feckin dae drugs!" Jimmy said offensively, once more finding that inner anger.

"Mr. Ferguson, you have three officers here, an ambulance crew and we have a duty of care to help you," one of the male officers said, but Jimmy was not listening. He lay there, staring hard at the shattered portrait lying on the floor.

"Do you have any family? Next of kin?" Lucy asked him, not wanting to lose the momentum.

"Thare is na ane, I have na family," Jimmy said.

"There must be someone. Someone from the army even?" Lucy said, bending down to pick up a photo. "Who is this?" she asked.

"He is na ane!" he said.

"He must be someone, Jimmy! You both have a huge grin on your faces and you are both in uniform!" she said, raising her voice slightly.

"Angus," he said.

"Angus who!" she asked.

"Angus Brown," he said, reaching for the photo and threw it to the floor.

"We are here to help you. Is anything else missing?" Lucy said, once more crouching down to hand Jimmy his wallet.

"Is any money missing?" she asked.

"Fifty pounds," he said.

"Okay, Jimmy. I can see you are exhausted," she said, deciding to give him a break and offered to find him a jersey.

Jimmy's head pounded like a hammer hitting a nail into a brick wall and he felt immense pain in his left arm as he struggled to push himself up.

"Here, let me help you," Lucy said, kindly helping him pull the jersey over his head albeit that he had shown the officers rudeness and had not been forthcoming.

"Would you like a drink of water?" she asked him.

"Aye," Jimmy said.

"Good," she said, and left him to get a drink and find something to wipe her shoes with.

"Jimmy, we will need a more formal statement from you of what happened, but you are in no state to do that tonight. You need to go to the hospital," Lucy said, arranging with her colleagues to travel behind the ambulance in case he kicked off again.

With his wheelchair folded and placed in the back of the ambulance, Lucy climbed in and took a seat. "Jimmy, I can arrange to have your front door locked once our forensic team has been and have an officer meet you back here when you are discharged," she said with kindness in her voice, as Jimmy's woeful eyes glanced briefly at hers before he turned his head away. He had felt immense embarrassment by his actions.

"I know how much this means to you, Jimmy. I will be in touch," she said, briefly touching his right shoulder and showing kindness in the gesture, before she stood up and left the ambulance crew and her male colleagues to deal with him.

* * *

Returning to the property, Lucy stood there for a moment and like Jimmy, stared at his portrait photo. That moment of sadness pierced at her heart once again. Her brother had stood proud too. Jimmy's home was filled with neglect and despair and he certainly looked like someone in desperate need of help.

She had driven down Rosetta road a hundred times, walked past Jimmy's property many times before, but she had never seen him or received any reports of disturbances, sending her on a guilt trip. Being a police officer for five years, she felt she should have known of him, if not in person.

"Lucy," Sergeant Steve Wilson called out, making her jump. She had lost herself in her thoughts whilst reading through the few notes she had managed to obtain from Jimmy.

"Sarge, what a night. I am taking some leave this year, come hell or high water. And shit...I stink!" she said.

"Yeah, you do. I was wondering what that smell was," her sergeant joked.

"Cheers for that. It's not all me, I might add. But seriously Sarge, this guy could do with some support," she said, updating her sergeant on what they had discovered; no forced entry and the medal stolen and explaining that Jimmy was in no state to give a formal statement and that she would speak to him later that day. A thorough investigation into the house-breaking would now have to take place.

"Hmm...Strange," she thought. "He would have accumulated more than one medal?" she questioned, and told her sergeant about Angus Brown. She needed to contact him, being Jimmy's next of kin.

Sergeant Wilson updated his officer with regards to the door to door enquiries, specifically the 999 caller, Jimmy's right side neighbour.

"Apparently, she heard two voices shouting and banging, but she had never seen any visitors to his property before, except his groceries delivered once a week," he said.

"By the look of him and the state of his mind, he takes his anger and frustrations out on himself. It is a sad society we live in," she said.

"Are you okay with this case? If you are struggling, come and talk," he said as her sergeant, but in a caring manner, knowing this case could stir up emotions, given the background with her brother.

"I will be fine, Sarge. It is close to home, but I will be fine," she said confidently.

"SOCO should be here shortly," he said, the forensic officer dealing with a knife attack in Galashiels.

* * *

It wasn't long before the Scene of Crime Officer arrived to carry out the forensic examination and Lucy left him momentarily to phone her male colleague and get an update on Jimmy.

It was now coming up to four hours since the incident. It was four o'clock in the morning and Jimmy had complied with both the officers and the A&E staff. He could not give a fuck! He had just slipped deeper and deeper into his world of darkness.

Firstly, SOCO conducted a visual examination of the point of entry through the ajar door. Using his torch, he examined the spots of blood, looking for fingerprints or tool marks in and around the frame. With a magnetic powder, he brushed for fingerprints and finding one set of distinctive prints, he lifted them off with adhesive tape and made a record of them.

In the lounge, he found more spots of blood where the broken glass lay shattered. Taking a photograph and swab to show its location, he recovered it from the scene and bagged it as evidence.

Another hour later and finally, SOCO had gathered crucial evidence, especially from the presentation box indicating the intruder had been rather blasé in covering up his tracks.

Concerned for Jimmy's well-being and knowing how upset he had been at seeing his army memories around him, Lucy showed respect by carefully removing the portrait from the broken frame and placed all Jimmy's army memories together with what looked like urgent documentation back into an empty drawer. She cleared the broken glass and pills from the floor before locking Jimmy's front door and made her way back to the station.

She was gathering significant information about the night's events and at the same time, getting to understand Jimmy's life.

CHAPTER THREE

Relieved to get home and soak in a hot bath, getting rid of the smell of Jimmy's despair and heartache, Lucy, who lived with her mother and helped her look after Molly, had a huge weight lifted off her shoulders.

She was grateful for a healthy home-cooked meal and savoured every mouthful while watching Molly giggle at her favourite television programme, Peppa Pig. The petite, almost two-year-old red-headed girl pointed at Peppa and turned to get her mother's approval. Lucy grunted playfully and bent down to join her daughter on the carpet as she embraced her with hugs and kisses and both giggled with the gestures.

"How was your day, love?" Lucy's mother asked.

"A busy shift, Mum," Lucy said, picking up her daughter and sitting on the couch. She told her mother about Jimmy, the state of his home, the strong odours and their confrontation.

"I do actually feel sorry for the guy. He seems so sad and lonely and bitter and angry, all at the same time," Lucy said.

"It sounds like he needs some help. Maybe someone who won't give up on him. Someone who will listen," Lucy's mother said.

"I can't be a policewoman and social worker, Mum."

"Lucy, you of all people should know what he is going through. His life has changed forever and he probably feels there is nothing worth living for anymore. Look at Tom and how proud and honoured he was…" Mrs. Harris half-heartedly laughed, "he was always the smartest little boy on the street and then he joined the army and his uniform was always immaculate."

"He was beaming from ear to ear the day he passed out," Lucy sniffed, stroking her fingers through Molly's hair.

"Yes, and Jimmy would have been just as beaming. Every soldier is proud to serve their country and is trained to be prepared for war. Then suddenly, the only life they know is taken away and they are just expected to fit into society. How often have we spoken about this…?" Mrs. Harris said, continuing to support but show Lucy that sometimes, someone could do with a little help and understanding.

"Imagine if Tom was in the same situation as Jimmy; a home filled with neglect and this proud young man unable, both physically and mentally, to help himself. I would be so hurt if I thought that no one was kind enough to help my son. Jimmy must be so alone, suffering a deep sense of loss for those who died and the army life he had. Lucy, darling," her mother said, standing up and cupping her face.

"You know what loneliness feels like. He must be so sad and alone. Maybe you can be a friend? Now, try to get some sleep before your next shift," Mrs. Harris said, giving her a motherly kiss on the forehead before picking up Molly, who had dozed off on her mother's lap.

* * *

Lucy sat at the end of her bed with her shoulders forward. Her mother's words and thoughts of Jimmy sitting in his wheelchair drinking himself sick, played on her mind. She thought about her brother, Tom. He was due to be promoted to Major on his return, but his career in the army was cut short in his prime. There were only two of them, Tom being the oldest by five years.

She had lost her father at an early age and her mother had dedicated all her life in giving her undying love to them and raising them to be good kids with good morals.

Lucy sighed heavily and stood up. She opened one side of her built-in cupboard and reached for one of the three shoe boxes that sat neatly on the top shelf. Placing the shoe box on the bed, she ran her fingers over it, reading the name and date she had smartly written on top in marker pen –

Tom Harris – 6th May 2010

She removed the lid and again ran her fingers over the tops of the letters that filled three quarters of the empty space. She had filled two and a half shoe boxes with Tom's letters, methodically sorting them and dating each box.

With every operational tour that Tom served, the siblings used every spare moment they had to write to each other. Lucy had kept every letter and this had been the first time

she had taken one of those three boxes down since his death.
Her hand trembled as she picked up the last distinctive 'bluey'
letter he had ever written

My sweetest Lucy   *6th May 2010*

We have always been open and honest with each other so know when I write this, it is hard and not good here, and there is a possibility I might not come home. I've been getting such bad feelings. We lost another guy today, and as I sit here resting, I can't help but find myself needing to write this letter to you, and although this will be the hardest thing I've ever had to do, know that you will always be loved.

Being your brother has been my finest accomplishment, from the girl who lit up my life with her smile and happiness, to the woman who has shown kindness and warmth to all those around her.

You are my best friend, we have shared our deepest thoughts, have cried with laughter, someone I have consoled in, and a shoulder to cry on. I am proud to be Molly's only uncle although I only wish I could be there to watch her grow and develop into a kind, caring and beautiful woman - just like her mother, (I'm smiling as I write this.) Always remind her that I loved her.

You are going to meet someone who needs their heart filled with trust and respect. Someone who needs your kindness and warmth. Someone is out there just waiting for you. You will be loved and respected for the beautiful woman you are. The happiest moments in my life were those spent with you and Mum, and I will always hold them close to me. If anything should happen I'm going to need you to be strong for Mum and look after each other.

So don't be sad my sweetest little sister, I will always walk alongside you.

I love you
Tom xxxx

The letter fluttered to the ground and Lucy wept, burying her
face in her hands.

CHAPTER FOUR

Monday, 2nd January 2012

Despite Constable Harris working nightshifts and feeling fatigued with Molly demanding her every need, she offered to work extra hours for Jimmy to at least see a familiar face, albeit that he had shown her despicable behaviour and it wasn't part of her job. Lucy had felt the need to help him, especially because it hit home and she hoped that if Tom should ever have been in the same situation, someone would have reached out and helped him.

Sitting at her desk, Lucy logged onto the internet and Googled Jimmy Ferguson. Twenty-nine thousand, eight hundred results were found. Scrolling down and reading the sub-titles that might resemble the army veteran, she found a link and clicked on it.

THE DAILY NEWS

www.dailynews.co.uk   Scottish Borders Local News   - Since 1879

Local War Hero Injured

After being blown up in Afghanistan, local war hero receives Queen's Gallantry medal for his bravery. Corporal Jimmy Ferguson from the 2nd Battalion The Royal Regiment of Scotland (Royal Highland Fusiliers) was injured when his vehicle hit an IED. Corporal Ferguson and three other soldiers were thrown from their vehicle with two of the soldiers being killed instantly.

Corporal Jimmy Ferguson who was abandoned by his parents, grew up within the care system and joined the British Army at age sixteen. He thrived and moved up the ranks. Top of his class, he lived for the army, finally having a sense of belonging and the family he so longed for.

He had immense pride in serving his country for ten years before the tragic incident.

Through Corporal Ferguson's bravery and disobeying his own injuries, he pulled himself along the ground to save the Junior NCO as they continued to come under fire. Finding some refuge from the burning vehicle, they sat and prayed for a quick rescue. "Corporal Ferguson was an exemplary soldier and had the potential to go all the way, he'll be sadly missed by his peers" his Commanding Officer said.

Sadly, the Junior NCO lost his life later that day in hospital. Corporal Jimmy Ferguson had both his legs amputated above the knee and has been left partially disabled down the right side of his body. He now requires a wheelchair to get around.

As Lucy read through the newspaper article, she started to understand some of the reasons for Jimmy's drinking. He had lived his whole life for the army, serving ten years and with the potential of going far. Lucy recognised the significance of Jimmy's army memories. "But why is he angry with his friend, Angus?" she wondered as she entered 'Glencorse Barracks' into the search engine and found a central telephone number. Getting through to reception and explaining who she was, Lucy made enquiries about an Angus Brown and was put through to his direct line.

A confident voice answered, "Good morning. This is Major Angus Brown speaking. Can I help you?"

"Good morning, Major Brown. I am Constable Lucy Harris from Police Scotland in Peebles. I understand you know a Corporal Jimmy Ferguson and thought you should know that he was beaten up last night and some property was stolen."

"Constable Harris, I have not seen or spoken to Jimmy in five years. Is he okay?" the major said with slight hesitation.

"Jimmy is fine, although he did go to the hospital last night for stitches and a more thorough examination. I have spoken to the hospital this morning and he will be discharged later today," she said.

There was a pause down the line. "Major Brown, I think Jimmy could do with some help. He is in a bad way."

"Do you know what property was stolen?" he asked.

"His Queen's Gallantry medal, but there could be others. I need to question Jimmy again. Also fifty pounds. We managed to find some crucial forensics and I am waiting for the results," she said.

"Constable Harris, I will see what I can do. Thank you for letting me know and please keep me updated?"

"Major Brown, I would like to meet you in person and get a better understanding of him."

"I can make time for you tomorrow, here at the barracks, say midday and we can talk over coffee?" he said.

"That would be great, thank you," she said, and they exchanged their mobile numbers before ending the call.

CHAPTER FIVE

J immy looked as tired as she felt. His hair was dishevelled and there were dark circles beneath his sunken, saddened eyes. His damaged right hand had been stitched and bandaged, and the laceration above his right eye glued. Being forced to go to the hospital with the supremacy visitors making that decision for him, he had been left feeling isolated with no self-control of his own body. But for those few moments, Jimmy was relieved to see the familiar officer waiting for him on his return.

"Hello, Jimmy," Lucy said kindly, offering to take hold of his wheelchair from the ambulance driver.

"Hello, Constable Harris," Jimmy said nervously, not quite knowing how to act around the officer. Her kind gestures were overwhelming.

"I thought if you saw a familiar face, it wouldn't be as daunting. How are you feeling, considering the circumstances?" she asked gently.

"Aye. Okay, thanks," he said, despite his head pounding sharply and heavily.

"I will make you some coffee and then I can update you on the case. I also need to ask you some more questions," she said, pushing him inside.

Jimmy's eyes fell directly where his army memories had been unceremoniously thrown to the ground.

"Jimmy, I can appreciate that last night was upsetting for you, so I have tried to clear as much as I can," she said.

"Thank ye," he said with his partially unfamiliar sobering actions.

Lucy gave him the coffee mug and took a seat at the table. "You put up quite a fight. We found some significant fingerprints on your presentation box, as well as prints by the door and spots of blood. Can you remember anything else?" she said, taking her notebook from her pocket.

"I remember someone being in my property..." The booze and anxiety often caused moments of blackouts. "I don't remember anything else," he said, fidgeting with his hands.

"You would have other medals for your years of service. Are they also missing?" she said, cautiously, as she watched Jimmy's body language quickly changing. The questions were hitting a raw nerve.

"Jimmy, I understand it is difficult to talk about your past...," but before Lucy could finish, he slammed his left fist on the table, making her jump and spilling his coffee everywhere.

"Ye know nothing about soldiering!" he said. Taken aback by the comment and almost letting her guard down, she wished she could grab him by the scruff of his neck and shake some sense into him, as her own anger now brewed inside her. She stood up and leaned in closer.

"You are not the only soldier who has fought for their country! My brother stood proud too! My brother died fighting for his country!" she directed.

What had been a moment of civilized conversation had now turned to anger. "You can lash out all you want! Shout your threatening, abusive language towards me! I do not give a shit! I have heard it all before!" Gesturing towards his body, she continued, "Do not think I feel pity for you just because you have no legs! Soldiers have died and you sit here feeling sorry for yourself!" she said, assertively, before storming out and slamming the door behind her.

Jimmy felt like a double-decker bus had hit him. A deep sense of guilt struck him in the gut and volcanic balls of fire exploded in his head.

"You fucking rude bastard!" he thought, and did what he did best, and went looking for a bottle of JD.

* * *

Taking in deep breaths, Lucy stood there for a moment and allowed herself to calm down before she re-entered the property. "I would rather you not drink at this moment in time," she said, wheeling him out of the kitchen and removing the new whiskey bottle from between his stumps.

"Listen, Jimmy. As part of the investigation, I spoke to Angus this morning and I am meeting him tomorrow."

"Whit the fuck! Why did ye dae that!?" he screamed at the woman with outrage. "A' don't want yer help! Or Major Brown's!"

"I am sorry, Jimmy, but it is part of the investigation," she replied, keeping her cool.

"Fuck yer investigation!" he said, slamming his fist on the table once more, as his face and eyes bulged with anger and his muscles tightened with every movement. "Get oot!" he screamed.

"You are right, Jimmy. I did not have to be here today, and would rather have spent the time with my family! I am working double time because of you! I will see you when I see you!" she said, knowing that once she left, he would be back on the booze, but it was not her place to say otherwise.

And so once again, Jimmy was alone. The start of another year. A new year filled with dreams and aspirations. But what hope and dreams did Jimmy have to look forward to? He was alone. It was just another day for him. Every day felt like an eternity. And listening to the silence creeping in and filling every space of his home, Jimmy's shoulders sagged and sadness engulfed his body.

With his jaw clenched and grinding his teeth in anger, Jimmy rocked back and forth in his chair, banging his head on the table as he fought a wilful battle against the tears that threatened to build in his eyes and his muscles tightened with each spasm.

"I want to fucking die!" he thought as the sadness just as quickly turned to anger and he lashed out, fist smacking his head, again and again. Thump! Thump! Thump! he thumped his stumps.

CHAPTER SIX

The unexpected phone call from Constable Harris earlier in the day had left Major Angus Brown feeling unsettled. He had not seen or heard from Jimmy since being medically discharged from the army. Angus had tried everything he could to be there for him in his recovery, but Jimmy's continued bitterness and anger towards his best friend eventually pushed him away.

He had suffered a deep sense of loss in losing Jimmy's friendship. He was suffering emotionally, if not physically. Angus was just as broken, but he was better at disguising it.

He stared at the photo sitting on his desk, which was taken fifteen years earlier at their passing out parade. They had both been looking forward to their futures in the army together. Jimmy was the brother he never had.

They had seen active duty over the years and were due to be deployed again on a six-month tour, when at the same time, Angus' sister was to be married. Sharing that brotherly bond, Jimmy had persistently persuaded Angus to apply for leave and attend the wedding.

Suddenly, the major felt uncomfortable and clammy. The memory left a queasy, unpleasant taste in his mouth and he jumped up, getting sick!

* * *

Briefly returning home after work, Angus changed out of uniform and found feeble excuses to waste time, despite his confidence in his ability to handle any stressful situation.

He hadn't driven down Jimmy's street or found any need to visit Peebles since he had pushed him out of his life. Managing to find a parking space outside Jimmy's home, he stood there hesitantly before he knocked and waited. But, there was no answer and he tried the door handle, finding the door unlocked.

The same strong stench of body odour and alcohol hit him as he entered and found Jimmy, his best friend, on the couch. The strong, confident and healthy man he once knew, was now battered, bruised and broken.

With a half-eaten microwave meal on the dining-room table and an empty whiskey bottle lying beside him, it was plain to see that Jimmy was in dire need of help.

Angus stood there for a moment. Jimmy's home was filled with as much neglect and bitterness as had been shown between the two best friends. No memories of their army lives together were anywhere to be seen. The house-proud, immaculate person that Jimmy once was, was now no more. Anyone walking into his home would not believe it was the same person.

Jimmy looked uncomfortable lying there. He was having a bad

dream. The stress in his face showed someone who had seen death a thousand times over, that no ordinary person would ever experience. He looked older than his thirty-one years of life.

A wave of emotions struck Angus one by one. Anger and detestation. Guilt and regret. He felt sick with revulsion at abandoning his best friend and with another urge to throw up, he stumbled to the bathroom.

Jimmy stirred at hearing the muffled sounds in his home. His body tightened with apprehension. "Fuck," he screamed and grabbed his wheelchair with rage, desperately trying to pull himself onto it as quickly as possible and fight the unwelcome invasion.

"Jimbo!" Angus said.

"Whit the fuck!" Jimmy screamed, bumping into the army major's legs, trying forcefully to push him out and desperately wanting to feel the satisfaction in slamming the front door in his face. Angus grabbed his wheelchair and shoved him backward as Jimmy's left arm reached for a dining-room chair and pulled it to the ground.

"Corporal, fucking control yourself!" the army major ordered as he grabbed Jimmy by the shoulders and shook him vigorously, pulling him to the ground.

Jimmy fought on as the possessed evilness within him took complete control over his actions and he head-butted the ranked officer. Managing to free his left arm, he swung a left hook and smacked Angus hard in the face.

Approaching Jimmy's property, Constable Harris could hear the commotion. With still some hours to go in her shift, she had felt this constant sickening and worrying feeling inside her and had felt the need to check in on Jimmy. This case was certainly hitting her hard and not bothering to knock on the door, she walked into a physical battle of outrage.

"Jimmy, calm down!" she demanded, kneeling beside them as the soldiers now noticed the woman in the room.

"Fuckin great. Ye called backup!" Jimmy said with a hint of sarcasm in his outrageous anger.

"Constable Harris is the only reason I am here, you pathetic piece of shit!" Angus said, assuming she was the officer who had spoken to him earlier in the day.

"He did not call me; I came to check on you," Lucy said.

"A' don't want yer fuckin help!" Jimmy's exhausted and cramped body spluttered.

"Do not speak to her like that!" Angus said.

"It is fine. Stop fighting, Jimmy. I am here to help you," Lucy said, trying to calm the situation. But Jimmy turned his head away. His body had given up on him.

"Please look at me, Jimmy," Lucy's kind and gentle voice said as she touched his right shoulder and his saddened and dejected eyes turned to look at her.

"I am not the enemy, Jimmy. I have a responsibility and it was my job to let Angus know your situation. You and Angus have your issues, but he has a right to know as your next of kin. You might not want to see him, but I need his help as part of this investigation," Lucy said with the continued gentleness in her voice.

Without interrupting, Angus had watched the police officer's kindness and reassuring words bring back some form of normality in Jimmy.

"Mate, I will help you back into your chair and then I will leave," Angus said bluntly.

"Please, Jimmy," Lucy said, and albeit reluctantly, his deflated body willingly accepted the help.

"I will leave you now," Angus said, sensing his friend's uneasiness.

"I am coming back, Jimmy," Lucy said, before she followed Angus out and closed the door behind her.

Angus Brown was tall, muscular, and broad-shouldered. "Major Brown, I presume?" Lucy smiled.

"Constable Harris, I do apologise for our behaviour earlier," he said with embarrassment.

"Please do not apologise. But, it is best you do not come back inside," she said.

"He truly hates me. I do not know if I can do this!" he sighed heavily, putting a hand through his cropped hair.

"Let us see what tomorrow brings. I want to know more about him," she said.

The usual confident, self-assured army major had clearly been shaken by the state of Jimmy's home and his appearance.

"I have been physically sick after receiving your call and seeing him today. Please understand, I am feeling mixed emotions at this moment," he said.

"I can appreciate that and I am truly sorry that this has happened," she said.

"He seemed to have moments of normality when you spoke to him," he said.

"That is why I felt the need to be here when he got home today. I want him to understand that I am here to help him and know how much his medal means to him," she said.

"Thank you for your help," he said.

"I am going to make him a strong coffee and see if he will talk to me. I will text you later," she said.

"Would you like me to wait in case he kicks off again?" he asked.

"Thank you. I would appreciate that," she said.

"I will be in my car. Thank you again," he said.

"My pleasure," she said, before entering Jimmy's property once again and finding him in his chair where they had left him. He looked defeated and demoralised, slumped forward. His sad face winced with every muscle spasm that hit him hard.

"Jimmy, are you okay?" she asked, with him only managing an uncomfortable nod before she went through to the bathroom to find a cloth to clean the dry blood from his face.

"A' don't want yer help!" he said bluntly.

"Tough luck, Jimmy!" gently wiping the dry blood from his face. "I am sorry," she said as he flinched with each gentle touch she made.

"Can I see your hand?" she asked in more of a gesture, rather than a question and took his bandaged right hand. "You are going to need your dressing changed. Did the hospital send you with any supplies?"

"Na," he said.

"Not everyone has someone to look after them. How do they expect you to change this on your own? Especially when it is obvious you need help!" she moaned, sharing a brief smile with him.

"I am sorry. That is my moan for the day. I have had an exceptionally long shift. I will bring some clean bandages tomorrow. Right, I will make you some strong coffee," she said.

"Thank ye," he said, fidgeting in his chair.

"You are welcome," she said.

Not quite knowing what to say to him, the police officer sat quietly. Maybe just having someone's presence would help Jimmy open more. But the longer they sat, the more she was drawn into his silence. His body slowly sagged forward with each heavy breath he took.

"Listen, Jimmy. As I said earlier, I am here to help you," she said, kindly, and he glanced up at her for a moment, but could not find the words to respond.

"We should get some results from the forensics in the next few days and I will keep you updated," she said.

"Thank ye," he said with some hesitation.

"I will bring those bandages tomorrow. Can I help you with anything else?" she said.

"Na, am guid," he said.

"Okay, Jimmy. Try to get some sleep," she smiled. There was nothing more she could do for him that evening.

* * *

Angus glanced up and climbed out of his car.

"Major Brown, thank you for waiting," Constable Harris said.

"Angus, please," he said.

"Lucy. I have given him a strong coffee, but I cannot guarantee he will not be back on the booze. I can pop in tomorrow and change his dressings. Hopefully I might have some news on the investigation," she said.

"Thank you for being here this afternoon and helping him. You have shown him kindness," he said.

"He needs help and I look forward to our meeting tomorrow," she said.

"Yes, I will see you then. Do you have a long shift ahead?" he said.

"Yes, some hours yet. I started earlier than usual so Jimmy has a familiar face to meet him," she said.

With an overwhelming sense of embarrassment and guilt, Angus rubbed his face in the palms of his hands and put a hand through his cropped hair. "Thank you," he said.

* * *

Amy had waited for Angus to get home. He had spoken to her soon after the initial conversation between him and the police officer and she knew he was in a state of shock and would need her support more than ever.

Captain Amy Rose Campbell from the 3rd Battalion The Rifles and part of The Adjutant General's Corps, met Angus a year after Jimmy's injuries, down at the local pub where soldiers had gathered to reflect and remember those who had lost their lives on 9/11. Angus and Amy knew of each other, Amy knew who Jimmy was, the news of his injuries, as was with every soldier affected, all who served.

There wasn't a day in their four-year relationship that Angus did not mention Jimmy's name. Whether it was in anger or a fond memory, he spoke about Jimmy and Amy was there supporting him through it all.

She knew it was important for Angus to talk about Jimmy, and had hoped that one day he could find the strength to be the bigger person and do the right thing by speaking to him. It even caused arguments between them for showing some support in Jimmy's favour, but even she was surprised by the unexpected news about the housebreaking.

Hearing Angus walk in, she got off the couch to greet him. Taking her in his arms, they fell against the wall and kissed.

"How are you feeling?" she asked, and Angus shook his head and threw his arms up in anger.

"What a fucking day this has ended up being," he said, angrily,

38

taking a beer from the fridge and collapsing on a kitchen chair.

"Speak to me," she said, pulling out her own chair and taking his hand in hers.

Angus took a long swig of booze. "He is on fucking death row. His home is a fucking sewer...," he continued rambling on in anger, explaining to Amy the state of Jimmy's home and the desperate situation he was in.

"I cannot do this, Aims," he said with heaviness in his voice and Amy stretched across and hugged her husband to be.

"You have got to do this. You have to help him now," she said.

"He pushed me away, remember!" he said, forcefully pushing his chair back.

"Angus, the time has come to help him," she said.

"There you go again, showing your support towards him! I have suffered too!" he said.

"And I have been there every minute of every day for you, trying to share the burden! But you do not always talk to me and I am just expected to understand what you are going through! He is there. In your mind. In our lives. Every day. We had only known each other for ten minutes and Jimmy had already been mentioned in the conversation. I practically know him as well as I know you," she said.

"He is angry and bitter," he said.

"Do you blame him? The army was his life. What about that stupid bitch? I too would be bitter," she said.

"I was there. He could have spoken to me and asked for help," he said.

"You are the brother he never had and yes, the army was his family. But that does not mean that suffering such a loss will not stir up emotions from his past. He was a very independent man, more so than you and now that has gone," she said.

Angus had listened to Amy's reasoning and he knew deep down inside his churning gut, that she was right. He turned and leaned against the kitchen cupboard, burying his head in his hands.

"Angus," she said, and reached out for him. Angus lifted her onto the kitchen counter and they shared a gentle kiss.

"Who is this police officer? She seems to be going out of her way to help," she said.

"Lucy Harris. She brought Jimmy back to moments of normality and she is working extra hours today," he said.

"That name rings a bell?" she asked.

"I remember a Harris at Sandhurst. We were part of the Military Skills Competition. I am sure he was from this area," he said.

"Let us see what tomorrow brings," she said.

"That is exactly what she said," he sighed.

"Well, that is it then! Take it from two outsiders looking in. Listen...," she said, cupping his face. "I want to marry you and I am tired of postponing the wedding because you hope that Jimmy will come to his senses and get help. You want him to be your best man. Now this is your opportunity to help him. Have that punch up and get it out of your system!"

Angus sighed exhaustedly. Amy was right. This was the opportunity to now do something about their friendship, albeit by the end of it, they never spoke or saw each other ever again.

CHAPTER SEVEN

Tuesday, 3rd January 2012

T he backfire from the modified vehicle sent a barrage of gunfire erupting down a back alleyway of desert brick buildings, breaking the thick stillness of death hanging in the air and Jimmy's stumps tensed.

"Argh, feck off!" he screamed with rage, punching his fist into the pillow, and smacking his head again and again. Thump! Thump! Thump! he thumped his stumps.

Why can't this God forsaken world take me now?

Jimmy's flashbacks were frequent.

Getting himself dressed in the morning, an image of kitting and gearing up would flash across his mind. Opening the fridge door, he'd hear the sound of clicks from loading and preparing his weapon. The clanking of the letterbox sent images of an explosion and the aftermath of his men.

06:23 hours, and Jimmy wiped his brow as an unpleasant

smell of perspiration seeped through his t-shirt. The endless wonder of endless wondering had once again kept him awake. The loneliness was as icy and chilling as the wintery claws that threatened to pounce on him. He felt this deep sense of tragedy, heartbreak and hurt. His open wounds and scars would never heal. He was suffering alone.

* * *

Constable Harris was ten minutes early. The guard on duty had been notified about her visit, and entry into the Glencorse Barracks was straightforward. She.had never been to the barracks. Tom had served in another regiment and her previous cases had never involved military personnel.

Jimmy served his country for ten years before the tragic incident, starting his career in 1997 at the Army Foundation College in Harrogate, where, at the same time, he met Angus. Both being the youngest in their section, they became inseparable, the best of friends and brothers in arms.

The forty-nine week course provided raw recruits with military training, personal development, and education. Following the course, the young recruits did a further ten weeks at the Infantry Training Centre, Catterick, where they were put through their paces training in survival, first aid and map reading, all the while building stamina and fitness and learning about the qualities of being a good soldier. Both soldiers also received their B category driving license before joining their regiment.

Jimmy thrived, pushing himself harder with every challenge thrown at him. His quick-witted, 'lad's lad' approach allowed him to get away with a lot more than he perhaps should have.

For both soldiers, it had been a proud moment on the day of their passing out parade. Jimmy was awarded The Marsh Trophy for showing the most endeavour whilst on the Combat Infantryman's Course, and Angus was awarded Best Recruit.

During a period of Regimental Duty and ongoing training, both soldiers completed Junior Brecon and were promoted to Corporal. It was during this time that the soldiers expressed their interest in joining the Special Forces Support Group and their Chain of Command approved them for P Company, where they successfully completed their PARA's course and gained their jump wings. However, it was then recommended that Angus apply for Officers Training and Jimmy continue moving forward with his transfer to the SFSG and was deployed to Iraq in 2004 on Operations TELIC 4.

While waiting for Major Brown to meet her, Lucy took the opportunity to look at the photos hanging on a wall of the reception area. "Would Jimmy be in one of them?" she wondered as a hand stretched across and pointed to a young recruit covered in 'war paint'.

"Here he is," the major smiled and shook her hand. "Good afternoon, Constable Harris."

"Good afternoon, Major Brown," she smiled. His stiff, starched, neatly pressed uniform and close-cropped hair showing a man with authority.

"That was a good day. Jimmy lived for the army," he said, before they made their way down the corridor towards his office.

"By any chance do you have a family member in the military?" he asked.

"My brother, Captain Tom Harris. He was killed two years ago whilst on tour," she said, swallowing hard.

"Oh God, Lucy! I knew your brother from Sandhurst. I am so sorry to hear that," he sighed heavily.

"He was due to be promoted on his return," she said with a hint of hoarseness in her voice. The major's presence was a hard pill to swallow.

"Tom and I were part of the 2006 Military Skills Competition," he said.

"Yes, at West Point," she confirmed. Tom had shared the enduring exercise with her in detail.

"He kept pushing and encouraging the team. He was a good leader and a decent guy. I am honoured to have known him," he said sincerely.

"Thank you, I appreciate that," she said as the major showed her into his office.

Of basic design; two aluminium desks and filing cabinet, a bookshelf and a heavy-duty printer, Major Brown's office was shared with another officer.

"Can I offer you a coffee and delicious Bakers original biscuits?" he asked.

"Yes please. One sugar," she said, taking the offered seat.

"Again, I apologise for last night's behaviour. It was a shock to see Jimmy in that state," he said.

"Please do not apologise," she said, and leaned forward to pick up a photo from his desk. "This is how I found you. Jimmy has the same photo."

"That was taken on the day we passed out. Jimmy was so proud," he said.

"He is not proud anymore, but then you saw that last night. He is in an awfully bad way, Angus, and the medal that was stolen is not helping matters. Jimmy has not been forthcoming and although I know about his Queen's Gallantry Medal, would he have accumulated other medals for his years of service?" she said.

"Yes. His Operational Service Medal for Afghanistan. So, you did not see any medals then?" he said.

"No. There was nothing else missing other than Jimmy's medals and fifty pounds. From what I have gathered, all his army memories were placed in one drawer.

"I tried so hard to help him, but he kept pushing me away. I eventually stopped trying and told him to contact me if he needed help, but he never did. I had to move on with my life. He received the Queen's Gallantry for his bravery, but he would not accept an honours reception or a visit from me," he sighed with a hint of sadness in his voice.

"Maybe he is embarrassed? Tell me more about him," she said, taking a sip of coffee.

Angus leaned back into his chair and took a moment before he started to tell Constable Harris about Jimmy.

"Jimbo and I met that very first day. Both sixteen, we were the youngest in our section so instantly, we stuck together. Jimmy beamed with confidence. Growing up in care, he was used to different surroundings, whereas I came from a loving home and good education. His quick off the mark, lad's lad approach allowed him to get away with more than most, whereas I often got our section doing an extra day on exercise in freezing conditions," he said, laughing half-heartedly.

"We were both competitive. If I beat Jimmy's time on a run, he'd beat me in push-ups," he said, sighing again, clearly finding it difficult to recall the memories.

"We both lived for the army. Jimmy finally had a sense of belonging and the family he always wanted. We were going to move up the ranks together and retire together. Our careers were sorted. We both expressed our interest in joining the Special Forces Support Group. However, it was recommended that I apply for Officers Training and Jimmy continue his way forward with the transfer. He was amongst some of the first guys to be incorporated into the role. He is the brother I never had," he said, gravely as he lost himself in his thoughts –

BREAKING NEWS - Soldiers killed!

*Receiving the phone call about Jimmy's dire condition
had left Angus choking for air, like someone had struck
him in the gut, leaving his body shuddering in fear.*

"Angus, are you okay?" she asked.

"Sorry. Yes, absolutely!" shaking his head and dismissing the thoughts that haunted him.

"There is not a day that goes by when I do not think of him. I am his next of kin, so I was the first point of contact. I received the call about the incident at my sister's wedding," he said, and explained further.

"We were to be deployed together on a six-month tour. Jimmy had insisted I apply for leave to attend my sister's wedding. All day, I had this bad feeling inside me. A sixth sense. I knew something was going to happen to him and receiving that phone call only made it a reality. The army granted me compassionate leave and I left on an emergency flight to be by his bedside. I was with him every day he was in the hospital, but he did not speak to me unless it was to throw abusive comments my way. I tried to encourage him in his recovery, but he kept pushing me away."

"I am truly sorry, Angus."

"I have never shed a tear, Lucy. I should have had his back. I suppose being a soldier, you learn to block your emotions. I have been lucky enough to have my fiancée, Amy, to support me," pointing to the photo that stood next to him and Jimmy.

"Does Jimmy know?" she asked.

"No, not yet," he said.

"Did Jimmy ever have someone special in his life?" she asked.

"He had been seeing a girl for roughly three years and they were due to be married on his return. But when she heard about his legs, she freaked. It broke his heart," he said.

"No wonder he is so angry. I truly feel sorry for the guy. Angus, I only met Jimmy two days ago and he has thrown just as much abuse my way. He vomited all over my shoes. I do think he could do with some help. When I found him he was lying on the floor. His dignity exposed, shattered glass and empty whiskey bottles lay around him. He did try to fight back, but his body is so out of it with alcohol. He is in a constant daze. Jimmy reeks of booze and body odour, but again, you have seen it for yourself. It is also none of my business, but I think Jimmy is having financial difficulties. I found sealed letters of payments amongst the mayhem," she said.

> *"Fuck! Why should he be in debt? Has Jimmy*
> *spent all his compensation pay-out?" he thought,*
> *leaving a sickening feeling inside him.*

"I did everything for him. I sold his car and made the necessary applications for benefits," he said with annoyance and stood up, putting a hand through his cropped hair. "Fuck you, Ferguson!" he said sternly and loud, without realising it.

"I apologise for the despicable behaviour he has shown towards you," he said, leaning forward onto his desk.

"Oh, do not worry. I can take as much as he gives. He lives on frozen meals and JD. He tried to kill himself, and I will not put it past him to try again. I want to help, but I could do with your help too. He does not lock his door, so anyone can walk in," she said.

"Okay, Lucy. I will do this for you. You have been kind enough, despite how he has treated you. I am off tomorrow. When I finish today, I will stop in and see him," he said, with Lucy standing up.

"Thank you, Major Brown, and for the delicious biscuits." They shared a laugh.

"No. Thank you, Constable Harris. I will walk you to your car. Heaven knows I can do with some fresh air.

CHAPTER EIGHT

1 9:30 hours – There was a knock at the door. "Fuck off!" Jimmy shouted as another knock came, but still, no one entered, and the knocking continued.

"Fuck off!" Jimmy screamed with his blood boiling over, and bumping into walls, he forced his wheelchair to the knocking door.

"Fuck you, Corporal. Don't you lock your door?" Angus shouted, dropping his duffle bag and pushing Jimmy's chair backward with force, allowing him enough space to close the door behind him.

"Whit the fuck are ye doin here? Did that bitch send ye again?" Jimmy spat.

"Look at you! You have no respect for yourself! You reek and you are rotten!" Angus barked. Grabbing the whiskey bottle between Jimmy's stumps, he pushed past him and placed it on the table, out of arm's reach, disarming any potential weapons that Jimmy could throw at him.

"If you ever fucking disrespect a woman again, I will smack the frigging daylights out of you!" the army major roared.

"Get the feck oot!" Jimmy screamed like a possessed demon.

Jimmy's hatred for his best friend showed in his bulging veins and every muscle that tightened, but his intoxicated body made him less capable of defending himself. Fighting against Angus' hold, he threw his head from side to side.

The unexpected fist left a sharp stinging pain to Jimmy's already battered and swollen face and Angus let go with guilt. He felt a suffocation of emotions pressing hard on his chest as Jimmy's haunted blank look stared back at him, but he was not going to be deterred by Jimmy's wretched and sorrowful life, so he wheeled him into the wet room and turned on the shower.

The icy water shocked Jimmy's drunken stupor into reality as he screamed abuse and his wheelchair rocked with uncontrollable movement –

SMACK!

Jimmy was thrown to the hard tiled floor.

"For fucks sakes, mate. I should fucking leave you here!" Angus shouted, pulling him up and lifting him onto the shower stool, but determined to fight on. Jimmy lashed out again, grabbing Angus by his t-shirt with his left arm and headbutting him. The major stumbled, almost losing his footing.

Angus forced his body weight and shoved him against the tiled wall, holding his left arm and making him totally immobile. "Now you will fucking listen to me! Get yourself fucking cleaned up and start taking responsibility for your fucking life!" he barked before he let go and changed the water temperature.

Helping Jimmy pull the drenched clothing off, Angus could feel his muscles tightening with each spasm, but no apologies were given.

Jimmy felt utterly deflated, embarrassed and ashamed by his deformed body being exposed, but his only escape was to hang his head and close his eyes as his muscles slowly relaxed with every splash of hot water hitting his naked body.

Angus slipped down and leaned against the tiled wall, pulling his knees up to his chest. Staring at his broken friend, he wished he could turn back time. All he wanted was his friend back.

* * *

An hour later, Jimmy was clean and as sober as his state of mind would allow him to be. There was no further backlash that night between the two soldiers, though the tone used was blunt and Jimmy had reluctantly accepted Angus' help in getting some warm clothing on and be carried to the couch while his wheelchair sat drying. He felt rejuvenated, despite the exhausting weight in his body.

Having changed out of his own wet clothing, Angus had ordered a Chinese take-away and both men were grateful for the distraction of the meal.

"Whatever happened to us mate?" Angus asked.

"Isn't it obvious? You moved up the ranks and became a fucking Rupert! You live your life and I got to draw the short straw!" Jimmy said.

"There are people who can help you. You are not the only soldier who has had their legs blown up!" Angus said.

"I don't want yer help...Major Brown! I should have died and maybe I will still!" Jimmy said bitterly.

Angus stood up and paced the room before taking a seat on the couch beside him. "I am getting married next year, mate," he said, ready for Jimmy's lashing out. But it did not come and Jimmy stared at his fidgeting hands sagging deeper with every breath.

"Her name is Amy. She is a captain with 3 Rifles," Angus continued carefully, seeing how Jimmy's posture and behaviour were quickly changing. "I want you to be my best man, mate, and Amy would love to meet you," he said, and Jimmy finally looked up.

"I want to go to bed," he said, bluntly.

"I have always been there for you! I have always been your friend! But where have you been? Where is my...?" Interrupted by a knock at the door, Angus threw his arms up in the air with annoyance. "For fucks sakes...!"

"Hello, Lucy," Angus said, surprised by her visit.

"Hello, Angus. I won't stay long, but I did promise to change Jimmy's bandage," she said with the first aid home kit in her hand, sensing the undoubted tension in the atmosphere.

"Thank you," Angus said.

"Mate, Constable Harris has kindly come to change your bandage," he said.

"Lucy, please. Hello, Jimmy," she smiled.

"Hello, Constable Harris," Jimmy said, trying to show the woman some respect and Lucy was grateful for his effort.

It had been the first time Jimmy had seen the officer without the distant dazed look in his eyes. Lucy was not in uniform, but instead wore an oversized jersey and skinny jeans that complimented her shapely body. Her auburn hair was tied up in a knot.

Seeing Jimmy in his depressed state of mind saddened Lucy and left a numb heartache deep inside her.

"Would you like coffee?" Angus asked."No, thank you. This is the first shift I have finished on time in a few days, and I want to get home to my daughter," she said, taking a seat beside Jimmy on the couch.

"Husband! Children! Lovely home! The perfect

life!" Jimmy thought with heaviness in his
heart, knowing he would never have that.

"Molly will be two next month," she continued speaking to both men, but focused on Jimmy, while gently removing the wet bandage and dabbing around his wound.

"You and your husband must be very proud," Angus said.

"Oh, I am not married. My daughter and I live with my mother," she said, slightly awkwardly, a look of grief flashing across her face while gently cleaning and drying around the stitches before taping the clean bandage end.

"All done!" she said, pleased with her attempt at first aid.

"Thank you, Lucy," Angus said.

Lucy had shown once again her caring side and went that extra mile to help Jimmy, who had slowly withdrawn. His anxiety dragged him down deeper into that dark, hollow crater of his soul.

"I will keep you updated with the investigation, Jimmy," she said, sensing his uneasiness as Angus walked out with her.

* * *

"Thank you for helping him," Angus said to Lucy as they stood

56

outside his property.

"How is he?" she asked.

"We have had another punch up," he said.

"I am sorry to hear that," she said.

"He certainly knows how to fight back. I will give him that much," he said.

"He is going to need his stitches removed next week, and will need to go to the surgery for that," she said.

"He looks a disgrace! This is not who he was," he said in his army major tone.

"He has lost his identity. Have you told him about Amy?" she said.

"Yeah, but he just withdrew even more. He detests me for still having my army career and hates me with a vengeance!" he said, deflated.

"I will do everything I can to help you both and can check up on him as often as I can," she said kindly and reassuringly.

"I cannot thank you enough and apologise enough for any disrespectful actions both Jimmy and I have shown," he said.

"I can pop in sometime tomorrow," she said.

"Thank you. Can I give Amy your number to contact you?" he said.

"Absolutely. Let us set up a group chat between the three of us?" she said.

"Fantastic idea. I will suggest to Amy that you meet up for a coffee," he said.

"I would like that," she said before Angus thanked her again and she left, walking back to the station to pick up her car.

* * *

"Mate, that was kind of Lucy to stop in and change your dressing," Angus said to Jimmy, who had remained in the same desperate state he was in.

"I want my chair. I want to go to bed!" Jimmy said abruptly.

"Seriously, mate. You are one selfish bastard! I do not know what shit is going on in your head, but if it is the last thing I ever do for you, tomorrow you will get a haircut and shave!" Angus said, furiously and helped him to bed.

Physically and emotionally drained, Angus closed his eyes and leaned back into the couch, hoping he could get some rest, but the distinctive smell of sterilisation filled his nostrils as consultants and nurses rushed to stabilise Jimmy.

Gripping his cropped hair, Angus tried to clear his head and remembered the photo Lucy had mentioned. Searching each drawer, he found the drawer of Jimmy's past. He saw photos he remembered clearly and others he had never seen, as well as discovering the letters of overdue payments.

"Fuck...!" he thought

CHAPTER NINE

Jimmy's eyes were heavy with lack of sleep, and every movement felt like there was a tonne of bricks tied around his neck.

"Mate, what the fuck is this?" Angus seethed, throwing the letters of a final notice on Jimmy's bed.

"It's none of yer fuckin' business!" Jimmy said with a surge of agitation and trepidation filling every muscle as he pushed himself up.

"It is my every fucking business! How dare you do this to me after everything I have done for you!" Angus said furiously.

"Phone them. I want to speak to them!" he said, and albeit reluctantly, Jimmy dialled the number and gave Angus permission to speak.

Slamming the lounge door behind him, Angus left a tide of hatred, disgust and embarrassment wash over Jimmy as he listened to his sharp and direct voice.

Ten minutes later, Angus walked in, clenching his jaw in vexation. "Five fucking grand, plus interest! What is that, a grand a year on fucking booze? Mate, you are ten days short of them knocking on your front door for payment. Fuck, you have nothing worth taking! Your AFC is there to help you with your physical needs, not fucking blow it on alcohol!" he said.

"It's not just fuckin' booze! Ye have control of my money. I must fuckin' live," Jimmy spat back.

"Live! Mate, I will be digging your fucking grave shortly! I did everything for you! It was all sorted and you were looked after! If I find out there is more…," Angus said, angrily, leaving the question hanging.

"Get the feck oot!" Jimmy screamed.

"I am gone mate," Angus sighed heavily, taking the letters he picked up his bag and walked out. Slamming Jimmy's front door behind him.

Jimmy's head throbbed with every Thump! Thump! Thump! he inflicted on his body, aggressively pulling himself onto his chair. He needed a drink.

❊ ❊ ❊

Physically shaking with rage and needing to clear his head, Angus left his car parked at Jimmy's, and welcomed the soft mist-like drizzle as he walked into town.

Giving the young woman behind the bar his table number, he

ordered a coffee and full English breakfast.

Angus texted, sending Amy a private message.

I cannot fucking do this!

Why? What has happened?

He is in at least seven grand debt! After everything I have done for him, claiming I had control over his money and he had to fucking live! What else has he spent his AFC on?

Where are you now?

I've left him. I'm having breakfast in town.

We had our suspicions. Pop into Citizens Advice, and get some info and I'll make some phone calls.

I'll phone you later.

Angus, you need to get back to him! We will talk later

But Angus did not reply.

* * *

"I have managed to find some information for you," the woman volunteer at the Citizens Advice said, returning to one of their private rooms.

"Thank you," Angus said, the woman explaining to him about consolidating the debt into one monthly payment and suggesting that he contact the various charities for ex-servicemen to get advice, while handing him some forms.

Popping into the bank, Angus spoke to an advisor about his options in setting up a debt repayment plan and asked, as next of kin, permission to look at Jimmy's account.

Going through each of the transactions on the screen, Angus confirmed each amount.

"Can we check any payments that have been paid into his account in the past five years?" he said, the woman clicking away on the keyboard. But with every year they went through, no substantial amount was paid into Jimmy's account by the Armed Forces Compensation Scheme, leaving Angus questioning his own abilities in taking responsibility for Jimmy's affairs.

"Why had nothing been paid into Jimmy's account?" he wondered while texting Amy a private message.

Aims, he has not received his AFC!

What? Did you send everything off?

I did, I'm sure of it!

*Just bring everything you have and we
can go through it together.*

* * *

Angus' purposeful walk back to Jimmy's flat showed an aura of confidence, despite the disappointment he was feeling inside and finding Jimmy on his second can of lager within a matter of two and a half hours of being away.

"Mate, you need to sign these!" he said, throwing the various applications on the table. "Have you received any paperwork from the AFCS? There is nothing to suggest you've received payment," Angus said bluntly.

"That was yer responsibility!" The stare was dark and bitter as Jimmy signed the applications.

"You're a fucking bastard, mate!" Angus said, taking the signed forms and walked out. Leaving Jimmy with his untouched greasy shoulder-length hair.

* * *

Not knowing of the earlier confrontation between the two men, Lucy texted the group chat.

How is Jimmy?

Her phone beeped ten minutes later. Amy had sent her a private message.

Angus has found out that Jimmy's in debt,
and has flipped! He has gone home.

Oh gosh, I am sorry to hear that.

Angus and I need to sit down and discuss our options.
Angus is going to need more convincing in helping Jimmy.

I will pop in after my shift and check upon him.

Thank you for all your help.

* * *

Lucy was relieved that her shift had ended with no last-minute call out. Knocking on Jimmy's door, she waited a few minutes, but he did not come. So, she tried the door handle and popped her head around the corner, finding him sitting at the table in the comfort of his beer cans, taking another long deep swig.

"Lucy," he said with no surprise or care for the world.

"Hello, Jimmy. I did knock."

"Did Angus send ye?" he asked with disapproval in his voice.

"No, Jimmy. I came to check on you. Please look at me," she said, briefly touching his arm before taking a seat at the table. "If you want someone to talk to in confidence, I can put you in touch with Victim Support. They are good listeners," she said.

"Na, A' don't want help," he said with a haunted, hopeless expression as his shoulders sagged even more.

"Okay, Jimmy. I do understand, but know that I am here to help you. Would you like me to make you coffee or warm up some food?" she said.

"Na, thank ye. Please leave," he sighed heavily.

"Try to get some sleep, Jimmy. I will pop in again when I have an update for you," she said, feeling herself close to tears while walking out of his property.

* * *

Amy tried Angus again, but her call went to voicemail. She had not heard from him in hours and had arrived home after work to find some signed application forms on the kitchen table, a dirty plate on the sink and tell-tale signs that he had already started drinking. He texted her, saying he was going out for a few more beers down at the pub.

The two army officers found the despairing soldier at their local sitting in a corner with a half-empty pint.

"Come on, mate. We are here to take you home. Amy's worried about you," the officers said, and Angus sighed heavily and stood up. Without Amy's love and support, his life would have turned out so differently.

Angus was drunk, but certainly not to Jimmy's standards and it did not warrant his excuse for not answering Amy's calls.

"How dare you not answer my calls!" she fumed as Angus stood helplessly in the kitchen. His two mates caught in the middle, but there to support them both.

"I am sorry I missed your calls, but I have had a fucking shit day and do not need to talk about it now!" Angus said with a raised voice.

"But that is just it! You never talk to me about what you are going through! I have had enough!" she said with anger and stormed upstairs, slamming the bedroom door behind her.

Angus collapsed onto a kitchen chair and buried his head in his palms.

"I will make us some coffee," a mate said.

* * *

An hour and a half later, Angus had allowed his temper to cool down before taking a shower and walking into the bedroom.

"Aims, I am so sorry," he said, climbing into bed and taking her into his arms. As the stressful situation got too much, she started to cry.

"I am there for you, but you do not talk to me. We blame Jimmy for his drinking, but you are heading that way too," she said, with Angus sighing heavily.

"See, you are not talking to me," she said sadly.

"I do not want to burden you," he said with a tearless stare.

"You are suffering just as much as Jimmy. I wish you would talk to me," she said, sitting up and cupping his face. "Who better to talk to? Jimmy has pissed you off today, but we have to try and you need to get him cleaned up and looking more presentable."

"I know. I cannot understand what has happened to this payment," he said, pulling her back into his arms.

"Are you sure you went through all his drawers?" she asked, sliding her hand under his t-shirt.

"There was nothing, Aims. I am now doubting myself on whether it was even sent off," he said disappointedly.

"Look, luckily we are still within the time limit and I will follow it up. In the meantime, we need to discuss how to clear his debt," she said.

"Yes, I know. What did Lucy want?" he said.

"She offered to pop in and check on him," she said.

"She has taken this case to heart," he said.

"And that is why we cannot give up just yet," she said.

"What would I do without you?" he said, pulling off his t-shirt and taking her into his arms as she let out a soft gasp.

Their relationship was strained at times, but they truly did love each other.

CHAPTER TEN

Monday, 9th January 2012

C onstable Harris, working the extra hours, had gone straight into her early shifts, and worked between cells.

Receiving confirmation from forensics, Sergeant Wilson updated his officer on the continuing developments of the housebreaking and theft.

With his details already in the system, for theft and the use of cannabis, the shy seventeen-year-old youth was well known to the police. Billy Smith, who lived with his parents in Galashiels was arrested and taken to the cells in Selkirk.

Lucy read the database report and prepared herself for the latest arrest and interview.

"Why on earth would this reprobate be in Peebles? Why is he here?" she pondered to herself and let out an audible sigh.

Lucy and her sergeant pulled out a chair in the interview room while the youth and his appointed lawyer sat opposite. Lucy pressed the record button.

"This interview is being recorded and may be used as evidence if the case is brought to court. I am Constable Harris and this is Sergeant Wilson. We will be conducting the interview today. You are currently under caution, may I remind you, that you do not have to say anything, but it may harm your defence...," and Lucy finished reading Billy his rights.

"You have been arrested on suspicion of theft. In the early hours of January, the 1st 2012, between 12 a.m. and 1:00 a.m., we believe you broke into a property with the intension to steal," Constable Harris said.

"No comment!" Billy said, and Constable Harris continued, expecting to receive the no comment response.

"We believe you stole some army medals and fifty pounds in cash," Constable Harris said.

"No comment!" Billy said again and folded his hands over his chest, giving both officers a smug smile.

Constable Harris watched the suspect carefully, desperate for something she could exploit to gain a confession. But the suspect sat just as equally determined to give the police officers nothing that could be used against him.

"We found an injured, disabled man beaten up on the floor. Do you have anything to add to that? We are conducting a search of your property as we speak. Will we find anything?" Constable Harris asked, but Billy continued to give the no comment response to the questioning and an hour later, the officers decided enough was enough.

"If you continue to go no comment, the courts may draw their own inference as to what this means," Constable Harris said, and for the time being, Billy was remanded in custody while officers continued to conduct the search on his parents' home.

* * *

Lucy texted the group chat.

> *We have arrested someone, but it is not looking promising. I will keep you updated.*

Angus replied.

> *Thanks for letting us know.*

Lucy texted back.

> *I will pop in and update Jimmy after my shift today.*

Amy joined the conversation.

> *Thank you. Can we meet up for a coffee sometime?*

Lucy replied.

I would like that. I will phone you later.

* * *

16:45 hours - Lucy took the leftover home-cooked cottage pie she had put in the fridge earlier that day, before starting her shift. Her mother had suggested dropping it off for Jimmy.

Lucy knocked and found a very distressing, broken-hearted man sitting on the couch. Jimmy was staring out the window and had not heard Lucy come in. A sealed bottle of JD waited for him on his left side table.

"Oh. Hello, Jimmy. I did knock," she said, putting the casserole dish and her bag on the table.

"Oh...um...aye...Hello, Lucy," he said in a shaky voice, man-oeuvring his chair to climb on while also pulling at his shorts to try and disguise his stumps.

Lucy, not wanting him to feel any more uncomfortable than he already did, smiled, kindness showing in her face as she continued to look directly at him. "I have brought you some home-cooked food if you would like it," she said.

"Thank ye," he said, looking down with embarrassment, pulling at his shorts once more, not realising his actions were making it even more obvious.

"I have also come to update you on the case," she said, taking a seat.

"We have arrested someone and he is in custody while we conduct a search of his property. But I will be honest with you. It is not looking promising," she said, calmly, hoping he would not lash out at her.

"Bring that bastard to me. I'll get him to talk!" he shouted with the anger building in him like a rampant bushfire, slamming his left fist on the table.

"Please do not get angry, Jimmy. I will not give up that easily," she said, with him looking directly at her while she spoke, although awkward at times.

"I'm sorry," he said in a clumsy voice.

"I am sorry if I went behind your back and contacted Angus, so I want you to know that I have arranged to have a coffee with Amy," she said, cautiously, watching him squeezing his damaged hand and rubbing his wrist.

"I can appreciate the tension between you and Angus, but I would give Amy a chance. You are going to need your stitches out next week, and if you do not want Angus to help you, it will need to be one of us," she said, and stood up to leave.

"I just want to help you, Jimmy."

Twitching nervously, he sighed a heavy breath. "Lucy can ye stay for a while?"

He needed some company, even for a short while, anything to take his mind off the booze that was calling and pulling at his desire strings.

All Lucy wanted was to get home and get a good night's sleep, but hearing the sadness and genuine need in Jimmy's plea, she knew that if she declined him now, he would never accept the help he so desperately needed.

"I can stay a while if you would like that. I will heat your meal for you," she said, pleased by the pleasantries.

"Thank ye," he said, trying to sound confident.

Lucy placed the hot meal in front of him and took her seat at the table once more, allowing him to enjoy what was his first decent meal in an exceptionally long time.

He savoured every mouthful, with each ingredient a burst of flavour. He could not remember the last time he had eaten a home-cooked meal. It was certainly before his injuries, let alone something that did not taste like plastic.

There was no further mention of the case or Angus, and Jimmy, having spent the past five years living in voluntary seclusion from the public and society, found Lucy's presence over-whelming. Unable to find something to say, they sat in silence, something Lucy knew all too well, after suffering the loss of Tom. But in a strange, bizarre way, they found each other's silence comforting.

"Would you like a hot drink before I go home to Peppa Pig?" she said with laughter in her voice, finally breaking the silence.

"Please, hou is yer wee lassie?" he said.

"Molly is good, thank you for asking," she said with pure joy and pride and pulled a photo from her phone. The beautiful petite girl staring back at him was a mini version of Lucy.

"She is lovely," he said.

"She is the sweetest little thing and she demands her mother's attention when I get home," she said, sharing a soft smile.

"Jimmy, I have to go. Is there anything else you want me to do for you?" she asked, giving him his coffee.

"I'm guid," he said with a sense of loneliness slowly growing within.

"I will visit again, but try to get some rest," she smiled, briefly touching his left arm.

With his life revolved around anger, loneliness and sadness, always lost in that moment of torment and pain, Jimmy screamed in frustration and fist smacked his head again and again. Thump! Thump! Thump! he punched his stumps, before forcing his wheelchair back to the couch, his best friend luring him towards his reward.

CHAPTER ELEVEN

Constable Harris was looking forward to her up and coming days off, when her sergeant informed her the following morning that Billy Smith had been bailed with conditions. No medals were found in his property and there was no evidence to point otherwise.

Lucy felt so disappointed she had let Jimmy down. "Sarge, can we make a public appeal in the local paper and social media? These medals mean so much to Mr. Ferguson. Someone always knows something and at this stage, it's our last option."

"Okay Harris, but unless new evidence is found, this case moves to the bottom of the pile," Sergeant Wilson said.

* * *

Saturday, 14th January 2012

The tension between the two soldiers was dire, and Angus did not think that Jimmy could be brought back from the brink of no return. But he knew Jimmy needed help and maybe he too needed that push from someone like Lucy to now do something about it.

He had suffered, and still was suffering, not in the same physical way as Jimmy, but mentally. He was fighting a constant battle of anguish and torment.

Waking up early, Angus popped into the Penicuik Tesco's to buy much-needed groceries for Jimmy, although he refused to spend his hard-earned cash on buying him a bottle of whiskey. The atmosphere between them was civil, even a little friendlier and Jimmy was grateful for a greasy fry up to help his pounding head.

After clearing the dishes and getting him showered, Angus followed through with his direct order from a few nights before and wheeled Jimmy out to his car, despite his surge of anxiety and stress.

Finding a parking space in Peebles, Angus helped the recluse and forgotten man into his wheelchair, exposing him to the world's beady eyes.

"People are looking at the chair, whispering, judging me", he thought.

"Breathe," Angus said, giving him a reassuring grip on his shoulder as a group of teenagers walked past and Jimmy bowed his head, clasping his sweaty palms.

Choosing the first barbers they saw with the typical red and white pole outside, Angus tipped the wheelchair backward and pulled it up the two steps leading into it. Inside, artistic frescoes and ornate mirrors hung on the walls while a rock song played on the surround sound. With the place virtually empty, save for the three members of staff and one customer having his finishing touches done, Angus insisted that Jimmy get the full barber treatment. A friendly slim-built man showed Jimmy to his chair and Angus helped him into it.

Jimmy's thin and gaunt body looked lost and insignificant sitting on the chair. He felt like it would swallow him whole. He wished it would, so he would be gone forever. Staring in the mirror, lost in its reflection, Jimmy could no longer see that inquisitiveness and the desire for life. He had lost the fire in his eyes. All that remained was the deceiving hollow soul that reflected at him. The damaged body taking over his true self, Jimmy was just a shell of a man.

He lay back with his eyes closed, as each stroke of the razor blade revealed a smoother skin. His greasy, unkempt shoulder-length hair would soon be cut to military standard.

"You look human again. Should we have a coffee before heading home?" Angus said enthusiastically, giving his mate a pat on the back.

"I don't feel like it!" Jimmy said bluntly.

"Just a coffee?" Angus tried again.

"No, I want to go home!" Jimmy snapped.

You could cut the atmosphere with a knife. The tension between Jimmy and Angus was on the verge of conflict, putting everyone in the shop on tenterhooks. Angus threw his arms in the air in defeat. He was struggling to understand Jimmy's mood swings.

One moment, Jimmy seemed like he was beginning to realise he needed to change his life and would accept some help. The next, he was rock bottom and angrier than the previous outburst. There was no conversation on the way home and Angus was not going to stay any longer than he needed to. When they got home, Angus would have a coffee and try one last attempt to have some form of conversation with Jimmy.

* * *

"Lucy is concerned about your well-being, and knows how much your medals mean to you. Please, mate. I ask that you show the woman some respect. She just wants to help you," Angus said, sipping on his hot drink.

"Feck the medals!" Jimmy said, with a hard and pointed stare.

"Fuck you, Ferguson! We knew what we were signing up for! Fuck! Yes, you lost your legs, but what about our mates who never came home? You are one selfish bastard! You still have your senses about you. Is that not better than no legs? There are guys a hundred times worse off than you and they are living their lives, doing the most incredible things, climbing Everest, walking to the South Pole! Fuck, mate. You could be doing that! I would fucking carry you if I had to!" Angus said with a forceful and somewhat resigned tone to his voice.

Jimmy looked directly at Angus as he spoke. Though no emotion showed on his face, Jimmy was being ripped to shreds inside. He so desperately wanted to show emotion, apologise to

Angus, ask for help, but he could not. He did not know how. He wanted his friend back, but his friend would not want him back now.

"Do not be your own lethal weapon, mate! I have to go," Angus said, turning Jimmy's chair to face him.

"Ask me! Fucking ask me for help!" he said, shaking Jimmy's shoulders, but no plea came and it felt like there was an ocean of despair and sadness between them.

CHAPTER TWELVE

Wrapped up in her thick woollen jumper, oversized coat, scarf, and gloves, the bitterly chilly air still found its way through to Lucy's bones, making her way to the top of the high street to meet Amy for a coffee.

"Lucy," Amy said, standing up to greet her. She had arrived a few minutes earlier.

"I really appreciate you and Angus helping me," Lucy said as a waitress took their order for two coffees and scones.

"We should be the ones thanking you. It has been a very disruptive and painful five years for Angus. Losing Jimmy's friendship was a kick in the teeth and I think we have all needed someone like yourself to give us that extra push. I have tried for so long, but his stubbornness and the hurt he feels inside have stopped him," Amy said.

"It could not have been easy for you as his partner and seeing it in a different perspective," Lucy said, supportively.

"I keep postponing our wedding because Angus hopes Jimmy will make that call for help, but to be honest with you Lucy, I have had enough now. I want to get married," Amy said, taking another sip of her coffee.

"I met Angus at the barracks to get a better insight into Jimmy's life and I am sure he has kept you updated in the investigation," Lucy said.

"Seriously, Jimmy is the third person in our relationship! In the first few minutes of meeting Angus, Jimmy was mentioned in the conversation," Amy said.

"I cannot tell you how many times I have driven or walked past Jimmy's property and not seen or heard anything out of the ordinary. No neighbours have ever reported any disturbances and as a police officer who makes it my business to know the area and local community, I feel a sense of guilt," Lucy said.

"Angus was saying that you have the ability to calm Jimmy down in his state of anger outbursts?" Amy said.

"I think that deep down inside, Jimmy is crying out for help. But I think he is embarrassed and he has lost that sense of pride. Losing his legs and then his fiancée freaking at the sight of him, that is just unbelievable," Lucy said with a lump in her throat.

"Angus was furious, practically foaming at the mouth! Jimmy was fighting for his life and that stupid bitch could think of nothing more but herself. Jimmy blames Angus for her leaving him and I think that is unfair," Amy said.

"I think Jimmy carries a lot of sadness in him and he lives this isolated life. It must be daunting to suddenly have people around you and see Angus for the first time in five years, especially as Angus gets to move up the ranks. Jimmy must be feeling like he is drowning in a life of no return," Lucy said, sadly, as a hint of tears welled up in her eyes, and Amy moved her chair closer and put a supporting arm around her shoulder.

"I apologise for not passing on my condolences earlier. Angus has told me just how much you are suffering and I did not want to hurt you any more than you already do," Amy said, giving her a gentle squeeze.

"Please do not apologise, Amy, but know I can sympathise with Jimmy's pain of loss, loneliness, sadness, all the emotions he is feeling right now. And I really want to help him," she said confidently.

"Angus told me all about your brother. Tom was a very respectful and dignified soldier. You can be immensely proud of him," Amy said, giving Lucy a well-needed hug.

"Thank you. I miss him so much. I reassured my sergeant that I would be okay with this case, but I am finding it tough," Lucy said with a heavy sigh.

"Well, Angus and I are going to help you. I think we have our work cut out for us," Amy said, and they laughed in agreement.

The women finished their coffees and scones, keeping the conversation light-hearted. "Do you have any brothers or sisters?" Lucy asked.

"I have a younger sister, Emma. She is in her second year of university, studying business and economics. I was the first in our family to join the military," Amy said.

"What interested you in the military then?" Lucy asked.

"You have seen a man in uniform, haven't you? I was attracted immediately," Amy laughed.

"And Angus has a sister?" Lucy confirmed.

"Yes, Laura. She married an Australian guy and immigrated soon after the wedding. Angus had loads to deal with in that year of Jimmy's injuries," Amy said.

"It has certainly been a challenging five years for all of you," Lucy said.

"You have had a challenging time too, and we will do this again," Amy said, interested in knowing all about Molly, and insisting they all get together, including Jimmy, in the summer for lunch at their house.

Lucy had enjoyed and had needed the coffee invitation. Angus and Amy were there for support, whether it was for Jimmy or to have someone to talk to in her own moments of need.

CHAPTER THIRTEEN

Jimmy had reluctantly agreed to Amy picking him up and taking him to the surgery to have his stitches removed. He was finding the sudden interest in his miserable, wretched life extremely intimidating and although Lucy had shown him that she was someone who could be trusted, showing empathy towards him and allowing him moments of reassurance, he could not help but feel utterly drained of self-belief.

Amy arrived as a home delivery van was pulling out, and took the free parking space two doors down from Jimmy.

"Jimmy, mate. It is Amy," she called out. Finding the door unlocked, she had let herself in, placing her bag and the various application forms on the table.

"Amy," he said, awkwardly. She found him unpacking his latest supply of frozen meals and booze.

Of average height, she had deep brown hair that complimented her olive skin and she had a slim, but fit physique. "It's guid to meet ye," he said, while Amy naturally leaned in to hug him.

"Lovely, you are practically part of the family. Angus talks about you all the time," she said, helping him put a bottle of JD in a lower cupboard, despite feeling disappointed in what she saw. A touch of embarrassment filled Jimmy.

"Cheers for helping me today," he said, struggling with his jacket that had gotten caught on his chair. Amy offered to help him.

"Lovely, I am here to help and support you, but both you and Angus are stubborn mules and eventually, you will need to talk," she said, boldly, making Jimmy feel immense discomfort with the comment.

"Do not lecture me today!" he said abruptly.

"Jimmy, I have not come here to start a war with you and I will not tolerate your rudeness towards me!" she said angrily.

"I'm sorry, but my life has suddenly been invaded and I'm struggling to deal with that!" he finally managed, sinking down in his wheelchair.

"Jimmy, both Angus and I have been there. We understand the consequences of war, and so does Lucy for that matter! Angus is there for you. He always has been, but you need to make that decision and ask him for help. It has to come from you!" she said, directly, but just as quickly, assured him that she was someone who could be trusted.

"I have taken a day off to spend time with you today and go through your AFC application and various others. I can change your bed linen and take out your rubbish. I am here to help and now we need to go. It is a beautiful crispy day and I do not feel like losing my parking space. Besides, you live so close. The fresh air will do us both good," she said, giving him a look that suggested she would win the battle if he tried to argue otherwise.

* * *

Besides his life-changing injuries, the last time Jimmy required medical attention was during his earlier years in the army, when he tore open his leg and needed stitches.

The drab, almost lifeless look and feel of the ice-cold white walls and the worn-out visitor chairs that had seen better days, much like the patients that sat on them, wasn't helping Jimmy's anxiety. Never mind the fact that his appointment was running late, and the extra fifteen minutes he sat waiting sent a surge of apprehension and dread through his veins, that feeling of being exposed to the world's beady eyes.

"Jimmy Ferguson," the nurse called out and Amy placed the magazine back on the table and pushed him through to the treatment room.

"I'm sorry we're running late. It's just been one of those mornings," the friendly nurse said.

"That is okay. He needs his stitches out and we could do with some advice," Amy said, knowing that Jimmy wanted the appointment over as quickly as possible, but she was determined to speak her mind.

"Just looking at your records, you have not seen a doctor in some years," the nurse said.

"Aye, I was registered with Dr. Aiken at Cademuir Central Surgery," Jimmy said.

"Okay, that makes sense. I am guessing you were living in Penicuik at the time. Have you received any emotional support? Has it been a struggle for you to arrange a visit with your GP?" the nurse asked.

"They moved Jimmy into the next vacant property, here in Peebles. It was a turmoil of emotions for my fiancée and Jimmy after his injuries, but we are trying to sort things out now," Amy said.

"I can understand that it's not easy," the nurse said.

"Jimmy is in constant pain, but he is also drinking very heavily," Amy said, continuing to speak up and say it like it was.

"Jimmy, you are going to need a follow-up appointment with your GP and he'll be there to listen and advise on pain relief. There is also an ambulance service that can pick you up. Just ask at reception on your way out," the nurse said while preparing herself to remove the stitches and Amy helped to hold Jimmy's hand open.

Jimmy's cut to his hand had required eight stitches and the nurse, happy that the scar should heal properly, placed a sterile adhesive plaster on the clean wound and recommended that he keep it clean and replace the plaster for a few more days.

❋ ❋ ❋

Amy unlocked the front door to find a note that had been pushed through the letterbox.

Hello, Jimmy.

I am sorry I missed you, and hope everything went well with the nurse, and your hand is healing nicely. I am currently on late shifts and will try and pop in, but if you want to talk to me or you desperately need help with something, please phone me.

Take care,

Lucy

"Lucy has been incredible. The kindness she has shown you has been overwhelming, even for Angus and me," Amy said, placing a hand on his shoulder.

"Lovely, talk to me," she said, pulling a chair out after seeing the sudden deterioration in his demeanour.

"I don't need the sympathy card," he said in a blunt tone.

"Jimmy, you are going down that road again! We are going to argue and I am going to leave! Today needed to be done and you can get angry with me for speaking openly to the nurse, but I have shown respect and know that today has been difficult. It is daunting. I know, mate! Your hand and scar are looking good, but we will need to make that follow-up appointment. We have the pamphlets now for the ambulance service and at least we know there is help. Come on, lovely, I am going to make us a cup of coffee and we are going to talk," she said, pushing his chair to the couch to get comfortable.

"I find all of this...," he said in exasperation, holding his mug of coffee and needing to express his frustrations. With his left hand, he gave Amy his mug, freeing his hand to wave in anger, "an invasion of my privacy!"

"Jimmy, an incident took place and the police got involved! Plain and simple! Maybe if you locked your door, you would not be in this situation!" she said annoyingly.

"Ye don't...understand!" he said with anger.

"Understand what, mate? That you have lost your dignity? Your career? Everything you lived for...? I get it! Angus gets it! You feel betrayed and life is not worth living for! You want to die! You live in isolation and now your shameful life has been exposed to the world! I get it, mate!" she said.

"I don't know if I can do this," he said, swallowing hard and choking back his tears.

"You have to try, lovely. Maybe Angus and I could have done

more and should have pushed harder in trying to help you, but I must support Angus too. He did try his darn hardest to help you!" she said, wrapping her arms around his neck to comfort him.

"Lucy is an angel. This is probably a blessing in disguise, as she has pushed Angus and I to now do something about it," she said, with Jimmy sighing heavily.

"Come on, mate. Let us finish these forms. I have filled most of them in, but I need your national insurance number and Angus will need to take you for passport photos to send off for your blue badge and bus pass," she said, giving him an encouraging squeeze.

"Aye. Thank ye...I'm sorry," he said, accepting the constructive lecture from her.

Jimmy's disconnection with society prevented him from having the confidence to speak out and open up. So, Amy 'getting it' put the matter to rest and she spent the day completing the application forms, changing his linen, and taking out his rubbish, all the while keeping the conversation trivial and Jimmy off the booze, even if for a few hours.

❊ ❊ ❊

"Mum and Dad have said they will help," Angus said, showing utter relief in his face, as he walked back into the kitchen later that evening, after Amy got home.

"Oh, my love. That is a huge help. I have gone over the accounts and we could not have paid for both. We will pay them back," she said, going through Jimmy's debts and weighing up their options.

"They do not want to be paid back. Consider it a wedding gift," he said, caressing her fingers.

"Angus! Jimmy has to pay us back!" she said.

"I know that, but...," he hesitated.

"But what? Why the hesitation?" she asked.

"Amy we can at least be grateful that he did not overdraw on his current account or credit card. The debt is solely on credit cards that are so easily obtained through the post," he said.

"Why the sudden change of heart? You were pissed off with him and half of the wedding money is mine," she said, annoyingly.

"You would have done the same for Emma and I would not have questioned my half of the money!" he said, as the threats of an argument brewed within them.

"My sister would not have drunk herself into debt!" she said, and just as quickly regretted her words as Angus forcibly pushed the kitchen chair back and stood up and leaned hard on the table.

"That is not fair! I am pissed off with him! I am not saying that Jimmy should not pay us back, but..." he said, with Amy wrapping her arms around his waist.

"I am sorry. I do not want to argue with you," she said.

"I feel guilty, Aims. Think of it as guilt payment. I am as guilty as he is and it was my responsibility to send off all the forms and look after him!" he said.

"Are you saying that Jimmy gets off scot's free then?" she asked as they both sat down once more.

"No, I am not saying that at all. What I am saying is that I do not think he should pay the whole amount. As much as we are angry with him and I am furious, believe me, I have thought long and hard about this and it is not him. He would have done the same for me," he sighed with a heavy heart and Amy leaned in to kiss him.

"Do you want to talk to me?" she asked.

"Another day," he said, sadly. He knew that not having the ability to talk to his future wife was causing a strain on their relationship.

"Okay...," she said with heartache. She could only hope he would one day soon, before it was too late.

"I do love you, Aims."

"Well, I should hope so," she said, finding his lap a lot more comfortable than the hard kitchen chair.

"I will transfer the money from the wedding fund into our joint account and pay off the debt that way, as well as set up a standing order with a reasonable payable amount from Jimmy's account into ours," she said.

"Thank you for understanding," he said.

"Angus, I do understand and I regret what I said earlier. It is just that now we have been hit with the realisation of it all," she said.

CHAPTER FOURTEEN

Friday, 3rd February 2012

After Jimmy's appointment with the nurse and his damaged right hand healing nicely, he was yet to see his GP. Reluctance and anxiety pulled and pushed at the constant negativity in his head.

Angus did not bother knocking on Jimmy's door and walked in and found him slumped in his wheelchair, taking another swig of whiskey. Empty cans sat on his left side table, where he had climbed onto the couch the previous evening and drunk himself into oblivion. With his bloodshot, sunken eyes lost to another world, Jimmy sat there without any protest towards his surprising visit. Not up for a fight, Angus sighed heavily and took a seat on a dining room chair, burying his head in his hands.

A spasm struck and every muscle tightened, "Fuck!" Jimmy screamed in a long drawn out tone and dropped the half-drunk bottle of whiskey. Thump! Thump! Thump! he thumped his stumps, regardless of Angus' presence.

"Jimbo!" Angus said, jumping up to grab his left arm. "Fucking hit me! Hit me!" he barked his orders, allowing Jimmy to fight his frustrations and use him as a punching bag.

Taking each punch to the chest, inside, Angus was screaming with rage and resentment. The ravages of war had changed their lives forever.

Jimmy's left arm fell to his side with exhaustion and he hung his head in shame. "I'm tired, pal, mentally and physically," he said with a deep sense of sadness in his voice.

"Let me help you," Angus said in a shaky voice, placing his re-assuring hand on Jimmy's shoulder. He wanted to support and make Jimmy realise he was there for him.

"I'm in constant pain. Look at my fucked-up body! What woman will want this?" Jimmy said with some anger.

"There are guys you can talk to. I can get you help," Angus said, but Jimmy just sagged deeper into his chair.

"Mate, I am staying the night. Amy is spending the weekend with her sister," Angus said, supportively.

Although both men needed to say more, they could not and did not know how. So, Jimmy, deflated, battered and bruised, allowed Angus to help get him showered and dressed in some warm clothing. Not wanting the leftover meal from Lucy, he climbed into bed and turned onto his left side, away from Angus, sinking deeper into his saddened world of anguish.

Not knowing what more he could do, Angus wiped the sticky floor where the whiskey bottle had fallen and removed the empty cans. Taking Jimmy's rubbish out, Angus struggled to focus and control his own inner demons. All he wanted was his best friend back.

He texted Lucy. He needed someone at that moment to help him with Jimmy.

✳ ✳ ✳

Lucy's car's headlights caught Angus sitting up against Jimmy's front door, with his knees to his chest. He looked sad and lost.

"Angus, are you okay? Is Jimmy okay?" Lucy asked as he stood up.

"Thank you for coming. I know it is late. Amy is spending the weekend with her sister and I just needed someone to help me with Jimmy. Maybe seeing you will cheer him up," he said.

"Is everything okay?" she asked.

"Neither of us are doing too good tonight. No punch up, but he is in a bad way and it is scaring me."

"I am so sorry, Angus. It cannot be easy for you either," she said.

"I am spending the night and he is showered and in bed now, but he did not want to eat anything," he said.

"I can make us a hot drink and we can sit and talk to him? I am getting cold," she laughed, and they let themselves in.

"Jimmy," she said, gently touching his right shoulder, and he turned his head to look at her.

"Lucy," he said.

"I have not seen you since your hair cut. You look quite different. You look good, Jimmy," she said smiling.

"Lucy has come to have a coffee with us," Angus said as Jimmy manoeuvred himself to climb out of bed.

"Do not get up, Jimmy. We can have coffee in bed," she said, with him and Angus showing a hint of amusement, watching the faint blush fill her cheeks.

"I will make us some coffee," she said shyly.

"No, I insist you climb into bed with Jimmy," Angus said with a mischievous grin spreading across his face and Jimmy let out a slight laugh.

"Let me help you," she offered Jimmy, seeing him wincing as he moved to make space for her on the bed.

"Hou is Molly?" he asked.

"She has been making biscuits with my mother all afternoon," she smiled.

"Yer should be at home with her," he said, rubbing his damaged hand nervously, a habit that had started only a few weeks earlier.

"She will be just fine," she said, grateful for his concern and pulled a video clip from her phone to show him.

"Look at her cheeky little face," she said with happiness in her voice, as both watched the little girl covered in flour helping her nanna mix the biscuit dough and both her and Jimmy shared a soft laugh.

Angus had deliberately boiled the kettle for a second time, standing in the kitchen, listening to Lucy's kind and reassuring words towards Jimmy and hearing the brief moments of conversation between them and it gave him hope.

"Coffee for two," Angus said.

"Thank you," she said.

"Are there any updates in the investigation?" Angus asked making himself comfortable at the end of the bed.

"The appeal on social media has been shared a few hundred times, but there have been no further leads. I am not going to give up," she said.

"You have worked more than your fair share on this case. We are grateful," Angus said.

"I am sorry, Jimmy," she said, giving him a look of disappointment.

"Na, it's fine," he finally managed, shaking his head.

"Mate, we can always apply for a replacement and Lucy can provide us with a crime report," Angus said.

"Tonight is not the night to talk about it..." Lucy very quickly followed up with, sensing Jimmy's apprehension as he sat there quietly.

"You are right," Angus sighed, knowing better. "I apologise, mate. Maybe we can arrange to do something with Molly in the summer?" he said.

"She would love that. Maybe we can go to a botanical garden or something?" Lucy said, smiling at Jimmy.

It did not matter who mentioned Molly's name, Lucy's face always lit up and Jimmy could see just what a caring woman she was.

Lucy spent an hour with Jimmy and her and Angus had kept the conversation flowing and light-hearted.

"I am going to have to go," Lucy said, looking at Jimmy.

"Drive safely," Jimmy said, awkwardly. The rubbing of his damaged hand played a huge part in the evening's conversation between them. But again, both Angus and Lucy were surprised by his consideration.

"I will. Thank you Jimmy. And try to get some sleep now," she said.

"Mate, I am going to walk Lucy out," Angus said as Lucy hesitantly waited to see Jimmy get comfortable and once more, he turned away from them.

* * *

"Thank you for your help tonight," Angus said, walking Lucy back to her car.

"You are welcome. Maybe by the summer, we can convince him to get out more," she sighed.

"Again, tonight he had those moments of hope. I could hear him asking you about Molly," he said.

"We need to appreciate that this whole situation; seeing you, Amy and my constant reassuring, must be so daunting for him and we should not push him into doing anything he does not want to do," she said confidently.

Angus would need a little more convincing and reminded himself that Lucy was seeing things differently.

"Tonight, I allowed Jimmy to use me as a punching bag, but I was not angry with him. I was angry with the way our lives have turned out, and each punch, Lucy, was justified. Every single punch!" he said with heaviness in his voice.

"I think deep down inside he is calling out for help, and not having much of a good upbringing, and losing that sense of belonging, he is no doubt feeling pretty lost right now," she said sadly.

"Amy has been a godsend. Did you ever get help?" he said.

"Not really. I concentrated on looking after my mother and daughter, and losing myself in my job. What about you?" she said.

"Probably not as much as I should have, and I would say that my anger for him and his actions towards me is more than likely what kept me from falling apart in that first year," he said, rubbing his face in his hands.

"We have to help him," she said, swallowing hard.

"You have a very good heart, Lucy, and between the three of us, we will help him."

"Thank you," she said, wiping a tear.

"Are you going to be okay?" he asked.

"I am fine. It is just sad and I feel so sorry for him," she said.

CHAPTER FIFTEEN

19th February 2012

I t was a Sunday, one of Lucy's weekends off, and her turn to pop in and visit Jimmy. She decided to give her mother a break from Molly and take the little girl to meet him, as she felt confident in his slow progress and pleasantries in allowing her and Angus to visit him.

Arriving, Lucy heard shouting and a loud bang coming from inside, and burst in to find Jimmy punching his head and thumping his stumps in rage. Beside him was his overturned wheelchair and an empty whiskey bottle.

She had not been expecting to see Jimmy in this state, especially as he had been doing so well. Lucy was absolutely horrified, and Molly's eyes widened and she tucked her head into her mother's neck and squeezed tightly.

"Jimmy, stop! My daughter is here!" Lucy screamed over the little girl's tears.

Jimmy, shocked by the little girl's appearance and what she had just witnessed, stopped immediately and looked at Lucy with utter horror while also struggling to hold his balance, his anger, shamefulness, and embarrassment fighting against him.

"Please, Jimmy. I had no choice. My mother needed a break. Please do not scare her, otherwise I am out of here and I will not be back!" she said in a calm, but direct voice, kissing and comforting her baby girl.

With the remains of tears and confusion written all over her face, Molly turned her head and rested on her mother's shoulder, watching Jimmy closely.

"I am so sorry," he said with deep regret, bowing his head in shame.

"This is Molly," she said, lowering her daughter. But the little girl protested and grabbed her mother's leg in fear.

"I am...," he tried, but another spasm hit him and Lucy, leaving her daughter, reached out to help him while Molly watched his every move.

"Lean against me and breathe, Jimmy," she said with kindness in her voice, gently rubbing his arms.

Jimmy's saddened and deflated body sagged with each breath he took. "I'm so sorry...," he said as Lucy reached out for Molly's hand, and the little girl moved forward to stand next to her mother, still not taking her eyes off Jimmy.

"I'm in pain...," he said with his head bowed.

"I wish I could make life easier for you," she said sadly.

"I'm embarrassed Lucy...," he said with a heavy sigh, "...aboot everything," but he was struggling to find the words.

"I know you are, Jimmy," she said, continuing to sit on the floor and rub his arms gently, with Molly still watching his every move.

"We are going to stay and have lunch with you, but please talk to me, Jimmy," she said, moving out from behind him while one arm still supported his back.

"Please don't tell Angus," he asked.

"I promise, but you need to trust me and let me help you," she said. Jimmy took another deep breath as they both sat on the floor a while longer. Lucy's kindness helped him to relax, and with her help, he pulled himself onto the couch.

She gave him a glass of water and momentarily left him, taking her daughter with her. They collected Molly's bag from the car, and put down her blanket and toys to play with.

"How are you feeling?" she asked Jimmy, touching his left arm in a kind gesture and taking a seat beside him.

"Lucy, the floor is filthy!" he said, fidgeting with his sweaty palms.

"Jimmy, please do not feel embarrassed. Molly is going to be fine. I have been to worse homes and seen horrific things in terms of how people live. Your home is sad and neglected, through no choice of your own," she said, smiling and touching his left arm again.

"This is not me...," he said with the continued embarrassment in his voice.

"I know that. I saw it the night I found you. You do not need to explain anything to me Jimmy," she said.

"Why help me? I'm a wasted drunk," he said.

"Because, Jimmy, I hope that someone would have done the same for my brother if he had been in the same situation," she said.

"I'm so sorry for disrespecting yer brother and ye," he said, succumbing to tears and burying his face in his left hand.

Able to control her own emotions, Lucy wrapped her arms around his neck as he choked on his sobs and for a moment, he took comfort before he kindly pushed her away.

"Sorry," he said awkwardly, quickly managing to dismiss his reactions.

"Do not apologise, Jimmy. I will make us some lunch." She smiled and crouched down to give Molly a reassuring hug and kiss.

Jimmy sat there, dominated by a sense of profound sadness.

His shoulders leaned forward and fatigue was engraved on his worn-out face, staring beyond the little girl, lost to the unknown. Sensing his pain, Molly looked up as Jimmy bowed his head, not wanting to scare her and although still nervous by his actions earlier, she approached him with caution as her small hand reached out and touched his stump. Jimmy smiled as her tiny fingers gently stroked the track marks left by his scarred reminders.

Lucy, who had been making the sandwiches, glanced over to see the tender moment shared between them. Still feeling touched by Jimmy's apology, she smiled and joined them. Acting as if nothing had happened, she picked up her daughter and took a seat on his left side.

"Molly loves animals, don't we," she said playfully, with the little girl's squeals of carefree happiness filling Jimmy with a sense of hope, and he smiled.

"Do ye have any pets?" he asked nervously, not really knowing how to initiate a conversation with a woman.

"We had a family dog called Toffee growing up, but we had to put him down last year. He really was like a family member, and I would like to get her a puppy one day," she said with some regret and remorse in her voice, whilst nodding in Molly's direction.

"Lucy," he said, fidgeting with his hands. He felt sick to the stomach with nerves, and at times looked away. "I am truly sorry aboot earlier..." He took a long deep breath and trying again. "I'm sorry for everything. I am so sorry for yer brother's loss. I wish I had known him."

"Thank you, Jimmy. I accept your apology. Despite our moments, I want to help you, and I am glad to be here today. Are you ready for lunch?" She smiled, overcome with a slight flutter within.

"Aye, thank ye," he said, getting ready to climb off the couch.

"Sit comfortably. I will bring it to you," she said.

Sitting on the couch opposite him, Lucy had made some sandwiches with the leftovers she had been bringing him, and he enjoyed the tasteful filling while Lucy fed Molly her mashed vegetables in between her own mouthfuls.

"You've been truly kind, Lucy. Thank ye for lunch," he said with a genuine and heartfelt tone.

"It is my pleasure, Jimmy," she said, stroking Molly's hair nonchalantly. The sleeping little girl curled up on her mother's lap.

"Yer wee lassie is lovely."

"She is my life. The only good thing her father gave me." She felt comfortable to finally explain to him.

"His name is Owen, my childhood sweetheart. But when I fell pregnant, everything changed. He was not ready to settle down, and could not accept the changes to my body. He went out every night, drinking and getting home in the early hours of the morning wanting to have sex. My refusals meant being punched and beaten, putting myself and unborn baby at risk. I got a restraining order against him and my colleagues had my back. Today, he is in prison serving a three-year sentence for assault on another girl, and several drug-related crimes," she uttered with a mixture of anger at not recognising something that would almost be a daily occurrence in her job as a police-woman, as well as sadness at living with the situation for so long before finally acting.

"I'm sorry to hear that," he said, sharing a look of sadness. The 'old' Jimmy would have gotten up and comforted her, reassuring her that everything would be fine, and offering any help she might have needed.

But sitting there, he could not! Certainly not physically! And it hurt! Right down to the core of who he was and what he had become.

* * *

Jimmy had enjoyed Lucy's and Molly's company all afternoon, with their voices filling the black void that consumed his daily life. Now they were gone, and the silence was more over-powering than ever before. He was used to the ghostly eerie silence of being alone and having no one to talk to. Now he was left with a jarring stab to the heart.

Lucy's sweet floral fragrance still lingered in the air like an aroma of freshness and goodness as Jimmy took another long deep breath. He was overcome by a desiring need.

Jimmy groaned.

What the fuck are you thinking, Ferguson? Look at
you! What woman wants your fucked-up body?

He loathed his deformed, wasted body. Thump! Thump! Thump! he thumped his stumps and fist smacked his pounding head, falling deeper into the dark endless hole, the hole to hell.

"Fucking piss off, all of you!"

"Stop! Do not do this anymore! I am tired!" Jimmy thought, and gave his already bloodied and bruised head one last fist smack. He took a long deep breath and lifted his head, only to stare hard at the drawer of memories.

With intense effort and every muscle in his body tightening, he climbed off the couch and dragged himself to the drawer. Shaking and sweating profusely, he fell back against the desk. He pulled at the drawer and opened it. His portrait photo lay on top. He stood tall, proud, and at attention in his neatly pressed uniform. The man that once was, was now no more. Jimmy picked up a photo of four men standing next to their armed vehicle, on the day of the incident.

There was a cloud of dust trailing behind the armed
vehicle as Corporal Jimmy Ferguson, Sergeant Nick
Taylor and two Junior Non-Commissioned Officers
from 2 SCOTS drove along the dry, dusty road, the full
force of the midday sun beating down on them as the
calls for backup echoed through their radios and US
Allies continued to come under fire in the distance. The

vehicle hit the IED with an exploding blast, throwing Jimmy in mid-air and hitting the ground hard.

Instinctively, a strong smell of burning fuel and human flesh filled the room and Jimmy's body shook uncontrollably, his muscles tightening with each spasm that hit him hard. The memories of that fateful day engulfed every emotion of Jimmy's mind, body, and soul, and he sobbed hard and long in need for Angus' friendship once more.

* * *

Curled up on the couch with Amy, Angus received the call for help just after 21:00 hours. Shocked by the caller ID, he was hesitant to answer, his own voice shaky and filled with apprehension.

He found Jimmy sitting on the floor, slumped against the desk. His army memories scattered around him with the photo of the day they passed out in his hand. His red-rimmed, swollen, watery eyes, hauntingly stared back at Angus.

Angus sat down next to him on the floor. Pulling his legs up to his chest, his own shoulders slumped forward, and the sadness filled his body with every breath he took. For what felt like an eternity, the two soldiers sat in silence, lost in their thoughts.

"That was a good day," Angus said with a sad exhalation.

"Ye are a guid friend pal," Jimmy said, taking a deep breath.

"I am your best friend! I have always been your best friend!" Angus said.

"I couldn't save them," Jimmy said, fighting to keep the tears at bay.

"Mate, no one could have saved them. You did your job and you did everything you could!" Angus said.

"I wish it had been me," Jimmy winced in agony.

Angus swallowed hard. What about his feelings and his loss? His world collapsed too! Losing Jimmy's friendship had been a kick in the teeth.

"You need help. You need to meet other guys who are suffering the same traumatic pain," Angus said.

Knowing and second-guessing what Jimmy was thinking, he pleaded, "Don't, mate!" while grasping his shoulders. "Let me help you! Please!"

Jimmy knew deep down in every fibre of his being that he needed help. Deep within, he had always known. But he was embarrassed, unsure, unready, and ashamed to admit it. He could not carry on the way he was for very much longer. He would die!

He pushed that deep dark thought to the back of his deeply tinged mind, an option he thought that would always remain open to him. He could still get his wish. Jimmy thought of

Molly and her tiny fingers stroking his scarred stumps, and how she had put her trust in him not to lash out at her. He was a melting pot of contradictions, anguish, hurt, and now hope.

"Come on, mate. It is time to accept some help. Amy and I are there for you, and Lucy is genuinely concerned about your well-being. I should still have my key, but I think Amy and Lucy should have one too. This would be for no other reason, but your own safety, in case you fall and we cannot get in," Angus said as Jimmy choked on his breaths and fought back the tears. He finally accepted defeat.

❊ ❊ ❊

Jimmy could not promise anything to Angus, but would at least try. He needed his friend back. So, between the three of them, they decided that Jimmy had to see at least one of them every day. Getting a key made for each of them at least assured them they could lock the door behind them. And so, between shifts, they popped in. Jimmy kept up with his hygiene and ate the meals Lucy brought him. However, conversations were always hard to come by, and he was embarrassed and ashamed by his appearance, making him feel very wary and aware of himself, as conflicting emotions often left him wondering –

What is she playing at? She is only feeling sorry for me!

CHAPTER SIXTEEN

*Saturday, 10th March 2012 – Two months
since the housebreaking*

C heers erupted as the lively pub belted out the National
Anthem captivating the rugby spirit of the Aviva Sta-
dium, where Scotland's Lock powered through to score
the try. Scotland's Brave determined to fight to the end and
not lose hope in their Six Nations dreams.

Drowning their sorrows in a flowing supply of booze, the loud
inebriated groups sought solace at the bottom of each con-
secutive pint glass.

"Gezz, what the fuck is your problem mate!? Why you spilling
drinks on me!?" the heavyweight twenty-something-year-old
male said.

"Bugger, pal. It wasn't mah fault!" the middle-aged regular
said.

"You got a problem with me!? You wanna fight!?" the heavy-
weight jabbed, with his chest pumped.

"Just feck off...!" the regular said.

"I'm asking ya, do ya wanna fight!? I'll smack ya!?" the smart-arse provoked.

"Feckin piss off!" the regular said, pushing his arm away, but the oversized male head-locked and pulled him to the ground.

Responding to a 999 call on Northgate street, it was evident that the altercation between the fuelled drunks had escalated out of control.

Constable Harris and her male colleagues scrambled to help break up the fight between the groups of shouting, shoving and pushing culprits.

While the male officers grappled with the wrestling heavy-weight, Lucy dealt with the pub's regular who had been punched to the ground and briefly knocked out.

"You have a nasty gash on your head. Just stay down. The ambulance is coming," Constable Harris said.

"Th' pumpin' prick assaulted ma!" the middle-aged male coughed, trying to force himself up.

"Mate, you're spitting blood all over the place. Sit down," Sergeant Wilson said, assisting Lucy.

"Ah will pumpin' murdurr him!" he spluttered.

"Listen, don't make threats!" the sergeant said.

"He hasn't done anything! Let him go...!" a drunken worse for wear woman whined hopelessly, trying to free the heavy-weight.

"You tell them, babe!" the boyfriend encouraged as police escorted him to the ASB van.

"Fucking let him go!" the girlfriend screeched and whacked an officer with her bag.

"Ouch! You stupid bitch!" she shouted as Lucy and another female officer pulled the woman away.

"Just calm down and stop whinging. I did not hurt you!" Constable Harris said as the woman fought against the officers and tripped on her heels.

"What was it, just a fist?" the sergeant asked while the injured man was being cared for in the back of the ambulance.

"Wis skelp wi' a pint," the bloodied man slurred.

"What glassed?" Sergeant Wilson asked.

"Aye, git smacked in th' coupon. Ah will pumpin' murdurr him!" he said.

"Mate, carry on like that and you will get yourself arrested.

Do you know him?" the sergeant continued to question the injured man.

"Na, pal. Whit urr ye aff tae dae aboot it? Ah, will git him 'n' ah will scar him lik' he's ne'er bin scarred afore!" The injured man was irritated and clearly showed intent on retribution.

"Fucking let me go!" the foul-mouthed woman wailed.

"Stop swearing and making threats. Do you want to be locked up?" Constable Harris said, restraining the woman.

"Fuck off, you stupid bitch!" the girlfriend sniggered.

"Come on. Swear at us again! Swear at me one more time and I will public disorder you!" Constable Harris said.

Arching her neck backward, the woman grunted and gurked, spitting the saliva at Lucy.

"Bitch!" she laughed.

"Bloody hell. You vile, disgusting girl! That is it. You're nicked!" Constable Harris said, cuffing her.

Sergeant Wilson also made the decision to arrest the victim who was clearly hell-bent on revenge.

Pub fight brawls and drunken behaviour always kept Lucy and her colleagues busy. People worked hard and then played hard. They socialised and enjoyed a drink and followed up with a good punch up afterward.

* * *

Back at her desk, a message had been left for Lucy to phone a Corporal Mackey from Portsmouth with regards to the appeal, leaving Lucy quite shocked as the appeal had been shared over a thousand times, but no one had contacted the station with new information. Dialling the mobile number, a woman's voice answered.

"Hello?"

"Good afternoon. I am Constable Harris from Police Scotland in Peebles. I have been left a message to call you with regards to the appeal on social media for any information on some stolen military medals," Lucy said.

"Yes, the appeal was forwarded onto me. It's my father. His own medals were stolen on Christmas Day, and has insisted on speaking to you. I'll pass you over," the woman said, before a proud, elderly man's voice was heard.

"...my home was burgled on Christmas Day. We were out with the family. The house was in shambles. Every room had been turned inside out, but after hours, even days of going through and sorting everything back to some form of normality, we found nothing other than my medals and a bracelet belonging to my late wife missing. It was almost like they knew exactly what they were looking for," the corporal said confidently.

"Mr. Ferguson is already in a desperate situation with his

medals having been stolen. This is not helping matters," Lucy said.

"They're invaluable. You can't put a price on them. They keep the memories alive for them and for us. Medals are stolen all the time and worn at certain momentous events by Walter Mittys, portraying this colourful army career when they don't even know what a battlefield looks like! It's an insult to all who have fought and died serving their country," the corporal told Lucy with anger in his voice.

"There have been several similar burglaries reported, all with one intention in mind; military medals!" he said, offering his opinion.

Before ending the call, Corporal Mackey gave his best wishes to Jimmy and offered any help he could give. He personally knew what Jimmy was going through.

The phone call had been a glimmer of hope. Not the full result Lucy wanted, but certainly a step forward in the right direction, and she decided to give Hampshire Police a courtesy call and have a chat.

Lucy texted the group chat.

Just to say that I had a call earlier with regards to the appeal on social media. An elderly veteran had his own medals stolen on Christmas day. This is not the full result I was looking for, but at least another step in the investigation.

Angus replied

*Thanks, Lucy. At least the appeal is being shared. I
am seeing Jimmy later and will update him.*

CHAPTER SEVENTEEN

Saturday, 14th April 2012

J immy had been up for hours. Not even total exhaustion could block out the constant nightmares. He had sat in his chair, staring out the window, and listening to the birds welcoming the start of a new day. It was a bright, cloudless mid-April day, though the sunlight beaming through the dirty greasy window had a feeling of strangeness to it, like a layer of tinted filtering had been added to the sky.

He was at least grateful for the bright day, as it meant less effort and struggle getting dressed. He'd wear just a pair of shorts and a t-shirt, although he was now regretting agreeing with Angus to spend the afternoon having lunch with him and Amy at their home. He wished he could just stay at home and be left alone.

He had not seen Lucy in over a week, as it had been agreed that Angus would pop in and see him every other day. Both men needed to build and repair their brotherly bond. In the meantime, Angus had organised a psychiatric evaluation for Jimmy, and was waiting to hear back from them.

Angus was pleasantly surprised to see that Jimmy had made some effort, but he also knew that today, Jimmy's highly-strung senses would be in full overload, not just because of seeing him and Amy together, but also the fact that he was getting out. And although he had not forcefully pressured Jimmy into having lunch with them, he had pleaded with him.

"Lucy will meet us there," Angus said while helping to lift him into the front seat. An acceleration of anxiety and nerves flashed across Jimmy's face. His vulnerability would be exposed to unfamiliar surroundings.

Even being around Angus made him nervous at times. He had become a total stranger to him.

Pulling into the driveway, Jimmy was on edge. The Afghan farmer stood beside his jalopy broken-down vehicle, posing as a decoy. "Jimbo," the muffled, ringing sound reverberated through the explosions and gunfire.

"Lovely, breathe. You are in a safe place," the calm voice brought him back from the disturbing vivid memory as he sagged into the car seat.

"Everything is okay, mate," Angus said.

"Breathe, lovely," Amy said.

"I'm guid," a drained Jimmy said.

"We will get you something to drink and you can enjoy the

sunshine and wait for Lucy to arrive," Amy said.

"Aye. It's guid to be here, but don't worry Lucy about this," Jimmy said, getting comfortable in his chair.

"No, lovely. We will not. I apologise, we do not have the most wheelchair friendliest of homes," Amy said as Angus tipped the chair and up the three steps leading inside.

Angus and Amy's home was beautifully decorated and had a feeling of carefree and ease to it. Modern art filled the walls. Photos of their travels and army lives were proudly displayed on coffee tables, sideboards and the mantel top. Jimmy felt a sting of embarrassment, knowing that he lived in a cesspit rather than a home. His stomach did triple somersaults while his congested mind of thoughts filled him with utter dread.

What will Lucy think? She will take Molly to the doctor, and have her checked for fleas and lice! She will stop visiting – she is already making excuses for not visiting! His demons were at full steam and at loggerheads with his sanity.

Jimmy really was trying hard, and although he declined the offer for a beer and opted rather for a cool drink, the thirst for something stronger and in the comfort of his own cesspit teased his taste buds.

Angus and Amy left him breathing in the warmth of the spring sun that soaked into his body and every muscle that creaked.

"Look who is here," Angus said joyfully, coming out with Molly in his arms. The little girl giggled with his playful tickles as a look of surprise filled her face at seeing Jimmy, and although still wary of his presence, her face was filled with kindness towards him.

"Hello, Lucy," Jimmy said as she followed Angus out. With her hair tied up in a ponytail, and wearing a comfortable floral blouse and jeans, Lucy's clothing reflected her casual, down to earth personality.

"Hello, Jimmy. I am so glad you came. It is so good to see you out," she said with genuine admiration in her eyes.

"Lucy, would you like a glass of wine? I am on driving duties, so we can always arrange to drop off your car," Amy said.

"I do not drink, but I will have what Jimmy's having," Lucy said happily, knowing that he had been controlling his drinking since their afternoon lunch together.

Lucy's admission of being a teetotaller took Jimmy by surprise, making him sit up and take notice both physically and mentally. It gave him another reason to feel comfortable and safe around her.

"Do you want a top-up?" Lucy asked, sub-consciously touching Jimmy's left arm before taking his empty glass.

"Aye. Cheers," he said, and shared a brief smile before she followed Amy back inside, leaving Molly engrossed in Angus' playfulness.

"It is so nice to see Jimmy out," Lucy said, helping Amy with the drinks.

"You have certainly had an influence on him. He is a different man compared to whom Angus described all those weeks ago. And he certainly washes up well," Amy said, nudging her gently.

"Why don't you go keep him company? We have another hour before lunch is ready," she said.

"Do you need any help with anything?" Lucy asked.

"No, not at all. Everything is under control. I'll join you shortly," Amy said, almost pushing her out the kitchen gently.

Sitting and watching Angus playfully chasing Molly around the garden, and hearing her joyful giggles sent Jimmy in a whirlwind of emotions. He felt a sense of hope for the future and getting his life back to some form of normality. But also, he felt a deep sense of yearning and hunger for affection.

Jimmy and Lucy smiled as she handed him his cold drink and took a chair beside him on his left side.

"Molly is such a happy wee lassie," he said as the little girl, now interested in her bottle of juice, waddled over to her mother who picked her up. Molly happily popped the bottle into her mouth and kept her eyes on Jimmy.

"She has a peaceful happiness about her," Lucy said, giving her daughter a kiss and doting on her baby girl.

Walking into the kitchen to get himself another beer, both

Angus and Amy listened to Jimmy conversing with Lucy, and although she had kept most of it flowing, they were surprised by his efforts.

"She might just be his saving grace," Amy said, leaning in to kiss him before taking another bowl of crisps, and they joined their guests outside, catching the remains of Jimmy's shaky laughs.

"Who's that?" Lucy asked Molly in a child-like voice, pointing to Jimmy and smiled at him.

Pulling her bottle from her mouth and making a popping sound in the process, "Jimmy," she said sweetly, giving him the cutest of smiles.

Jimmy stretched across gently, taking her little hand in his and kissed it lightly, their eyes sharing a twinkle of playfulness.

Choking back the tears and grateful she could hide behind her shades, Lucy would always cherish and hold the memory close as an adrenaline and surge of warmth so strange and overwhelming filled her veins.

Why am I feeling like this? Am I falling for Jimmy?

Angus and Amy shared a smile with her. Neither of them expected the tender moment just shared.

Amy had put up a delicious spread, and Jimmy had thoroughly enjoyed his meal, grateful that no knife was required and as such, no extra help was needed. He was embarrassed enough. He had managed to put the flashback behind him and enjoy the day's hospitality, but now as Angus and Amy sat cosy on the couch and holding hands, Lucy and Molly opposite, he felt separated and disconnected. He felt alone, and was overcome with a deep sense of loneliness.

He listened, trying to show interest and enthusiasm in Angus and Amy's stories about their travels. He had tried hard all day. But hearing of the places they had always discussed and planned to visit together as friends, and now that it wasn't going to happen, hit Jimmy hard and drained every ounce of energy out of him as not to physically lash out.

He watched as Angus and Amy's fingers intertwined, the tender strokes they made, and the passionate glances they shared and the love for one another. In a brief second, Jimmy glanced at Lucy. Their eyes locked, and they were both overwhelmed with a sense of longing.

With his hands clasped tightly and cold sweat glistening on his furrowed brow, the tiredness and sadness slowly dragged Jimmy down, and he bowed his head.

"Can I go home?" he asked.

Angus swallowed hard at seeing Jimmy's look of soul-deep sorrow, the etchings of age and pain upon his friend's face.

❋ ❋ ❋

Amy and Angus dropped Jimmy off soon after 17:25 hours, but

despite the encouragement and reassurance that they were there to help and support him, all Jimmy wanted was to be left alone. Angus and Amy respected his wishes, although they knew that after they left, he would be back on the booze.

Thump! Thump! Thump! he thumped his stumps as his face received another strike and Jimmy slammed his fist on the dining room table.

The temptation had got the better of him and he took another swig of whiskey.

*　*　*

Kneeling beside the bath, mother and daughter shared a fit of giggles as Lucy blew another soapy bubble and Molly's little claps popped them in return. She had decided to give Molly an early bath, and spend the last few hours of her days off with her precious little girl.

Lucy had thoroughly enjoyed her day and could not remember the last time she had been invited out. Seeing Jimmy and Molly's touching moment had left a powerful mix of emotions inside her. The euphoria was so intense, she ached deep down in her gut. The uncertainties and fear of letting her guard down sent thunderstorms of breaking waves crashing down on her.

*　*　*

20:45 hours and Angus and Amy had also decided to have an

early night. Jimmy's gradual decline had affected Angus and he had not been up for much conversation.

Cuddled up in bed, they had chosen something on TV, but neither were paying much attention and both were lost in their thoughts.

"We need to get Jimmy to meet other guys," she said, caressing his bare chest.

"I know," he sighed heavily.

"It would be good for you too. Angus, hear me out," she said, sitting up on her haunches. "You do not talk to me, but we both know you need to get some help."

"Aims, I have a job to do. I cannot allow my emotions to cloud my judgement," he said.

"We have started the process of organising psych therapy, but we could all benefit from this and I think talk therapy between the four of us would be good too," she said.

"What if I cannot handle what Jimmy's going through? Or if you want me to sit down with you afterward and pour my heart out? I do not know if I can do that," he said.

"I love you, but I do not know how much more I can take. You are slowly pushing me away. I need the help too," she said, wiping her tears as Angus pushed himself up and took her into his arms.

"Aims, I am nervous and I am scared," he said, kissing her lips lightly.

"That is the first time you have been honest and open about your feelings. Allow me to carry some of the burdens. There is nothing better than talking about it, especially to someone who understands it," she said.

"I have never shed a tear," he said.

"I know and I am not expecting you or Jimmy to sit down after each session or talk therapy and pour your hearts out. We have our discussions together and we leave it at that. Unless, you or Jimmy needs to talk about it further," she said.

"I need to think about it," he said.

"That is all I am asking," she sniffed.

CHAPTER EIGHTEEN

Wednesday, 9th May 2012

After lunch with Angus and Amy, Jimmy very quickly slipped back into his old habits of drinking and lack of hygiene.

Amy took the initiative and made enquiries with different organisations in getting Jimmy out and meeting other guys in the same situation as him. While exploring her options, she came across an upcoming exhibition and event in London for a group of wounded veterans. The guest speaker was to be a wounded veteran who had already conquered the South Pole, as well as numerous other enduring challenges that most able people would no doubt have struggled with, and Amy went ahead and bought Angus and Jimmy tickets.

The unexpected arrangements had left Jimmy's mouth dry, and the colour drained from his face as the thought of travelling all the way down to London and being around and seeing other veterans, other people for that matter, made his anxiety levels rocket. However, instead of allowing it to drag him down, he reminded himself that he needed Angus' support, and he accepted his invitation, albeit reluctantly.

Spending the night at Jimmy's, Angus had become accustomed to sleeping on the floor. Though being in the army, you learned to get shut-eye at any time of day, and in any position and situation.

Jimmy and Angus would catch the 9:34 X62 bus from Peebles to Edinburgh, and arrive with more than enough time for Angus and Jimmy to make their way down to Edinburgh Waverley station and catch their train at 11:30.

"A few of the guys are also going," Angus said as the bus drove through Penicuik.

"Still looks the same," Jimmy said, trying to sound optimistic and nonchalant at seeing the barracks for the first time in five years. The distinctive brick buildings, the recognisable accommodation sections, the guard on duty, all reminded him of the life he once had and Angus could see the heartache he was feeling inside. He

too wished Jimmy had his army life back, serving alongside him, together where they belonged.

Piling Jimmy's lap with his bag and the two suits in their protective covers, Angus pulled along his own suitcase whilst manoeuvring Jimmy's chair through the hustle and bustle of Edinburgh's streets towards the station.

Not needing to organise assistance before, Angus made enquiries at the information desk and was pointed in the right direction, and they popped into M&S with time to waste and buy a meal deal.

Wanting to feel more comfortable for the four-hour journey, Jimmy insisted on climbing out of his wheelchair and onto one of the reserved seats.

Despite knowing that he was nervous and anxious about the whole experience, Angus was pleased with Jimmy's efforts in trying to enjoy the trip. Folding the wheelchair and placing their bags in the extra space that having a wheelchair provided, Angus took his own seat on the aisle.

"Mate, I should travel with you more often," he said.

"Aye. It certainly has its advantages," Jimmy said, laughing and feeling slightly more at ease as he plugged his mobile charger into the socket, and Angus helped peel open their sandwiches and opened their soft drinks.

As the train pulled out of Waverley station, leaving behind the historic dark stone buildings, it slowly picked up speed, passing through seaside towns and rugged coastlines as Jimmy and Angus sat back and admired the panoramic vistas of the rolling hills and castle ruins. Scotland would always be their home.

Jimmy had just finished the first half of his sandwich when his phone lit up and Lucy's name came up on the screen.

Hi, Jimmy. I hope you have a wonderful time with
Angus and enjoy the dinner. I can't wait to hear
all about it when you get back. Take care.

Thanks, Lucy. Have a lovely day with Molly.

"Lucy is a really kind woman," Angus said. No sooner after taking his last mouthful, Jimmy's phone lit up again.

"I don't know how to react around her," Jimmy sighed, showing Angus the photo of Molly in her summer hat playing in the garden.

"You should just be yourself. Lucy is the most down to earth person I have met and she likes you, mate," Angus said with Jimmy leaving the suggestion hanging as the train pulled into Newcastle station.

Watching the countryside rush by, they were both happy to sit back and enjoy the view of the beautiful town of Durham and its notorious cathedral in its highly strategic position over the River Wear, and passing through towns and cities filled with their own historic secrets.

About to make a comment, Jimmy looked back at Angus, only to see he had dozed off. And not able to settle and shut-eye himself, desperately needing a slash, he decided to log onto the free wi-fi and look at the different organisations out there helping veterans, a process he had blocked and avoided since his injuries.

Reading the individual testimonies of veterans going through their own struggles, both physically and mentally and missing that competitiveness and camaraderie of being part of a team all rang true with Jimmy. But whereas they had benefited from seeking help and support, Jimmy's drinking and self-rejection had prevented him from ever seeking the help he so desperately needed.

He read about the achievements of the extraordinary veteran who would be speaking at the dinner, how he spent months and even years preparing himself physically and mentally to take on various gruelling challenges, only then to find himself needing to pull out halfway through the challenge in fear of further injury to himself, but then coming back even more determined and stronger than before, and completing the challenge. With Angus sleeping through the various stations, Jimmy had sat watching the green valleys of England passing by, his thoughts often trailing towards Lucy.

She is kind and down to earth, and maybe I do feel something for her, but she deserves more. Someone who could look after her.

"Sorry, mate. I must have dozed off. Where are we?" Angus said, rubbing his face in the palms of his hands.

"We're here, pal," Jimmy said as the train chugged along the outskirts of Kings Cross.

Jimmy felt relieved to finally arrive as the aches and pains of sitting in one position had slowly taken their toll on his body.

With the station assistance already waiting for them, they waited for the other passengers to disembark before once more, Angus piled Jimmy's lap and pulled his suitcase behind him towards the taxi pick up line.

It was not long before a black cab pulled up and Angus pushed Jimmy up the ramp and took a seat beside him.

"Park Plaza Riverbank please, mate," Angus said to the cab driver.

With years of knowledge and experience, the cab driver sliced through the chaotic streets of London's rush hour traffic. The bright early evening sun peeked through the breaks where skyscrapers towered towards the sky.

Not being to London in many years, Jimmy and Angus took in their surroundings of a city that was a constant development of movement and growth.

Situated on the South Bank of the River Thames, overlooking Westminster, the hotel was a modern-looking multi-floor hotel with a sleek modern and chic décor. A huge screen display of striking purple LED lighting filled a wall where escalators ascended to higher existences and expectations, leaving both Jimmy and Angus in awe of the hotel's modernisation of the future world.

"Welcome to the Park Plaza," the friendly receptionist said.

"Afternoon. We have a reservation under Brown," Angus said while the young woman typed in the details.

"For two nights?" she confirmed.

"Yes, we are here for the charity event tomorrow evening,"

Angus said.

"That's right and I am to give you this," she said, handing Angus an envelope.

"Thank you," Angus said, giving it to Jimmy.

"It's a welcoming letter for all who are staying at the hotel and are attending the event," she said.

"That is great," Angus said.

"You'll be in room 545 on the 5th floor and these are complimentary passes for the executive lounge on the 15th floor. The views are amazing," she said in her continued friendly manner.

"We will definitely go up and have a look," Angus said, sharing a friendly laugh with the young receptionist.

"Daniel will help you with your bags and should you need anything please let us know," the woman said, before Daniel took hold of the bags and they headed towards the lifts.

With its smart LED televisions, universal power sockets and free wi-fi, the ultra-sleek spacious rooms and fully tiled bathrooms complimented the chic décor throughout the hotel.

"I hope the room will be comfortable for you," Daniel said, showing them the accessible bathroom.

"This is great. Thank ye, Daniel," Jimmy said, feeling relieved by the accessible facilities, and grateful for Amy's consideration.

"Mate, there is no pressure to fill the hours exploring the city streets tonight or tomorrow morning," Angus said, finding the tea and coffee hidden away in the glossy stylish dresser as both men made themselves comfortable on their beds.

"Cheers, pal. I appreciate that," Jimmy said, attempting to open the envelope, but his damaged hand proving useless.

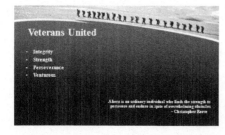

Dear Jimmy and Angus,

We are delighted to welcome you both to our annual charity event in supporting our veterans.

David served as a Royal Marine for eight years, before being medically discharged from the army with sustainable injuries to his shoulder and leg.

Unable to cope with the sudden change of lifestyle, he woke up one morning and walked away from his family, leaving his parents in desperate concern for his wellbeing.

For two years, David was homeless, sleeping in hazardous conditions and searching in rubbish bins for his next meal.

The little money he was given, David spent on cheap cans of beer, drinking his already spiraling out of control life into oblivion.

"You don't care after a while. You just drink and drink."

One evening, while seeking shelter in a doorway, a week before Christmas, David was brutally attacked and left for dead. His last few belongings were stolen. However, through the support of the emergency services, David was put in touch with Veterans United.

Today, David is back with his family and has completed a course that helps ex-service personnel find employment and has recognised his new skills.

"Without Veterans United, I doubt I would be alive today."

David's story is just one of many successful case studies that Veterans United has been involved in and through the continued support we receive from generous donations, we will continue to help and encourage all veterans to live an independent life outside the army.

I look forward to seeing you at the dinner and catching up.

Kind Regards,

Mike Tully

Date: Thursday 10th May 2012

Venue: Park Plaza Riverside Hotel – Thames Suite, 1st Floor
Time: 18:30 – Champagne Reception

* * *

Jimmy raised his eyebrows and shook his head. David's story was just another reason why he knew he needed to get his life back in order. He was not the only one out there struggling with their demons.

"Mate, Mike is speaking tomorrow," he said with Angus reading the letter. And like Jimmy, Angus knew that veterans were out there fighting their inner demons, too proud to ask for help.

"Mate, I have not been to one of these either," Angus said.

* * *

Both exhausted from the long journey, the men showered and freshened up. They decided to make use of the complimentary passes to the executive lounge, and take in the spectacular views for themselves before heading to a nearby pub Angus had found on Google.

The lift opened on the 15th floor, greeted by the same LED feature wall and escalators that had finally found their destination. Just like the receptionist had said, the views of Westminster overlooking the river Thames were breath-taking.

Other than Angus and Jimmy, the room was filled with its city bankers and high-flyers, all prepared to negotiate a good deal.

They found a table with a perfect eye view of River Thames snaking its way up to the horizon with countless centuries of history on either side of it; the Houses of Parliament with the infamous London Eye behind.

The whole experience of travelling down to London and the anxiety of tomorrow's event had shown itself through Jimmy's body language and Angus was prepared to accept that he might need a stiff drink.

"Mate, would you like a whiskey?" Angus asked, coming straight out and asking him and taking Jimmy by surprise.

Jimmy had not had a drink in days, but the craving consumed his every waking moment and being thrown out of his comfort zone and into a tough, harsh world that could not give a shit, made those temptations even more mouth-watering.

"Mate, if I have one now, I might never have the strength to stop," Jimmy said, the thoughts of Lucy helping diminish those cravings.

"I admire your courage mate. Coke?" Angus said.

"Aye. Cheers," Jimmy said.

Jimmy and Angus sat enjoying their drinks and complimentary snacks as they soaked up the atmosphere of a city that never sleeps, nor is aware of its allure and cold, harsh, unforgiving engine of constant change.

* * *

A few drinks later and losing track of time, Angus and Jimmy hoped they could still catch the kitchens open and enjoy a hearty pub meal. Walking out into the reception area, a group of people were checking in. Their look and luggage suggested they were part of the charity's event, though Angus was yet to see any familiar faces.

The Rose was a traditional English pub with oak panelled walls. Old traditional oil paintings depicting kings and queens hung on the walls, and a distinct smell of lager and ales hung in the air.

A central bar was served by your usual crop of Uni goers who needed the cash of an evening job and with Wednesday being the new Friday, the pub was buzzing with city-goers and people alike as Jimmy and Angus were shown to a table and given a menu.

CHAPTER NINETEEN

Veterans United Annual Charity Dinner
– Thursday, 10th May 2012

T he lift doors opened on the first floor with a huge pop-up screen representing 'Veterans United' welcoming them to the event.

"I'm nervous," Jimmy said, rubbing his damaged hand.

"We need to do this, mate. You are going to be fine. I am nervous too, but I want you to hear what Mike has to say," Angus said, giving him a reassuring grip on his shoulder.

A pre-function area with a built-in bar, the Thames suite mirrored the same stunning views over the river Thames while atrium-style ceilings gave you the sense of stargazing.

With an orchestra playing in one corner, groups of people mingled and celebrated a vibrant atmosphere of conversations. Recognising some mates from the barracks, Angus made their way to them.

"Jimmy, mate. Great to see you," they said, shaking his left hand with respect, knowing exactly how much it meant to Angus.

The events coordinator made her way through the groups, confirming names and table numbers with them. "A new face," she said to Jimmy excitedly. She had been part of the charity from the beginning and always made a point of remembering those who came to the events.

"I am Loraine," she said.

"Jimmy Ferguson," he said with bouts of nerves as she searched down the list for his name.

"Angus Brown. I'm with him," Jimmy said, pointing to the name on the list.

"Fantastic. Another new face," she said, introducing herself to Angus.

"You are on table twelve. We are all family and it is going to be a great evening," she said to Jimmy.

"Thank ye," he said, before she moved on.

With precision, guests were asked to make their way to their tables. The twelve tables, each seating ten guests, represented all walks of army life as Angus and Jimmy took their seats and introduced themselves.

Each table, with its gold chairs, was elegantly decorated in white tablecloths and supplemented with dark grey textured runners to cut through the starkness. Copper cutlery with printed menus and votive candles complimented the elegant centrepieces of lilies and roses. Each table had a bottle of red and white wine, together with a jug of water. Pledge cards to encourage donations were placed at each setting, and Angus made a mental note to donate on behalf of him and Jimmy.

Forty-inch LED televisions were spaced around the room, with a projector screen displaying screenshots of the charity's successes.

Jimmy's anxiety prevented him from finding that ability to hold a conversation longer than five minutes, and the screenshots were a welcoming distraction.

Despite the room being filled with wounded veterans and their own physical impairments exposed, each course required Angus' help in cutting Jimmy's food, leaving him feeling extremely defenceless. He truly did not know how to react around other people, wounded or not. He had disconnected himself from the rest of the world.

As the plates from the main course were being cleared, the announcer introduced the guest speaker of the evening, and cheers erupted as a confident, broad-shouldered man walked onto the stage. The only difference was his prosthetic legs.

"Thank you for that introduction. What a fantastic evening it has been so far and seeing old and new faces can only remind us why Veterans United are vital to helping ex-servicemen and women retain their independence.

It is easy to forget what an amazing gift life really is. How

can life be great when your closest friends are being blown
up in front of you? 'Living with your wasted body, day in,
and day out. What is so amazing about that?' you ask.

Of course, there are those challenging times, dark
harrowing times, those suicide attempts, the
physical beatings, the constant rejection.

I have been through it all. I am no different to any of you
sitting here tonight. But changing the way you think and
feel about yourself, including your beliefs and expectations
about what is possible for you, determines everything
that happens to you. When you change the quality of
your thinking, you change the quality of your life.

Losing my legs made me feel less of a man.
What can a man do with no legs?

A man is expected to support his family. I was ashamed
by my appearance, and embarrassed to be with my wife.
But through their love and support, and organisations
that supported me through my rehab, I found solace and
inner strength to accept my life for what it is today.

Life has been an incredible journey for me. Few people
can say they have conquered the South Pole. I did this.
And with no legs! I have achieved the impossible!

And I will achieve the impossible again by
climbing Kilimanjaro next year.

I certainly would not have accomplished any of those
incredible journeys if I still had my legs today."

Mike Tully could not have been much older than Jimmy, but
his confidence and acceptance of his injuries filled the room
with inspiration and hope as everyone, who could, gave a
standing ovation.

"How amazing was that!?" Angus said, giving Jimmy a huge
manly hug, knowing that he needed it.

"Mike," a close friend of Angus said, approaching him, and
took a seat at his table not far from Jimmy and Angus.

"I know someone who could do with your help," he said to
Mike, and explained briefly about Angus and his struggles
with Jimmy.

"With pleasure, mate," Mike said, only too pleased to offer any
help he could, looking over at Jimmy and seeing the impression of someone truly out of their depths. Five months on and
Jimmy still showed signs of someone who was haggard and
washed out.

"Jimmy, mate. Welcome," the voice said, approaching him,
shaking his left hand with pride and taking the empty seat
next to him. Angus receiving a friendly reassuring pat on the
back, looking up to see his mate walk past him.

"Mike, great speech," Jimmy said with true admiration towards the extraordinary man sitting next to him.

"It's a team effort, mate," Mike said.

"The evening has been great," Angus said.

"The reception we've received these past four years has been amazing, and the charity is there to help. I understand you've had a tough time," Mike said supportively to both men.

Jimmy sighed heavily.

"Neither you nor Angus should suffer in silence," Mike said.

"I'm a shameful drunk, and embarrassed," Jimmy said, finding himself opening to Mike's encouragement and understanding.

"Mate, there is nothing to be ashamed about. Everyone in this room has suffered mentally and physically.

We've been there. You are not alone," Mike said as Angus listened and saw Jimmy for the first time in a different aspect. Jimmy was reaching out to someone who had also suffered the physical impact of life-changing injuries.

"I fight my demons daily, mate. I have good and bad days. Some bad days, I just need time to get through it on my own. Other days I need someone to talk to. Someone who will listen. I had to watch my best friend die lying next to me and there was nothing I could do. I have those haunted memories, but we survived, mate, so they will never be forgotten," Mike said.

"Jimmy is suffering and blames me for still having my career. We need to sort ourselves out and talk openly about our disagreements," Angus said.

"Aye, I know that," Jimmy said in agreement.

"Have you organised any therapy or joined any support groups?" Mike asked.

"I have organised an evaluation and am waiting to hear back from them," Angus said.

"Is this for yourself too?" Mike asked Angus.

"I am considering it, although I have my job to do," Angus said.

"Mate, it would be beneficial for yourself to take part. The organisations are out there, but we can all be too proud to ask for the help that some of us so desperately need. They are there to help you through the transition and train you in new skills. Recreational sports are so beneficial to recovery," Mike said.

"We have also considered talk therapy," Angus said.

"They are greatly beneficial, and highlight the importance of having friends around you. That way, you go through the healing process together," Mike said.

"I refused further support after being discharged," Jimmy said.

"It did not help that Jimmy was due to be married and her attitude towards him was disgraceful," Angus said.

"I am sorry to hear that, mate. Your best bet is to focus on getting your strength back and working towards something physically and mentally challenging. It's a form of coping mechanism, and reminds you that you are still alive and capable of living," Mike said, giving Jimmy a good pat on the back.

Every emotion washed over Jimmy listening to Mike, and he took every word to heart. He felt ashamed by the way his life had turned out. He was a wasted drunk, a pathetic loser. He shut everyone out of his life and yet, everyone still came up to him and showed their respect, and treated him like one of their own. He was still part of the family he always wanted.

"Please contact me anytime you want to talk. It helps, mate," Mike said to Jimmy, but directed it to both men.

Exchanging numbers, he gave them the reassurance they needed to hear as Jimmy's facial features lightened. His body relaxed and his shoulders lifted. He had been inspired and felt humbled by the wounded soldier's advice.

Angus stood up and shook Mike Tully's hand. "Thank you," he said with gratitude.

Pledging a hundred-pound donation, Angus and Jimmy stayed and had one more drink. Jimmy drank coke in between glasses of water, and was undoubtedly the soberest one of the evening.

With the wine flowing during dinner and a percentage of the

bar takings going towards the charity, pledge cards were generously filled, and the celebrations went on till late.

* * *

Mike had certainly left an impression on Jimmy and Angus, but they found themselves restless and unable to sleep. Angus saw and heard another side of Jimmy, and Jimmy heard from someone who understood him in a different way from Angus.

"Mate, do you want some coffee?" Angus asked, turning over for the hundredth time in his bed.

"Aye, cheers. Gussie, thank ye for bringing me," Jimmy said slightly awkwardly. He had not appreciated something from Angus in an exceptionally long time.

"This is a good start to build bridges, and hearing what Mike said tonight, we can both do with the help," Angus said while they drank their coffee and reflected on the night's events.

"Let's go to the Cenotaph before we leave tomorrow," Jimmy suggested, with some hesitation to his voice.

"Mate, are you sure? We do not have to do this," Angus said, taken aback by the unexpected suggestion.

"I want to go," Jimmy said.

"Okay, great. We will do it," Angus said.

* * *

Falling in and out of sleep for the next two hours, Angus and Jimmy were up at 5 a.m. Getting dressed and doing their toiletries, they left their bags in their room, knowing they would be back with enough time to have breakfast and check out.

As the soldiers took a slow sombre walk, the streets of London started to rise. The men breathed in the fresh early air and lost themselves in their thoughts, as they admired the different views of the river Thames while crossing Lambeth Bridge and seeing Parliament Square Garden with the renowned Big Ben on the right. Bearing down on them with his distinct determined and knowing look of authority, they walked past the statue of Winston Churchill staring out over Westminster, down towards the Cenotaph.

Realising where they were, both men swallowed hard as Angus stood beside Jimmy's chair.

"I want yer help, Gussie," Jimmy choked, succumbing to his fears. He was scared... scared to admit that the tragic stressful situation he was in was also empowering him to reach out and realise he needed help.

"I will help you every step of the way," Angus said, giving Jimmy, once more, that reassuring grip on the shoulder.

CHAPTER TWENTY

Friday, 25th May 2012 – Psych Therapy begins

F-E-A-R has two meanings: 'Forget Everything And Run' or 'Face Everything And Rise. The choice is yours – Zig Ziglar

Hilary Hinton "Zig" Ziglar was an American author, salesman, and motivational speaker – Wikipedia

I t had been a long-drawn-out afternoon of various health checks and GP appointments, and Jimmy's head throbbed as though his skull was being compressed. His body cramped and was exhausted as he sat with Angus, waiting for his last appointment.

Angus wheeled Jimmy into the consultation room, looking as nervous as he did. He never expected the psych therapy to involve him, but he had also realised that by being a confidant for Jimmy, he would be receiving his own form of help.

An accredited psychiatric nurse with twenty years' experience to her name, Rosalind Anderson was a woman in her early fifties. Her empathetic nature and professional mannerism provided a warm and supportive atmosphere to work in.

"Good afternoon, gentlemen. I am Rosalind Anderson, a psychiatric nurse here at the surgery. What would you like me to call you?" Rosalind said.

"Angus and Jimmy are fine, thank you," Angus said, glancing towards the nerve-wrecked veteran.

"Aye, Jimmy is guid," he said.

"Jimmy, I have also spoken to your GP and will keep him up to date with your progress," Rosalind said.

"It has been some time since Jimmy last received medical advice, and we have all agreed that any medication is not an option at this moment, because of his drinking," Angus told Rosalind.

"It is an option that can be discussed later. Jimmy, how are you feeling with today's evaluation?" Rosalind said.

"I'm nervous," Jimmy said.

"And Angus, same question," Rosalind said.

"There is always more to be said between us, and I am there supporting him through it all, but I will not deny I am nervous too. We have never spoken about the incident and I am scared to hear it for myself," Angus said.

"That's understandable. For you both, it is especially important you discuss your feelings and how the past five years have affected you," Rosalind said.

"We have discussed doing talk therapy as well," Angus said.

"You'll find this easier to cope in everyday life, feel less alone with your problems, and share the burden amongst each other. I would most certainly encourage it," Rosalind said.

"Are we going to see you with each session?" Angus asked.

"Yes, I will be involved throughout this process. I will adapt the sessions to work for you and with you, and guide you through a process of solving the problems that are currently tormenting you. Feel free to interrupt me at any time, or steer the conversation to where you need it to go. Be honest, swear and raise your voices if need be, but no fistfight gentlemen," Rosalind said with some humour, and both men laughed nervously.

Psych Evaluation

"I would like to start by asking Angus to give me a narrative of who Jimmy was before," Rosalind said.

The little colour Jimmy had left in him now drained from his nauseated body, and he choked on a dry heave.

"Take deep breaths, mate. We need to do this," Angus said supportively. "It's been a long day," he told Rosalind, before going into more detail about Jimmy.

"If you can imagine a hall of around a hundred and sixty young blokes going through this massive cultural change, from being at home with their parents and a nice warm house, to many of them crying and doubting themselves on whether they had made the right decision to join the army.

And then there is one who stands out from the crowd.

This composed, determined and focused young sixteen-year-old.

Jimmy approached every situation free of doubt and full of assurance. He was decisive with a body of strength and a mind of knowledge and experience. Jimmy was a born leader," Angus said with confidence, despite this overbearing sense of sadness that tore him apart inside.

"I am not fucking him anymore!" Jimmy coughed and spluttered, trying desperately to hold back the rancid vomit. But with a heaving lurch, he grabbed the disposable pulp bowl and gagged.

"I know that! That is why we need to do this and get you the help with some form of fucking normality back into you!" Angus said.

"Jimmy, I know how daunting this process is going to be and we can work through it slowly," Rosalind said.

"What we see and what we do changes you forever. Do I think Jimmy will ever be that quick-witted, self-assured mate I once knew? No. But you will always have the traits of a soldier, mate," Angus said, giving Jimmy a big pat on the back. "He needs help," he almost pleaded.

"Have you ever received help before?" Rosalind asked.

"No," both men said.

"Jimmy, have you considered attending any meetings for The Twelve Steps Programme?" Rosalind asked.

"Coming here today and going through this process has been incredibly challenging, and I'm going to need time to get my head around it," Jimmy said with exhaustion and frustration in his voice.

"Can we see further into the process?" Angus suggested.

"The organisations are out there, and only a phone call away. They listen and are non-judgemental, and you can speak to them in confidence. How are you feeling, Jimmy?" Rosalind said.

"I'm exhausted," Jimmy said, fidgeting in his chair, clearly uncomfortable in his surroundings.

"I have a few more questions I need to ask and then we can finish. What is the problem from your viewpoint?" Rosalind said.

"My drinking," Jimmy admitted.

"It is not just your drinking, mate! You are depressed, angry, bitter, and in debt. My problem is that I do not speak to my fiancée, Amy. I have never spoken to her about my feelings of that day, and it is affecting our relationship," Angus said.

"What makes the problem better?" Rosalind asked.

"Alcohol," Jimmy said.

"Mate, it is not just the alcohol. You thump the hell out of your body," Angus said, slightly annoyed.

"For me, it is having Amy's support, despite not being able to talk to her," he said.

What positive changes would you like to make happen in your life?" Rosalind asked.

"To stop drinking," Jimmy said.

"To have the ability to speak to Amy," Angus said.

"Overall, how would you describe your mood?" Rosalind asked.

"Angry and bitter," both men agreed.

"In that first year of Jimmy's injuries, our anger and bitterness towards each other are what held me together," Angus said.

"What do you expect from this process?" Rosalind asked.

"Being able to speak to my future wife and getting my best mate back," Angus said.

"What would it take to make you feel more content, happier, and more satisfied?" Rosalind asked.

"Show us how to work through our differences and get Jimmy's life back on track," Angus said, giving him a huge pat on the back.

"Jimmy and Angus, I apologise for the long day, and as I've said before, this process will get easier. I would suggest that you have a talk therapy about how the past five years have affected you both," Rosalind said, and ended the day's evaluation.

✳ ✳ ✳

18:10 hours -

Jimmy had felt somewhat trapped in a conflicting emotional state of doubt and relief after the day's assessment, and needed the continued support from Angus.

"Hello, my lovely. You look totally washed out," Amy said, taking hold of Jimmy's bag.

"Aye. Feckin frustrating," Jimmy said.

"I am pleased you decided to come and now you can just relax and have a nice evening with us," she said.

"It has been a long day," Angus said, putting an arm around her shoulder.

"Before we all settle down and get comfortable, are you going to get us a takeaway?" she asked Angus.

"But we can phone for a takeaway?" he questioned.

"Yes, I know. But I have been craving a KFC all day," she smiled.

"That means I have to go out and get it," he said.

"My love, please," she said, giving him a flirtatious fluttering of the eyes.

"Are you trying to tell me something?" he grinned.

"I am saying that I am hungry," she laughed, wrapping her arm around his waist.

"Mate, how can I resist?" Angus said, grabbing his keys and kissed her before walking out.

"He falls for it every time," she smiled.

"Aye, you've trained him well," Jimmy said.

"How are you feeling?" she asked.

"Feckin frustrated and pissed off with this whole process!" he said, palm smacking his head.

"Come on, Jimmy. Today is over. You know you need the help and we are here," she said.

"Ah cannae feckin handle the constant rollercoaster of mood changes! Ah dinnae feckin get it!" he said angrily.

"It is going to be tough in the beginning. You have these unprocessed memories to deal with," she said.

"It's everything! Home environment! Not fucking being able to have a conversation with Lucy! I feel incapable and weak!" he said, sighing heavily and hung his head.

"You are not weak, mate! Out of practice maybe, but not weak! Why not allow me to come and clean your place, spend time with you and just have a good chin wag?" she said.

"Whit be my squaddie for the day?" he said, feeling a little more relaxed.

"You cheeky bugger!" she laughed.

"Aye, I would like that," he said.

"Good. We will make some arrangements," she said.

"Any news on my AFC?" he asked, taking a drink of coke.

"No, lovely. But I spoke to someone earlier this week, and they are going through each section with a fine-tooth comb. In a sense, it is a good thing that this has happened, because now we can explain in full detail the effect of your injuries, and I am rather good at doing that," she said, smiling confidently.

"Anytime you want to, come and stay, even if it means going back to basic training and dragging you up the stairs and helping you in the shower. Mate, I have seen it all before. Although, there are limits and I refuse to wipe your arse...," she said, with Angus walking into the remains of laughter.

Jimmy was grateful for Amy's sense of humour and her no-nonsense approach.

Angus had bought a selection of chicken pieces, corn on the cob, and fries. Sitting at the table, they heartily tucked into the food and enjoyed the takeaway, where afterwards all three moved into the lounge and got comfortable. Jimmy happily climbed out his wheelchair.

Amy texted Lucy a private message while the men watched some inane documentary on engineering skyscrapers.

It's been a long day, with Jimmy being sick during

*the assessment, but Angus convinced him to
come and spend the night at ours*

Shame, I'm sorry I couldn't help. How is he feeling now?

*He's frustrated and pissed off with this whole process, but
we've had a good chat and he knows he needs to do this.
Angus and Jimmy are slowly sorting out their differences
but have not pushed either of them for answers*

*Jimmy is probably feeling so many conflicting
thoughts right now and doesn't realise it,
but he's already making progress*

You truly have a soft spot for him

Lucy replied with a blushing face.

*I have said he can stay whenever he wants if
it means I must help him, but I said there were
limits and I refuse to wipe his arse LOL*

Ha-ha you get gadgets for that

Really!

Amy laughed out loud and interrupted the guys' attention.

I will find the link and send it to you. Do you have the date for the next session? If it coincides with my shifts I can pop in and see him

I will find out and let you know. We must arrange another coffee date

Definitely. Please tell Jimmy I say hello

Amy ended the text messages with

I'll give him your love.

Leaving the two men engrossed in the next episode of the documentary, she headed upstairs to have a bath.

❊ ❊ ❊

Hearing the base tunes of both Angus and Jimmy's snores told her it was time to send them to bed and after shaking Angus gently, she got him to helping Jimmy. "Lovely, count yourself privileged. I have never been carried up these stairs," she said, laughing out loud at the absurdity of Angus carrying Jimmy upstairs and over the threshold. Jimmy planted an amusing kiss on Angus' cheek and the three soldiers laughed hard.

He felt somewhat relieved and at ease. Agreeing to spend the night had been the right thing to do, and it had certainly helped take his mind off the booze.

"He looks much better and more relaxed," Angus said, climbing into bed.

"I am not going to pry, but are you feeling okay?" she asked.

"It has been a tough day, but I am okay, Aims. I know I need to do this, and I know I need to talk to you," he said, taking her into his arms.

"She wants us to have a talk therapy about how the past five years have affected us," he said.

"Would this be between you and Jimmy, or would you like me to be involved?" she asked.

"This first chat should be between Jimmy and me," he said.

"I agree. You guys need to talk alone. How did the GP appointment go?" she said.

"They did blood tests and took blood pressure. We have agreed that while he is still drinking heavily, pain medication is not an option," he said.

"Do you remember my uncle and how addicted he got to his medication for his knee?" she asked.

"Yeah, I remember that. You could see him agitated and counting down the minutes to his next fix. Your mum and aunt eventually stepped in and put their foot down," he said.

"With the extent of Jimmy's mental and physical injuries, he probably will need some form of medication to help him, and we can only hope that with our support, he can manage his intake safely," she said.

"He needs physio," he said.

"Yeah, he does, but he is more than likely to finish the psych sessions before he even gets an appointment with the physio on the NHS. That alone took long enough. Jimmy's best bet is to go private," she said.

"He needs an assessment at Redford," he sighed.

"Let us get through a few more sessions and see how he progresses. I will make some phone calls and see what options we have," she said.

"I could not have gone through this without you," he said, pulling her closer and kissing her.

"I keep meaning to ask, did you take him to have his photos for his blue badge and bus pass?" she said.

"He found some old ones tucked in the back of a drawer. We used them," he said.

"I suppose they are better than nothing. He no doubt looks healthier in them too. I have said to him that I will arrange a day to go around and clean his place, spend some time with him and just have a good chat," she said.

"Thank you," he said, and they shared a moment of tenderness.

CHAPTER TWENTY-ONE

Talk Therapy –

Emotional pain is not something that should be hidden away and never spoken about. There is truth in your pain, there is growth in your pain, but only if it is first brought out in the open – Steven Aitchison

Steven Aitchison is the UK's top personal development blogger and has a BSc in Psychology.

"**...F**uck I cannae do this!" a frustrated Jimmy said, continuing to smack his head.

"...Come on, mate. Take a deep breath. You have been on edge these past few weeks, and if we are going to do this as part of your process in finding that inner peace, then God forbid, let us have this conversation! Why do you think you have had a bad day?" Angus said, trying to calm him down.

"I fuckin don't know! I can't control this constant negativity! I have no fuckin control of my life!" Jimmy sighed heavily.

"It has not been fucking easy for me either, mate!" Angus said, momentarily getting up to get them a cold drink.

"The structure of the military is changing. Aims and I will move with our units, and whether you are aware of it or not, I have had to consider my options moving forward. You have always been a part of my life, regardless," Angus said.

"I fuckin know what's going on and I don't expect ye tae look after me pal!" Jimmy said.

"Mate, it is a different world out there and unfortunately, you will need to learn to adapt. But you are a fighter and there are opportunities for you to do good and make changes for the better," Angus said.

"I'm na fuckin pen-pusher!" Jimmy said.

"Do you think I fucking want to be a white-collar in one of Amy's father's companies? That is neither of us," Angus said.

"I fuckin don't recognise me anymore, pal," Jimmy said.

"You are still alive! Your soldiering has ended, but your life does not have to end there! Remember what Mike said. We survived so they will never be forgotten. You survived, Jimbo! Jock Strong! It is going to get tougher before it gets easier, and she will ask some awkward stomach-churning questions, but it needs to be addressed. I am going to have those same questions thrown at me, and I am just as nervous. We have never spoken about that day, and how each of us is suffering. You have never asked me what I am going through or how receiving that phone call also changed my life forever," Angus said.

"Ye get to keep yer career. There's no comparison!" Jimmy said bitterly.

"Seriously, Jimbo. I will fucking smack you if you are not careful! You think that because you sit here in your sorrowful state, the rest of us who try to function in a normal environment are perfectly fine! I am not fine! I am suffering, so do not try your pitiful excuses with me!" Angus said furiously.

"I don't want to feckin do this!" Jimmy said.

"I am not leaving until we sort this out! You still blame me for that stupid bitch leaving you! You are angry and bitter with me, throwing callous comments my way! Everything has been my fault!" Angus said.

Listening to Angus, Jimmy realised just how much bitterness he had spewed towards his best friend, and the suffering he was going through.

"Pal, I'm alone. I have no companionship. I have gone through endless days not seeing a face or hearing a voice and unless you've been in that situation, you can't imagine it. But my default feeling is aggression. I'm frustrated and angry at having no control over my life! I can't do a fuckin simple task like taking down that fuckin picture falling off the wall!" Jimmy said, showing a frustrated gesture towards the picture before slamming his fist on the table.

"Mate, I did not even consider that. Fuck!" Angus said, annoyed with himself, and immediately took the broken frame down and placed it at the front door to remind him to scrap it.

"I'm physically and emotionally broken. I don't sleep and I'm scared to fall into nightmares that are so real, where I've woken up with the smell of something still in the air, sounds, a full-on scream in my sleep, and waking up and still hearing it echo," Jimmy said, palm smacking his forehead in frustration.

"Mate, I am struggling too. I have this constant battle inside my head just to keep me grounded. It is exhausting to have to concentrate on controlling my emotions, or these racing thoughts that are going in directions that I do not necessarily control" Angus said, waving his hands as he spoke.

"I have the nightmares too. The distinctive smell of sterilisation that is so potent, it burns the back of my throat. The continuous beeps of machines hooked up to your body. I am suffering, mate! I am suffering too!" he said.

"I lived this rigid, focused life. Now I'm suffering the depression, anxiety, sleep issues, physical pain and anger. Feck, I have this overwhelming sense of sadness and I do not know how to control it," Jimmy said.

"I could have been right there with you, had it not been for Amy. I know what I am supposed to do, and how a normal human functions. I am very aware of what normal should look like and every day, I act normal. But it is nothing like how I feel, and I do not know if you understand that. I suffer inside while you beat the hell out of your body," Angus said with a heavy sigh.

"I do not speak to Amy about how I feel, and if I do not do something about it soon, I am going to lose her," he said.

"Drinking was my only escapism," Jimmy said.

"I miss my feckin life. I did push ye away, but then it was too late to ask for help. I am ashamed," he said.

"Mate," Angus said, placing a reassuring hand on his shoulder, "every day, I wear the uniform for you," he said, swallowing hard.

"I miss our friendship. Ye have always been a good friend. Ye are my best friend, Gussie, and I will be yer best man at yer wedding," Jimmy said, succumbing to tears.

Angus heaved a heavy sigh, and his shoulders sagged. For the first time in five years, he choked, and Jimmy reached out to his best pal.

The soldiers hugged and cried hard. They finally allowed the weight they had carried for so many years to be lifted.

❊ ❊ ❊

21:30 hours –

The overload of weight had finally been lifted, and the pressure from the cooker was released. Angus and Jimmy had shared their emotions, and now their friendship could start to heal. But also, now Angus could not ignore the uncertainties of the foreign territory he felt himself walking into.

Will this now affect my role as a soldier? Will this make me weak? Is this how Jimmy feels?

A whiff of roasted vegetables and chicken hit Angus as he walked into the house. Dropping his keys in the bowl, he could hear Amy upstairs talking to her sister, and made his way up.

"Emms, Angus is home. I will speak to you tomorrow," Amy said as he entered the bedroom.

"Are you okay?" she asked him as he sat down at the end of the bed.

"He said yes to being best man," he said, showing a hint of tears in his eyes.

"Oh my love! That has made my day!" she said.

"How are you feeling? Are you ok?" she asked.

"I am okay, Aims. We had a good meaningful chat and I do feel elated. I just do not know if this whole process is going to benefit him. He agreed he needed help after meeting Mike, but these past few weeks feel like we have taken a step backward rather than forward," he said.

"You know my feelings about talk therapy and how they will benefit us all. Maybe the controlled environment is a good thing, but together we can speak freely and have that understanding of what each of us has been through. Let us see how the next session goes, and together, we will organise a talk therapy," she said.

"You are right," he sighed, trying to hold it together. The emotions he was trying to control were something he was unfamiliar with.

"It will be good. I know you are feeling slightly apprehensive, and today has been tough. You think you have let your guard down by allowing your emotions to surface, but you have not, and this will not affect your job. Just know I am here if you want to talk to me," she said with a lump in her throat.

"I love you, Aims, and I will find a way to talk to you," he said, taking her into his arms.

CHAPTER TWENTY-TWO

Psych Session

"Jimmy, you weren't very well the last time we met. How are you feeling today?" Rosalind said.

"I feel this is not working for me," Jimmy admitted.

"He has been making progress, but these past few weeks have been a struggle, and his moods are all over the place," Angus said.

"Did you manage to have a further conversation between yourselves?" Rosalind asked.

"We needed to talk, and although I initiated the conversation, we realised we were suffering the same pain and anger, just in different ways," Angus said.

"I just can't find the once confident and focused man I once was. The soldier! Am I ever going to feel like that again? I

can't fucking understand why this doesn't connect with this!"
Jimmy said, stabbing at his head and gesturing towards his
wasted body.

"Why doesn't it work anymore!?" he literally screamed in
frustration.

"Mate, just accept you have had a traumatic ordeal. Why can
you not accept that?" Angus said.

"Jimmy, you've suffered these life-changing injuries that will
affect how you feel and respond both physically and mentally.
As we explore these issues you will start to notice the difference and feel a sense of worth again," Rosalind said.

"Have you met any other injured veterans since your injuries?"
she asked.

"Aye. Angus and I went to a charity event in London a few
weeks ago. It was the first time I had seen any vets, injured or
not, since my injuries. If I saw anyone during my stay in the
hospital I do not like to remember, I block that out," Jimmy
said.

"Amy took the initiative and bought the tickets. We are trying
to get Jimmy out and meet other vets," Angus said.

"Did anyone inspire you?" Rosalind asked.

"Aye. I suppose meeting and listening to Mike, and hearing
how familiar that fateful day was for each of us, made me realise I needed help," Jimmy said.

"He lost both his legs, and has since conquered the South Pole. He is now taking on the challenge of climbing Kilimanjaro next year," Angus said.

"He sounds amazing," Rosalind said.

"I think he is going to be a good support network for Jimmy," Angus said.

"By speaking to Mike and meeting others, do you feel that moving forward, you could get your own prosthetics fitted?" Rosalind asked.

"I'm never going to walk again!" Jimmy said.

"Mate, there is no fucking reason why you should not walk again! Why are you so angry and negative about everything?" Angus said.

"I'm scared to make that move," Jimmy said.

"Jimmy, are there times when you feel separated from your surroundings, detached from your life, or struggle to explain how you feel?" Rosalind asked.

"Aye, I don't understand it," he said.

"There are different calming and breathing techniques that I think will benefit you both. They are simple, easy techniques to help you whenever you're feeling anxious, stressed, or overwhelmed. They will help you feel calmer and more grounded. I would like to start with the counted breathing. To do this, you must exhale for a few more counts than the inhale. It is also helpful that with every inhale, you think positive thoughts, and with each exhale, you release the negative stresses. Jimmy and Angus, I would ask that you close your eyes and take a moment to breathe," Rosalind said in a soothing, pleasant voice...

"Inhale, two, three, four, hold. Exhale, two, three, four, five, six, hold. Think about breathing in calm and peace and breathing out pain and stress," she said.

Speaking in a soft tone, Rosalind continued the breathing technique for a few more minutes.

"Okay, Jimmy and Angus. Take a deep breath and open your eyes. How do you feel?" Rosalind asked.

"I don't know about you, mate, but a few more minutes of that and I would have fallen asleep," Angus said, sharing a laugh.

"I don't know what I'm feeling. It's something I have to get used to," Jimmy said.

"It's going to take some time getting used to, but I would suggest you try this at home. Another simple and easy exercise to do is place your hand on your chest over your heart, and then start rubbing in a circular motion. You don't need to press awfully hard, but firm enough where you can feel it. And as you begin to rub, say out loud - Even though I am feeling anxious, I am going to be okay. Even though a part of me is feeling stressed or anxious, I can calm down. I have the strength to do this.

Always start with 'even though a part of me is feeling'...and you can say whatever you want.

Release your negativity and remind yourself of the positives" Rosalind said.

Jimmy and Angus followed Rosalind's lead, rubbing their chests in circular movements.

"Even though a part of me is feeling overwhelmed, I know I am going to be okay," Angus said.

"Even though a part of me is very angry right now, I know I have the strength to calm down," Jimmy said.

Again, Rosalind continued the technique for a few more minutes.

"Right. Take a long deep breath, and exhale. How do you feel?" Rosalind said.

"I feel okay," Jimmy said, slightly strangely.

"I am definitely going to continue doing this. It will be good for us, mate," Angus said.

"I am pleased to hear that. You both look more relaxed. In our next session, I would like to begin the Eye Movement Desensitisation and Reprocessing with Jimmy.

"Can you explain how the process works?" Angus asked.

"When doing the eye movement, I will move my fingers in a horizontal or diagonal direction whilst focusing on the visual image, negative beliefs, and bodily sensations. I will also guide you in focusing on a healing light that is something you feel comfortable in going to at any time you want to stop, or whilst going through the target processing.

'What are you noticing now?' is also a question we use often during the process, and is intended to be very open-ended.

As we work through the negative beliefs, any new material gained then becomes the focus for the next set of eye movements.

Jimmy, throughout the process, you will be in control and in a safe environment," Rosalind said.

"Just do what needs doing. I am here for support," Angus said.

"Thank you, Angus. I can appreciate that this will be a difficult and emotional experience, but if you can remember you're in a safe environment, nothing can harm you. Jimmy, how are you feeling?" Rosalind said.

"Aye, I won't deny I'm nervous," Jimmy said.

"I am feeling nervous too, mate," Angus said.

"We will start with the counted breathing and work through

the questions slowly, and at any time you feel like stopping, we will," Rosalind said reassuringly.

"We need to do this, mate," Angus said.

"I know that, pal" Jimmy said.

"It's been a good session, Jimmy and Angus," Rosalind said.

* * *

16:15 hours – "Mate, it has been a long day. How are you feeling?" Angus said.

"Aye. I'm exhausted and already flipping tense with this idea of the next session," Jimmy said.

"Mate, you cannot allow this process to pull you down. Do not allow yourself to get into a state that you cannot get yourself out of again," Angus said.

"I know, pal. I know I need to do this. I'm just mentally drained," Jimmy sighed.

"You can do this, Jimbo! I need your strength as much as you need mine. I do think the breathing techniques are going to help you, so please try them," Angus said.

"Aye. I'm going to try to get through this," Jimmy said.

"That is good to hear, mate. I know you can do this. Lucy should be here shortly, so I am going to take this opportunity to get home and spend some time with Amy," Angus said.

"Aye. That's guid," Jimmy said.

"If you need to talk, I am on the phone," Angus said.

"Aye. Cheers, pal. I appreciate that," Jimmy said, with Angus giving him a supportive pat on the back before leaving.

❉ ❉ ❉

With the help of knowing that Lucy was about to arrive, Jimmy felt a sense of accomplishment, being able to diminish the urge for a swig of whiskey.

He had barely manoeuvred himself into the kitchen to get a cool drink when Lucy's kind voice called out, "Hello, Jimmy."

"Lucy," he smiled, pushing himself out the doorway at hearing her arrival.

"I have just seen Angus drive off. How are you, Jimmy?" she said, placing her bag and casserole dish on the table before giving him a light hug with shyness showing in the gesture.

"Aye, I'm guid, ye?" he said.

"I am good, thank you. I have been off today, so have spent time with Molls," she smiled.

"Ye should be at home with her," he said.

"She will be fine. She has a playgroup this afternoon, and I can get home to give her a bath and read a bedtime story," she said.

"Wad ye like a cauld drink?" he asked.

"Thank you. I have brought you some chicken casserole," she said, taking two glasses from the cupboard, and helped Jimmy reach for the 7 Up cans in the fridge.

"Yer kindness is overwhelming," he said, sighing heavily as he pushed himself out.

"Jimmy, do I make you feel uncomfortable?" she asked cautiously.

"Na, Lucy. I'm just embarrassed," he said.

"Don't be. I enjoy cooking and visiting you. It is an outing for me too," she smiled.

"Yer visits do help. I'm grateful," he said.

"I am so happy to hear that, because it is only a pleasure," she said, feeling a hint of rosiness in her cheeks as her eyes met his.

"Whit shifts are ye on?" he asked with interest.

"Finishing my late shifts. I was off yesterday and today and then tomorrow I start my early shifts again," she said.

"Whit time do ye start?" he asked.

"At 07:00 hours, and should finish at 16:00 hours. I will bring you a rota of my shifts," she said.

"Aye. That would be great," he said.

"Jimmy, would you mind if I asked how today's therapy went?" she said with slight hesitation.

"Aye. No worries, Lucy. She's given us some breathing techniques to use, and wants to go into more detail about that day in the next session," he said.

"Are you feeling apprehensive and confused about this whole process?" she asked.

"Aye, exactly! I'm nervous that this does not work," he said.

"You are such a strong person, and you will get through this. I know you will. Does it help to have Angus involved in the sessions?" she said.

"Aye. I don't know if I could sit in that room alone," he said.

"How did Angus find the breathing techniques?" she asked.

"He reckons he could fall asleep," he laughed.

"And you Jimmy?" she asked.

"I might have felt a little more relaxed afterward, but everything is so short-lived. I feel like my own prisoner inside," he said.

"Maybe we can do the breathing exercises together?" she smiled.

"Have ye done meditation?" he asked.

"I have tried yoga a couple of times and only since Tom's death, but I can't seem to switch off either. Can I ask you something?" she said.

"Aye," he said.

"Do you feel like a drink now?" she asked.

"Aye, very much so. It's frightening me, but I'm glad yer here," he said.

"I thought you did really well in finding that courage to spend the night with Angus and Amy after your evaluation," she said.

"Aye, it helped diminish the urge to have a drink," he said.

"Jimmy, without putting pressure on you and making you feel uncomfortable, you are always welcome to stay at my house if after the sessions you are finding the need to be around some company. We do not have a shower, but we have a sofa bed and I know you will manage fine," she said.

"Thank ye, Lucy," he said, letting out a sigh.

"Would it help if I phoned you later and read you a bedtime story?" she asked light-heartedly, and Jimmy laughed with ease.

"Seriously though, Jimmy. Please phone me if you want to talk. I am a good listener. I am really grateful to you for being so honest and putting your trust in me," she said.

"I appreciate that," he said, sharing a smile despite quietly feeling a sense of anxiety spreading through his veins, knowing that Lucy's visit would soon come to an end.

Whereas some people would have found her thoughtfulness quite intimidating, months earlier, Jimmy would have been one of them. But he was beginning to realise that Lucy was the most caring woman he had ever met.

* * *

"You are home early," Amy said, finding Angus sitting in the garden, drinking a beer.

"Lucy was popping in to see him, so it gave me the opportunity to come home," he said, pulling her onto his lap and she wrapped her arms around his neck.

"How are you feeling," she asked calmly.

"Besides it being a long drawn out day and times when Jimmy's despondence got to me, I thought the therapy was good. She has given Jimmy some breathing exercises to do, and wants to talk about that day in the next session," he said.

"What was Jimmy's reaction to that?" she asked.

"He does not think this process is going to help him. He is convinced that he will never walk again," he said.

"I have managed to book a day's leave to spend time with him and clean his place. I can also have a chat with him," she said.

"We have seen the effects of broken men, but Jimmy's has hit me hard," he said.

"That is because he is like a brother to you," she said.

"I hope he does not have a drink tonight," he sighed.

"Listen, we all know he is trying, and we must be there to support him," she said.

"You are right. At least Jimmy and I are talking about it more," he said.

"Not just you and Jimmy. This is the first time in our relationship that you have actually shared any emotions on how it has affected you," she said.

"Always know it was not my intention, Aims," he said.

"I know that," she smiled, leaning in to kiss him.

"Did you do the breathing exercises too?" she asked.

"Yeah. They were good, although I was close to falling asleep," he said.

"Did you start to snore?" she laughed.

"A few more minutes, I reckon I would have been," he grinned.

"Honestly, what are you like?" she laughed.

"Well, you kept me up all night," he said.

"Oh really now. It takes two to tango. Now you can help me with dinner," she said, giving him a teasing look.

* * *

Lucy pulled up to the house where a cheerful little face stared back at her from the lounge window, and mother and daughter blew air-kisses as she made her way inside.

"Mummy," Molly's excited sweet little voice said, with Lucy dropping her bag and sweeping her baby girl into her arms, twirling and swaying, "Hello, Mum." Lucy smiled in between the squeals of pure happiness.

"How is he," Mrs. Harris asked, putting the kettle on.

"He is struggling, Mum. I think he will have a drink tonight," Lucy said.

"He will get there and all you can do is support him," Mrs. Harris said.

"I know, Mum. I just wish we could all spend more time with him," Lucy said.

"He is always welcome to come here," Mrs. Harris said.

"I did say that to him, but I think he is embarrassed to ask," Lucy said, offering the mashed food to Molly, who was quite happy to sit on the kitchen floor and eat her dinner.

"You just need to continue supporting him," Mrs. Harris said.

❊ ❊ ❊

After Lucy left, it wasn't long before Jimmy found himself craving that urge for a potent drink. Finding himself very quickly being drawn into the deathly silence of his never-ending grim situation, and with a forceful push into the kitchen, he reached for the cupboard.

Holding the open bottle between his stumps, he took a long deep breath. The woody oak aromas filled his nostrils. The smooth liquid dragged at the back of his throat. He was desperately fighting that thirst in lifting the bottle to his lips.

"Fuck, do not do this!" he thought, with the desperation fighting a tug of war against his mixed emotions, and he phoned Angus.

* * *

"Jimmy, how are you?" Amy said, after seeing his name come up on the screen and answering Angus' phone.

"Amy," surprised at hearing her voice.

"Lovely, Angus is in the shower. Are you okay? Do you want to talk to me?" she said, hearing his hesitation through the connection.

"I'm desperate for a drink," he said.

"Listen, I am going to phone you back on FaceTime," she said, ending the phone call.

"Hello, my sweet," her face appeared on the screen soon after.

"Amy, I don't know what to do," he said.

"Truthfully, do not have a drink, lovely. You did the right thing by giving us a call," she said.

"I find myself reliving that day over and over in my head and worrying a lot about things that might happen in the future," he said.

"Remember, we do get it. You just have to start believing that life will get better...," she said, momentarily interrupted by Angus entering the room.

"What has happened? Mate, are you okay?" Angus asked, appearing on the screen.

"Aye, I needed someone to talk to," Jimmy said.

"Mate, have you had a drink?" Angus asked.

"No, my love. Not yet. That is why he has phoned us," she said.

"Please do not have a drink, mate. You did really well today," a pleased Angus said.

"How is Lucy?" she asked.

"Aye, guid," Jimmy said.

"Did she bring you food again?" she asked with amusement.

"Aye," Jimmy said, the muscles in his face slowly relaxing.

"Honestly, she is like a mother hen around you," she said, and all laughed at the idea.

"Mate, have you eaten?" Angus asked.

"Na," Jimmy said.

"Have something to eat. Maybe read a book and allow your mind to escape," she said.

"Aye," Jimmy said with his mind considering her suggestion, and a few minutes later, they ended the call.

Jimmy had needed the FaceTime conversation and found the inner strength to place the whiskey bottle back into the cupboard before he tucked into the hearty home-cooked meal.

❉ ❉ ❉

21:30 hours and curled up in bed, Lucy's phone beeped.

Amy texted sending Lucy a private message.

> *Just wanted to let you know that Jimmy phoned us earlier. He was fighting the urge to have a drink and I think we have convinced him not to*

> *Thanks, Amy. I was worried when I left him, but I am*

pleased he found the strength to pick up the phone and call.
That is brilliant! I will pop in after my shift tomorrow

Thanks, Lucy, night

Goodnight

CHAPTER TWENTY-THREE

*Hang On, Pain Ends. You Have The Strength You
Need To Get Through This – Michael Josephson*

*Michael Josephson is a former law professor and
attorney who founded the non-profit Joseph and
Edna Josephson Institute of Ethics – Wikipedia*

After speaking to Amy and Angus a few days earlier,
Jimmy had controlled his drinking at manageable
levels and had stayed off the hard-core whiskey, despite the constant cravings that consumed his every solitude
moment.

He was 'chin strapped' spending the night thumping his
stumps and fist smacking his head, trying desperately to block
out the aching pain that endured him, and was grateful to have
Amy spend the day with him.

"Mate, why not take paracetamol and ibuprofen? I am here.
You have not had a drink and it is not going to affect you," she
said, enjoying her morning coffee with him.

Jimmy had attempted suicide, overdosing on legal and easily available pain relief, but the thought of taking that same legal drug to help him, rather than kill him, was terrifying.

He was an alcoholic. He considered the legal drugs a betrayed ally.

"Have you got any?" she asked.

"Aye, in the drawer by the kettle," he said, appreciating the familiarities of Amy's direct and controlled approach.

"It is going to be a good day, and once we are on top of things, it will be easier to manage," she said, giving him the tablets.

"Cheers. I'm ready to give my orders now," he grinned.

"Forget that you are not sitting here like Lord Muck on toast, twiddling your thumbs all day. We are in this together," she said, making Jimmy relax with laughter.

Jimmy's home wasn't cluttered, far from it, but years of neglect and denial had made the place feel haggard. It looked and felt just like he did.

"Lovely, can I leave you to clean the kitchen surfaces and throw out what you can?" she said.

"Aye, I'll do that," he said.

"Great, and I will start with the windows, finishing the kitchen and lounge last," she said.

It was the first time that Jimmy had put any physical effort into getting his home cleaned since his injuries, doing a half-hearted attempt of any sort only when it was an absolute necessity. He saw his right arm more of a weight bearer and taking on today's task was certainly going to test his abilities.

"Put more elbow grease into that!" she joked through the window.

"Ha-ha, I only have one elbow," he laughed.

Wiping down the kitchen surfaces and scrubbing the microwave, whiffs of cleanliness sent conflicting thoughts running through Jimmy's mind like a congested highway of vehicles going in opposite directions, but he had to admit he was enjoying the challenge.

Amy started the inside by sweeping and gathering the dust pile in one corner for a quick vacuum, before allowing herself to then start with the more thorough cleaning. With every scrub and wipe, the smells of bleach and lemon citrus soon eliminated the dull smell of alcohol and body odour.

"How are you doing, lovely?" she asked, walking into the kitchen.

"I know it needs to be done and I'm embarrassed and feckin annoyed with my lack of ability to sort this...!" he said tensing his left hand and shaking it at his head.

"We could have organised a one-off professional cleaner to come in and do it, but I felt you would be more accepting of the idea if I took on the challenge and at the same time got you involved and spent time talking to you," she said.

"I've needed your push. You're one iron-willed woman," he said.

"Absolutely. We are very much the same, mate, and we will get you sorted. I am going to get into your room, and then maybe we can have some lunch," she said.

"Aye, that sounds guid," he said, using his attached weight bearer to tear off a new bin bag.

With the noise of the vacuum cleaner and the clatters of ex-pired tins being thrown out, there was a lively activity within Jimmy's home, and two hours later, one half of his flat looked and smelt pristine.

Amy had worked fast and efficiently, and he respected her qualities as an army officer.

"Did the tablets help?" she asked as they sat enjoying a well-earned lunch break.

"I don't know. I can't say," he said.

"How about taking another two after lunch?" she suggested.

"Amy, I don't want to be reliant on tablets!" he said.

"Jimmy, there is a possibility you will need some form of pain relief or antipsychotics in the near future," she said.

"I'm na fuckin psycho bastard!" he raised his voice.

"I did not say that! Lovely, we are not going to argue. We are just talking," she said.

"Aye, I know that," he said.

"What are you afraid of?" she asked.

"Fuckin everything! They will willy-nilly put me on these drugs and label me some crazy shit!" he said.

"I am on your side, lovely, but just keep an open mind. I will also say to you that there is no harm in taking paracetamol or ibuprofen. Why not take some when one of us is visiting? Think about it. Right, just the lounge and kitchen to finish and you can keep me company," she said.

"Cheers," he said, pondering on her thoughts.

"I am impressed, mate!" she said.

"Do I get my promotion?" he grinned.

"It is a pass," she smiled.

Jimmy sat, taking in a long deep breath as Amy was coming to the end of her last job for the day. His home looked and felt different, and everything felt so strange to him. Amy had done a decent job in five hours.

"That will be a hundred and twenty-five pounds, thanks," she said.

"What a feckin rip off!" he laughed.

"This is an accomplishment, lovely. You have done good and be proud," she said.

"Yer a great support. Thank ye for helping me," he said.

"I am not going just yet. I need a coffee. Lucy's working the late shifts this week," she said.

"Aye, I know," he said.

"Have you asked her about her brother?" she asked, giving him his coffee.

"Na, I don't know what to say to her," he said.

"Just talk to her. You will find the appropriate time to ask her," she said.

"What if it triggers any memories for her? For both of us?" he asked.

"Lovely, Lucy is already suffering the memories. And so are you. It will be a form of talk therapy," she said.

"Is Lucy going to be involved in any of the talk therapies?" he asked.

"Lucy needs the help as much as we do, but she also understands that there will be times when you do not feel comfortable talking in front of her," she said.

"Are ye and Gussie talking?" he asked.

"We are talking more, but we still have a long way to go. He is concerned with you moving forward and nervous about the next session," she said.

"How can triggering memories help! I just think it's feckin 'bone'!" he said.

"You need to go back to that day to move forward," she said.

"What if I fuckin never recover? Mike and the guys just seem to accept their new lives like it's the norm! It's not fuckin normal!" he said angrily.

"You think Mike and hundreds of other guys have not, at some point, felt exactly what you are going through? Just because Mike has conquered the South Pole does not mean getting there was easy!" she said.

"What if prosthetics don't work for me?" he said.

"You have lost a lot of body muscle because you did not continue through with your recovery, but this does not mean you cannot get back into it. It is going to be a whole new experience, and terrifying in the beginning. It might take a year or two before your body is strong enough to carry your weight. And yes, you are going to always be weaker through your right side, but that is the reality of your life. Have you looked at any electric wheelchairs?" she said.

"Na, I can't afford one now," he said.

"No, but there is no harm in looking. This is a whole new world for all of us," she said, grabbing her mobile off the table and started scrolling through the internet for disabled equipment.

"Are you thinking of a scooter, or electric chair?" she asked.

"The scooters are too cumbersome for inside," he said.

"Going by the descriptions, a rear-wheel-drive would be easier to manoeuvre," she said.

"Gussie and I can go in and put them to the test," he said.

"You should go in pretending you both disabled," she laughed.

"Aye, Gussie can be blind and I'll give him directions," he said, sending them both into hysterical laughter.

"Who determines these bloody names? Quickie, Pride, Freedom. How about a Sunfire Plus GTX," she said as they continued to laugh.

"Does it come with a V8 engine and beatbox?" he asked.

"Check. You can get a polyester canopy cover that protects you from the rain and sun. Oh my God. You could be the new royalty to Peebles, going down the high street, waving like His Royal Highness," she said.

"I'll be some fuckin hard arse dude! What's this?" he said, pointing to a link on the same website.

"Intimate rider love chair…!" she said as both her and Jimmy struggled to hold back their laughter at watching the demonstration of sexual positions.

"Wait until I tell Angus," she snorted.

Jimmy was enjoying having Amy spend the day with him, and in turn keeping him off the booze. He would never have found the motivation in getting his home cleaned without her continued push.

CHAPTER
TWENTY-FOUR

A man is known by the silence he keeps – Oliver Herford

*Oliver Herford was British born (but American),
a humourist writer, illustrator, and well known
for his poems and quotes – Wikipedia*

Psych Session

"**H**ow are you feeling about the EMDR today, Jimmy?" Rosalind asked.

"Not too good," Jimmy said.

"You need to do this mate," Angus said.

"Aye, I know pal," Jimmy said.

"Remember, Jimmy, you're in a safe environment and in control of this whole process. If at any point you want to pause, is there a stop signal you want to use?" Rosalind said.

"I'll use my voice," Jimmy said.

"That's great, and will likely clarify with you first. Let's start with a couple of counted breaths. Inhale, two, three, four, hold. Exhale, two, three, four...Breathe in calm and peace, and exhale your pain and stress...," Rosalind said in her monotonous voice.

Jimmy tried to find that inner calmness, but the pain and suffering crept in with every breath.

"What are you noticing now, Jimmy?" Rosalind asked.

"I feel some tension in my back," Jimmy said.

"Stay with that for a moment. Let's test the eye movements by following my fingers," Rosalind said, moving her fingers in a horizontal motion.

Jimmy followed Rosalind's fingers...

"Take a deep breath and let it go. Were you able to track?" Rosalind said.

"Aye," Jimmy said.

"That's good. What are you noticing now?" Rosalind said.

"A sharp, burning pain," Jimmy said.

"Okay, stay with that. Now, imagine if that sharp, burning pain had a shape," Rosalind said.

Jimmy felt this torturous and suffocating pain running through his body as the intense heat pushed him deeper into the scorching ground.

"Could Armageddon be a shape? A black hole?
A planet that has died?" he thought.

"What's coming to mind, Jimmy?" Rosalind asked.

"A dying planet," Jimmy said.

"Now, imagine if this dying planet had a size. What size would it be?" Rosalind said.

"The fuckin size of a landlocked country!" Jimmy said.

"Imagine if it had a colour. What colour would it be?" Rosalind said.

"What is fuckin darker than black? Could a world of non-
existence be classed as a colour?" Jimmy thought.

"Black," he said.

"If it had a temperature, what temperature would it be? Hot or cold?" Rosalind said.

"Fuckin melting-of-the-skin hot!" Jimmy said.

"If it had a texture, what texture would it be?" Rosalind said.

"Fuckin grit!" Jimmy said.

"If it had a sound, what sound would it make? The high or low pitch?" Rosalind said.

"A crucifying sound," Jimmy said.

"Okay, Jimmy. Let's stay with these thoughts whilst following my fingers again," Rosalind said, now moving her fingers in the diagonal motion.

Jimmy followed her lead...

"What are you noticing now?" Rosalind asked.

"Anger," Jimmy said, rubbing his damaged hand with force.

"What words would best describe your negative belief about yourself?" Rosalind asked.

"I am a failure! I let my men down! I fucked up!" Jimmy said.

"If you had to think about what you would like to believe about yourself instead of 'I'm a failure', would it be 'I did the best I could'?" Rosalind said.

"With all due respect, there was no fuckin positive outcome!" Jimmy said.

"Now, focus on your last mission. What image represents the worst part of that incident?" Rosalind said.

A terrible anguish struck Jimmy's heart, a feeling of dreadful ache, like something was being torn inside of him. And for a moment, he sat there quietly, his head bowed.

"My men died! I could not fuckin save them! There's no fuckin part of that day that was good!" Jimmy said angrily.

"What image represents the incident?" Rosalind asked.

"Fuckin mayhem!" Jimmy said.

"When you think of the incident, what do you get?" Rosalind asked.

"A loud explosion...BOOM! It all really went so fast at that point, and then it just slowed down, and it was like everything just stopped. My ears are ringing. I wake up on the ground, a taste of blood and dirt in my mouth. I try calling out to my sergeant, but I'm choking on my own vomit and struggling to breathe. No one responds. I can see a Junior NCO lying a few metres to my left. I manage to pull myself towards him.

His right leg is gone. He is still breathing," an agitated and dis-jointed Jimmy recalled.

"Fuckin stop!" he screamed.

"Jimmy, can I clarify you want to stop?" Rosalind confirmed.

"Aye, please," Jimmy said.

"Take a drink of water and a few moments," Rosalind said.

Despite himself serving on the frontline and knowing the con-sequences of war, Angus was left with a penetrating mental anguish, hearing Jimmy's account of that day for the first time.

"You are doing good, mate," Angus said, trying to reassure him.

"Before you continue, can I say something please?" he asked Rosalind.

"Please, Angus," Rosalind said.

"Mate, we go out and do our best. No one is going to judge you for not saving them. No one could have saved them. You did everything you could. You survived for them," Angus said.

"Jimmy is suffering `survivor's guilt`," he told Rosalind.

"This is something we will work with as we go through the process. Are you okay to continue Jimmy?" Rosalind said.

"Aye," Jimmy sighed heavily.

"Jimmy, what are you feeling at that point?" Rosalind asked.

"I am feeling fuckin mad. I am scared. I am feeling pain in my back and in my right arm. My whole body is shaking. I know something is wrong with my legs," Jimmy said.

"You mentioned a Junior NCO. Where is he now?" Rosalind asked.

"He died! They all died!" Jimmy said, fidgeting in his chair.

"How do you feel about that?" Rosalind asked.

"My men were my responsibility! I fuckin let them down!" Jimmy said.

"Who decides if a person lives or dies?" Rosalind asked.

"It is my fault! Why am I alive!? Why are they not!?" Jimmy said, struggling to find even one positive belief about himself.

"Staying with that, follow my fingers," Rosalind said, moving her fingers in both a horizontal and diagonal motion.

"What are you noticing now?" she asked.

"I'm confused," Jimmy said.

"Stay with that," Rosalind said, moving her fingers a little faster... "Take a deep breath and let it go...

Now, imagine some healing light coming down from above, and moving in through the top of your head and through your veins. This wonderful light of peace and comfort is directing itself towards the shape in your body. Give this wonderful healing light your favourite colour, and different to the colour of your shape. You can decide whether this light is warm or cool. Notice how the healing light resonates with the shape, vibrates with it, in and around it. Notice as it does this, what happens with the shape," she said, allowing Jimmy to digest the information as all three sat in silence.

Trying to process the information, the thoughts of Lucy and Molly came to Jimmy's mind. If there was ever a moment of inner peace, it was time spent with them.

*"Could they represent the form of healing
light?" Jimmy thought.*

The colour purple came to mind for some reason.

*"It could be a little girl's favourite colour? Maybe
a colour he could borrow?" he thought.*

"Does it have to be my favourite colour?" Jimmy asked.

"No, as long as your colour feels warm and comfortable," Rosalind said.

Jimmy felt this warmth of purple light filling his head, spreading through his brain and the billions of nerves that sent his mind on a constant warpath. It filled his eye sockets and the back of his throat, across his shoulders and down his arms into the tips of his fingers, filling his chest and opening his airways, spreading a warmth of adrenaline through his heart and a numbness through his stumps.

A little hand reached out and touched his stump.

"I can't do anymore," Jimmy choked, the emotion getting the better of him, as Angus showed his support and Rosalind quietly walked out, closing the door behind her.

✻ ✻ ✻

21:35 hours –

"Angus, you have been very quiet since getting back from Jimmy's," Amy said.

"It was a tough day, but all is good," he said, trying to avoid any further discussion on the matter.

"My love, you need to help me understand what you are going through," she said, making herself comfortable beside him on the couch.

"Aims, I do not know if I can," he said.

"I also need this. We need to talk about us and help each other in finding a solution with good coping mechanisms," she said.

"It is not that I do not want to talk. I am afraid that if I do, it will break me. I have a responsibility to hold down my job and look after you," he sighed heavily.

"And I have a responsibility to look after you! We need to talk. We are constantly treading on eggshells and a small disagreement over the most ridiculous thing like not putting your dirty shirt in the wash basket can escalate into a full-blown argument. And it always ends up being about Jimmy. He is mentioned in almost every conversation we have, but let me show just a touch of support for him and you fume. Yet, you will not share any of your own suffering with me. I am just expected to understand. I sometimes dread asking you how your day was because I do not want it to turn into an issue. I am going to be your wife and you cannot even share something that is literally common ground between us," she choked.

It had been the first time that Angus had listened and acknowledged what Amy was going through. She was carrying an overwhelming load of pain and unhappiness.

"Aims, I am so sorry," he said, taking her into his arms to comfort her.

"I just want you to share your feelings. Tell me about today's session," she said.

"The session was mostly directed towards Jimmy and the EMDR," he said.

"How did you feel about that?" she asked.

"He needs the help and if I can gain anything from hearing his account of that day, it will help me," he said.

"Talking to me will help you too. What sort of questions did she ask him?" she said.

"They started with the counted breathing before she went on to ask him to think of a shape, the size of it, whether it had a temperature, and all the while taking notice of whatever came to mind," he said.

"What were his thoughts?" she asked.

"He more or less described Afghanistan with a sense of Armageddon," he said.

"I guess that is a fairly good description. My love, are you okay?" she said, seeing the colour drain from his face.

It had been an emotional ending to the session and despite Angus being able to hold his dignity and find an inner strength to help Jimmy regain his composure, the manifest of desperation and responsibility now compressed him like an intense sudden cramp.

"He was my responsibility! I should never have abandoned him! I let him down!" he said, hysterically clenching his cropped hair.

"Angus, stop!" she said, taking hold of his arms. The unexpected outburst took her by surprise and she had never seen Angus this vulnerable.

"Why has this happened!? Why!?" he said, breaking down in her arms.

"Just breathe. I am here for you," she said gently.

"I sit there watching him going through this process and visualising his traumatic experiences and I feel out of control and helpless. I built a wall of anger and bitterness, a steel enforced barrier to hold me together and protect you. Now a fucking mortar has hit it and I am losing the strength to keep it stable," he said with a heavy heart.

"My love, never ever think yourself as less worthy and out of control. You have always been there for Jimmy. You guys always had each other's backs, whether he was on tour or you were stuck on a training exercise. The whole incident was not helped by that fucking bitch! If you should blame anyone, it is her," she said.

"My men expect me to be their leader, not some fucking wuss!" he said.

"Angus, you are not some robotic machine. You, your men, the Company, the Regiment. You are all human beings with feelings," she said.

"I wish he would put his photos on display. He should be proud for serving his country," he said.

"Give him time. It is a big ask of him," she said.

"This is the first time we have had any form of conversation regarding the predicament we find ourselves in," he said.

"We are all struggling in some way or other and talking about it will help us get through it," she said.

"I am sorry about earlier," he said.

"My love, never apologise for showing your feelings. It is okay to not be okay," she said.

CHAPTER TWENTY-FIVE

L ocated in the hills of the Scottish Borders, Dawyck Botanic Garden had an esoterica collection of trees and plant life, crossed over by pathways and footbridges that captured bursts of fragrant colours of seasonal displays from all directions.

Lucy had organised with Angus and Amy to have a picnic where Molly could enjoy the free-spirited squirrels and ducks. This was something she had suggested months earlier to Angus, hoping that Jimmy would get to a stage where he felt comfortable being out in public with them.

Both Angus and Amy could smell the transformation, not just in his home, but in Jimmy too. Angus knew that for Jimmy, sitting through the sessions and talk therapies was going to be difficult at times. And, his army memories still lay in a drawer. But he hoped that one day, Jimmy would find the courage to have them on display and he will not be prouder of him for trying.

Lucy had just gotten Molly's pram out when Angus parked up beside her. A deep sweet floral scent filled Jimmy's nostrils and he smiled at her through the window.

"I have not seen you in ages," Lucy said, with her warmth and kindness helping put Jimmy at ease.

"Aye, it's lovely seeing ye too," he said, giving Lucy a light hug before reaching out for Molly's little hand to kiss her.

Offering to be pack donkey, Jimmy held the picnic basket on his lap as the two men walked in front and the women tagged behind, often stopping to admire the variety of plant life and exchange ideas.

Crossing a pathway, they found a quiet location under a tree and close enough to watch the ducks on the pond. Angus helped Jimmy out of his chair and onto the spread-out blanket, with the lushness of the grass underneath it making him feel a little more human again.

Edging ever so closer to hold on to her mother's leg, Molly watched Jimmy's every move. The last time she saw him on the floor, he was thumping the hell out of his body.

Jimmy saw the concern in Molly's eyes and looked up at Lucy. They shared a mutual understanding and he reached out for the wee lassie's hand. The little girl slowly approached him and placed her tiny hand on his shoulder. His tickles lit up her face with joy and her infectious giggles made everyone laugh out loud.

Lucy and Amy put out a delightful spread of picnic sorts. They all ate the delicious hand-held delights and drank the welcomed cold drinks as the afternoon rays spread across the cloudless sky and they felt blessed for the shadiness of the tree and the light breeze.

They enjoyed Molly's entertaining chatters and kindness in sharing her half-eaten leftovers with Jimmy. Her tiny pearly white smiles were enough to melt anyone's heart.

Angus watched the relationship forming between Jimmy and Molly. He had seen it the day he had come for lunch. The little girl seemed to help bring him out of his shell. He had seen the brief glances, the awkwardness and shyness between him and Lucy. There was something there. A deep sense of longing, but neither knew how to express their feelings.

"Why don't we take Molly for a walk?" Amy suggested to Angus.

"Should we go feed the ducks, Molls?" Angus said, giving the little girl a broad smile and sending her into squeals of delight.

"I'll stay here," Jimmy said, happy enough to sit and enjoy the surroundings.

"I'll stay with Jimmy," Lucy said, subconsciously brushing his arm. She felt her face flush and Amy and Angus desperately suppressed a laugh as Jimmy, who had kept quiet and given the impression he hadn't noticed, burst out laughing at seeing Lucy's blush deepen.

Laughing nervously, she gave Amy Molly's bottle of juice before Angus lifted the little girl onto his shoulders and Amy took hold of the empty pram, leaving the flirting singletons to enjoy time alone while they went in search for squirrels and ducks.

"It is lovely seeing you laugh, Jimmy," Lucy said.

"Ye and Molly have kept me entertained," he smiled.

"It is so beautiful and peaceful here," she said.

"Have ye been here before?" he asked, taking a sip of cold drink.

"No, but it is strange how you can grow up in an area and never visit a place," she said as Jimmy winced as a spasm hit him hard and losing his balance, he fell backward.

"Are you okay?" she asked, quickly moving forward to help him as he fought the need to thump his body.

"Lean against me and breathe," she said, supporting his weight. Her reassuring words of comfort helped him to slowly relax.

"Do ye know how hard it is not to swear in front of ye right now?" he said, trying to laugh at the situation.

"Swear all you want, Jimmy. Darn, if it were me, I would swear every thinkable word," she smiled, leaning over to look at him.

"I'm sorry," he said.

"Don't be sorry. Just relax and breathe. My mother would love the variety of plant life here," she said, rubbing his arms as he leaned against her.

"Ye sound like ye know yer flora?" he said.

"I only know the common varieties, but I like anything with colour," she said while continuing to rub his arms.

"Tell me about yer mother," he said with a genuine interest in Lucy's life.

"My mother is a retired headmistress from the local primary school in Eddleston," she said.

"So, ye live in Eddleston?" he asked.

"Not far from the school actually, which will be convenient for Molly when she gets older," she said.

"Yer mother sounds like a lovely woman," he said.

"She is remarkable. I would never have managed without her," she said, and Jimmy turned his head and smiled at her.

Giving him a gentle squeeze, Lucy's own nerves now caused one flutter after the other to roll over inside her as the sounds and smells of nature faded and Jimmy breathed in her subtle perfume.

* * *

Molly had fallen asleep not long after leaving the ducks, but Angus and Amy decided to explore the grounds further. Walking down paths of hybrid azaleas and through canopies of giant Redwood trees, they passed carpets of Himalayan blue poppies, all in spectacular displays of colour and tranquillising scents.

"You should bring Lucy back and explore the gardens," Angus said to Amy, as they turned around to make their way back.

"I will. I don't think she gets out much either," she said.

"Have you noticed the relationship between Jimmy and Molly?" he asked.

"It is very sweet and they would be perfect for him," she said, looping her arm around his.

"Molly needs a little friend," he said with a mischievous grin.

"Babies! We should offer to have Molly for a sleepover," she said.

"She loves animals. We should go to the zoo and make a day of it?" he said.

"I will speak to Lucy. Maybe on her next days off, she can look after Jimmy that weekend?" she said before making a detour and popping into the gift shop to buy Lucy some plant seeds.

"Thank ye for a lovely day," Jimmy said as Angus approached them.

"I will come and visit you tomorrow," she smiled, moving out from behind him.

CHAPTER
TWENTY-SIX

*One Kind Word Can Change Someone's Entire
Day – The Golden Rule*

J immy sat in anticipation, waiting for Lucy to arrive. The
very act of watching the door hurt his eyes. He felt an ex-
citing wave of adrenaline wash over him, but he was scared
and nervous too.

When would be the right time to ask Lucy about her brother?

Jimmy barely heard the knock at the door. Lucy popped her
head around the corner and instantly breathed in the remains
of freshness and cleanliness of lemon citrus and bleach. She
was absolutely delighted and filled with admiration for him
in trying to get his life back on track despite the setbacks.

"I've brought us some home-made soup," she said, placing her
handbag and a carrier bag with the flask of vegetable soup and
fresh scones on the table, before leaning in and giving him a
light hug.

"Thank ye. I've put on weight," he said with a cheeky grin.

"You look good," she said.

"Aye, I'm getting a six-pack," he said as her giddily actions made him laugh hard.

"I'm kidding. You've been truly kind in bringing me food," he said with the remains of laughter in his voice.

"How are you feeling after yesterday?" she asked.

"Better, thank ye," he said.

"You look much better. I'm glad," she smiled.

"It wis a lovely day, yesterday," he said.

"It was and we have been blessed with the weather," she said.

"Aye," he said.

"Shall we eat?" she asked, taking the carrier bag through to the kitchen.

"Thank ye," he said, briefly touching her arm.

"Whit has ye an Molly done today?" he asked, taking a bite of his dunked scone.

"In the morning, we planted the flower seeds Amy bought me and we made the soup and scones in between her afternoon nap," she said with joy.

"You're very easy-going," he said.

"I don't take my work home and everything I do is with Molly in mind," she said.

"I admire ye, Lucy. Our job roles were at different aspects of the spectrum, but we have both been in distressing situations," he said, swallowing hard at hearing himself say the words aloud.

"And I admire you, Jimmy. You have come such a long way and I know it is not easy," she said.

They sat, enjoying the hearty meal and each other's company. And although there was never any pressure for a continuous conversation, the conversations between them flowed smoothly and naturally, helping him to forget his loneliness, even if for a short while.

"How long have ye been a police officer?" he asked as she handed him his coffee and took a comfortable left seat beside him on the couch.

"Five years, this year," explaining further, with excitement in her voice.

"I always wanted to be a police officer. I joined the police cadets having this excitement within me every time I heard a police siren go past. I'm not an office, sitting behind a desk, day in and day out, looking at figures on the computer screen kind of person," she said.

Jimmy was genuinely interested in what she was telling him and seeing her passion for something she absolutely loved doing. He admired the woman sitting beside him.

"Every job is different and you are helping people," she said.

"Are ye going to do yer sergeant's exams?" he asked.

"When Tom was killed, thinking of doing my sergeant's exams was the last thing on my mind. Maybe when Molls is a bit older, I will consider it again," she said.

"I'm truly sorry, Lucy," he said, touching her arm.

Lucy pulled a photo from her phone and showed Jimmy the last photo ever taken with her brother. A tall, broad-shouldered man with the distinctive look of a soldier, stood with his arm around her and holding his baby niece. Taking in another long deep breath and fighting back her tears, she began to tell him about the dreaded phone call.

"Molly was three and a half months old when we received notice for Tom's deployment, so we rushed around trying to find a priest who would have her christened before he left," she said, swallowing hard and took Jimmy's offered hand, squeezing it tightly.

"Two weeks after this photo was taken, he was killed. I had already gone back to work that day and was working a late shift. The weather was dreadful. Roads were closed due to flooding and despite the warnings that people should not travel, they did. So not only did we have the already stranded vehicles to deal with, but we also had the stupidity of enthusiastic rubberneckers to deal with. It was chaos, soaked to the bone and with little resources. I did not even feel my phone vibrating continuously in my trouser pocket."

She hesitated briefly and went on, "The worst thing is, I could not even bring myself to tell my mother straight away. I blamed my tiredness during the long hours I was working. I only told her five days later, with the help of my sergeant. The moment my mother saw him, she knew. What daughter does that to their mother?" she said, choking with grief and tears still running down her cheeks, a visible weight on her shoulders.

Lucy went further, "I felt I had to continue to go to work as we all needed a reason and purpose to carry on. I ploughed my grief and inner turmoil into my job, thus giving my mother the chance to pour her love into looking after Molly. With Tom gone, we were all so very alone and lost."

"Lucy, darling," he said, stretching across with his left arm and pulled her towards him.

"He knew, Jimmy. He knew he was going to die," she said through her tears.

"Ye don't deserve this," he said, feeling his own emotions surfacing and Lucy wrapped her arms around him.

With no words needed, they took comfort in the closeness of each other.

CHAPTER TWENTY-SEVEN

Psych Session

"**I** would like to start today's session by asking Angus a few questions before continuing with the EMDR," Rosalind said.

"Sounds good," Angus said.

"The last session was mainly directed towards Jimmy. What are your thoughts?" Rosalind said.

"Just being a part of the sessions whether the questions are directed towards me or Jimmy is helping me. I am pleased with his progress," Angus said.

"Tell me how that fateful day affects you." Rosalind said.

"It affects me. I am angry. If not physically, psychologically. It is a constant war zone and I find it extremely testing to hold down my job as an officer, knowing the physical battles of daily life that Jimmy goes through," Angus said sadly.

"It's okay, pal," Jimmy said, giving Angus an encouraging clap on the back.

"Are you managing to speak to Amy?" Rosalind asked.

"We are talking more and doing the talk therapies have helped. I also know though, that I can do more," Angus said.

"Have you found it less forceful?" Rosalind asked.

"Yes, definitely. We had a good chat after the last session. However, I did have a moment's meltdown and was angry with myself for allowing it to happen," Angus said.

"Can you tell me about it?" Rosalind asked.

"It is always the same intrusive memories. A distinctive smell of sterilisation. An organised chaos of surgeons working on Jimmy. The constant beeping of medical equipment," Angus said.

"Have you experienced these memories from day one of the incident?" Rosalind asked.

"Yes but I do not think I was aware of them as much. Again, I think the anger and bitterness as well as losing myself in my job helped to block them from taking over my life" Angus said.

"Do you now feel you've let your guard down?" Rosalind

asked.

"Yes, I used to be able to control my focused mindset. Now, I have moments of doubts in my ability as a soldier," Angus said.

"Angus and I are experiencing a combination of life experience clashes," Jimmy said.

"Yeah. I totally agree with you, mate," Angus said.

"Angus, I'm going to suggest a guide of self-help techniques like the questions put across to Jimmy and are doable without the eye movements. This can be an exercise you do with Amy," Rosalind said.

"Yeah. I will do the exercise with Amy," Angus said.

"Angus has a good woman. She keeps both of us in line," Jimmy laughed.

"Jimmy, do you feel you're making progress?" Rosalind asked.

"I have completed the set goals with good days and bad days. I have laughed and even joked, but I also find that very quickly, I begin to question myself as to why I am laughing, or why I should be allowed to laugh," Jimmy said.

"You can laugh sometimes. You've laughed now and can I confirm it made you feel good?" Rosalind said.

"Aye," Jimmy said.

"Mate, we can all see the difference in you," Angus said.

"I would now like to pick up where we left off in the last session. Jimmy, did you find the healing light something we can come to that would help you with a sense of calm and peace?" Rosalind said.

"Aye, it's something I can go to," Jimmy said.

"That's good. Did you notice the shape changing in any form during the experience with the healing light?" Rosalind said.

"The shape did not change, but the light filled and surrounded me," Jimmy said.

"How did that make you feel?" Rosalind asked.

"I felt a sense of relief. I felt safe," Jimmy said.

"Let's stay with that and do a couple of breaths," Rosalind said.

"Inhale, two, three, four, hold. Exhale, two, three, four...Breatheing in calm and peace and exhaling your pain and stress...," she said.

Jimmy followed Rosalind's lead, holding his breath for a period. Breathing outward from his lungs, he brought his body back into balance, giving his organs a much-needed oxygen boost.

Angus found himself doing the breathing with Jimmy and bringing his body into a deep sense of relaxation. He was finding the sessions a useful tool that could be used in times to come.

"What are you noticing, Jimmy?" Rosalind asked.

"More of settling into my wheelchair. I felt more aware of my body in the chair," Jimmy said.

"Okay, let's do another set of eye movements to strengthen that as you notice the settling into your wheelchair and the awareness you felt in your body," Rosalind said, moving her fingers.

A few minutes later.

"Are you okay talking about your injuries?" Rosalind asked.

"I am fucking mad! I hate my fucked-up body! I am in constant pain! I don't sleep! I'm living this bad dream every day! I'm not capable of doing things and it makes me feel like a loser! Like I'll never really take care of myself!" Jimmy said.

"On a scale of 0 - 10, where 0 = no disturbance and 10 = high disturbance imaginable, what score would you give that emotion?" Rosalind asked.

"Feckin ten!" Jimmy said.

"Where in your body do you feel that pain?" Rosalind asked.

"In my heart, but everywhere really. I'm mad!" Jimmy said.

"Staying with those thoughts, now follow my fingers…," Rosalind said.

"Let it go and breathe. What are you noticing now?" she said.

"I just get so feckin mad! It takes me double the time just to make a sandwich, triple the time to have a feckin shower!" Jimmy said.

"Jimmy is also concerned with his fucked-up body and not having the ability to function properly with a woman," Angus said.

"Ah coudnae cut my food at the dinner!" Jimmy said, forming a fist with his left hand.

"And mate, there are guys who have completed challenges, but still need help tying their fucking shoelaces! I can guarantee there were vibrant banter remarks being exchanged!" Angus said with a slight annoyance in his voice.

"Jimmy, there are vets out there needing twenty-four-hour care. Their minds are perfectly capable of understanding how to look after themselves, but their bodies don't connect. It must be extremely difficult to carry this constant frustration and not have the physical ability to change it," Rosalind said.

"No one prepares you for a life outside the military," Angus said.

"Again, let's stay with these thoughts and follow my fingers," Rosalind said.

> *"I'm not the only one suffering. I'm not the only one who's lost a limb. I'm not the only one going through the mental anguish." Jimmy thought, following her fingers.*

"Let it go and breathe. What are you noticing now?" she said.

"I'm not the only one suffering," Jimmy said.

"What SUDs would you give it?" Rosalind asked.

"Nine," Jimmy said.

"That's good. It's getting better. I would like you to start paying attention to the messages that are going through your mind. If you start to notice yourself feeling sad, mad, bad, angry, frustrated, or discouraged, lonely, whatever it is, take a second and tune into those thoughts and what's happening as you're feeling those emotions...

I want you to write them down. For instance, if you are thinking 'I'm a loser', what are you feeling and how do you behave? Do you feel angry and behave by lashing out...?

But I want you to go further and write down what you would change. For instance, if you are thinking positively, do you feel happier and behave by doing exercises...?

Let's end today's session by bringing in your healing light, coming down from above and moving in through the top of your head and through your veins, a wonderful light of peace and comfort directing itself towards the shape in your body" Rosalind said.

Jimmy closed his eyes and focused on his surroundings more.

The extinction of life began to creep into every part of his being, all around him, washing over him like a wave of death.

The doomsday planet began to become parched, arid and bone brittle dry beneath his feet. The incessant and scorching rays of the sun beat down upon him like a heavy weight of strength-sapping metal, his existence struggling to breathe.

He noticed the ominous bolts of purple lightning striking in the far distance, beyond the parched land.

Crack!

They were getting closer and stronger with every strike, more piercing and threatening. Jimmy watched with trepidation as the forces of this doomed planet clashed in an almighty and ethereal maelstrom, this electrifying power of good and evil and dark and light fighting to their inevitable bitter end.

It was the end of another world.

The hard, desolate and arid ground shook violently and with unhindered power. Cracks spread and rippled out like a spider web of torn earth. Canyons appeared and widened as a warm inundation of purple light caught him, just as the ground beneath his feet fell away and his legs were lost forever.

The healing light filled his head like the warmth of a sunrise on a crisp spring day, spreading through his brain, into all its dark recesses and cavernous voids of despair and then on into his whole body, filling his chest and opening his airways, surrounding and protecting him.

"What are you noticing?" Rosalind asked.

"I can't explain it," Jimmy said.

"Is it a good feeling?" Rosalind asked.

"Aye, I feel calm," Jimmy said.

"Are you noticing any changes to the shape?" Rosalind asked.

"Aye, there is plenty of shift in the shape," Jimmy said.

"Staying with that feeling of calm and the shape's vision, follow my fingers," Rosalind said, moving her fingers in a horizontal motion.

Jimmy followed Rosalind's fingers…

"Take a deep breath and let it go. What are you noticing now?" Rosalind said.

"I'm still feeling the calmness," Jimmy said.

"That's good. It's only going to get better, Jimmy," Rosalind said, and ended the day's session.

CHAPTER TWENTY-EIGHT

As Jimmy worked through his psych therapy, he thought the progress was slow and doubts on whether he was improving often crossed his mind. But, he did feel a sense of relief and they were all seeing an improvement in him.

Constable Harris knocked on the door, giving her sergeant a smile while they waited patiently. It had been early evening and Jimmy was not expecting Angus till much later. Besides, Lucy and Angus usually popped their heads around the corner.

Counting down the hours to Angus visit, Jimmy had managed to keep his mind active and stay off the booze. He had streamed the latest news and hype of the country's excitement and preparations for the London 2012 Olympics and Paralympics. He also looked at future aspects of finding a job, something he was petrified of doing. He only knew how to be a soldier.

A surge of apprehension filled his gut as he struggled to move his wheelchair and open the door.

"Who would be knocking on my door?" he thought.

"Hello, Jimmy," Lucy said.

Her professionalism stopped her from showing him more affection.

"This is Sergeant Wilson. He wanted to meet you. We have an update on your case," she said.

"Hello, Constable Harris. Nice to meet ye, Sergeant Wilson," he said nervously, shaking the officer's left hand. He respected Lucy for being in uniform, but felt intimidated by the officers standing in front of him.

Inviting them inside, he offered the officers tea, but both declined and took a seat on the couch. Sergeant Wilson was a man in his early forties, a man with authority and was in decent shape and even good looking.

Lucy took out her notebook, feeling Jimmy's apprehension, sitting there watching her every move as her sergeant started explaining to him where they were in the case.

"We have had reports of another military medal being stolen in the Glasgow region. Unfortunately, we have had no further leads in finding your medals and we had no success on social media or the newspaper appeal. Our suspect was re-arrested earlier today for other offences and we questioned him again, but we also believe he is just an opportunist," he said.

The conversation was interrupted by another knock at the door. The officers took Amy by surprise.

"We have come to update Jimmy on the case," Lucy said, introducing Amy to her sergeant and Amy pulled out a chair to sit next to Jimmy.

"There have been no cases of medals being stolen around the country in as many years and they normally only resurface on a significant date. We have not closed your case and I am sure Constable Harris has kept you updated," the police sergeant said.

"We are grateful for everything you have put into the case," Amy said.

"Aye, thank ye for the update," Jimmy said with a touch of confidence in his voice, although the brief glance towards Lucy showed some doubt.

The officers got up to leave and Lucy wished she could lean in and give Jimmy a hug. She had felt immense reassurance and affection the night she cried for Tom, and he had held her tightly against his chest. He had made her feel safe, and she longed to feel that again.

Amy showed the officers out, pulling Lucy back as her sergeant walked on. She gave her an encouraging smile, knowing just how much she felt for Jimmy. Lucy gave her a phone gesture with her hand and both women nodded with an understanding.

"Lovely, how are you?" Amy asked, hugging Jimmy.

She had suggested to Angus that she pop in and visit him. She wanted to do her share in helping him and maybe having someone other than his best friend and the woman he clearly had feelings for might just help him open more.

"Aye, guid. Do ye want a coffee?" he said, relieved to have her company. It was just what he needed after seeing Lucy.

There had been an uneasy tension watching the two officers sitting on the couch together.

"Was Sergeant Wilson Lucy's type? Why wouldn't he be? They worked together, he was good looking and with all his body parts!" he had thought.

"I will make it. Go sit down," she said, checking her phone that had just beeped.

Amy, I do not think Jimmy was incredibly happy with me

Hmmm...I saw that. He is out of practice. I will talk to him

*I want to invite him over for lunch. Maybe
I can pop in after my shift*

That would be wonderful. Leave it to me, I will

make sure he is expecting your visit later

Thanks, Amy

Jimmy and Amy's relationship was relaxed, warm and they spoke with ease. She just fitted in and treated him like the soldier he once was.

"I was starting to feel left out," she said, giving him his coffee and taking a seat beside him.

"What took you so long?" he said, giving her a cheeky grin. With Amy, there were moments that Jimmy showed his old self. He did not have to feel the shyness and awkwardness around her, like he did with Lucy and even Angus.

"I needed your company tonight," he said, taking a drink of his coffee.

"Do you think the psych sessions and talk therapies are helping?" she asked.

"I have guid days and bad days. Honestly though, I am scared for the future. What happens when the sessions end?" he sighed heavily.

"Lovely, you have come so far in what, seven months. We are so proud of you. You have been able to manage your drinking and speak to someone when that craving gets too unbearable. That is true willpower and determination. That was a huge step forward and you did that, all on your own," she said.

"Aye, but it's difficult, Amy. What happens in a month or two?" he said.

"Lovely, Angus is taking that day off. Someone will be with you," she said.

"What if I'm on that verge of no return?" he asked.

"It is going to take time. You have had five years of deep depression, and your life changed in an instant. You cannot expect to feel better overnight. You have also got to understand, there will be good days and bad days. I cannot promise you will be rid of depression forever, but you will learn how to manage it. I will promise you this though. Lucy, Angus and I will always be here for you," she said, giving him a supporting arm around his shoulder.

"What am I going to do about a job? I can't fuckin sit behind a desk. That's not me," he said with frustration.

"Angus and I have spoken about this and we understand your frustrations, mate. But let us cross that bridge when we get to it. Mike has been keeping in touch and is determined to get you involved, but we all want you to get through the sessions and concentrate on your recovery first," she said, with Jimmy nodding his head, and she continued to offer her thoughts.

"We know you miss army life and if Angus could change that, he would. But we know what we sign up for. I lost some good friends too, but life goes on. We are never going to forget them and in fact, because we survived, they will not be forgotten. You will always be a soldier, Jimmy. No one can ever take that away from you," she said, supporting him as he choked on his tears.

"I will be honest with you. Angus at times had his doubts, but you are proving him wrong. He wishes you could display your army memories, but he also knows that will come with time. You should be proud of yourself. I live with him, and I have seen a difference in his appearance. Not having you in his life left a painful void. He was close to breaking point, but he will never admit it. He never stopped talking about you.

You are the third person in our relationship and he does not want to lose your friendship again," she said, squeezing his hand.

"Will ye be my psych nurse?" he laughed through his sorrow.

"You can always talk to any one of us. That was Lucy messaging me earlier. She wants to invite you over for lunch and I think that would be lovely. She is going to pop in after her shift. You looked awkward around her tonight, mate. You know she was only doing her job?" she said.

"Aye, I don't know what I'm feeling," he said with his anxiety in overload.

"Lucy is a lovely person. Just give her a chance. She has been through so much and all on her own. Molly's father is a total bastard and what happens when he is released from prison?" she said.

"Aye, I would feckin fight him, but this...," he said, gesturing towards his body, feeling his muscles tightening with his own anger for the situation Lucy was in.

"It worries Lucy. She is always on alert, scared someone he knows might come knocking on her door. She misses her brother terribly and the only thing keeping her going is Molly. Lucy is suffering a deep sense of loss and loneliness. She does not get out much and her mother and daughter come first," she said.

"I'm scared. I've been burned once before and now look at me. What woman wants this?" he sighed heavily.

"Lucy is not her! That stupid bitch had no comprehension of how to be a soldier's partner!" she said, raising her voice slightly, in support of his pain.

"Lucy cares for you. I know how you treated her in the beginning and believe me, she is strong enough, especially because of her job. She could have walked away and treated you like any other case, but she saw someone who truly needed help and went that extra mile. Angus and I can see you have feelings for each other. You are both scared to show it. You have both been burned. Accept her invitation to lunch and enjoy it. You should also invite her over one evening. Take her out for a meal or order a takeaway," she said, nudging him and looking at her watch.

"That is our talk therapy over for today, corporal," she said, and Jimmy laughed hard.

* * *

22:55 hours –

Angus had dozed off in between watching something on TV.

"How is he?" he asked, hearing Amy walk up the stairs and into their bedroom.

"...and hello to you too!" she said, slightly annoyed.

"I am sorry. It has been a long day," he said, taking her arm as she sat down on his side of the bed.

"I am exhausted too. Lucy and her sergeant were with him..."

"What the fuck has he done now?" he asked, throwing his arms in the air and cutting her off.

"Angus, do not cut me off like that again!" she said angrily and stood up.

They were both feeling the exhaustion in the extra man-hours visiting and taking care of Jimmy, but knew it had to be done, and they were grateful for having Lucy's help.

"Aims, I am sorry," he said, climbing out of bed to apologise.

"Another medal has been stolen in the Glasgow region. They were there to update him," she sighed, sitting on the end of the bed.

"What was his reaction?" he asked.

"I think he was more concerned about Lucy being with her male colleague," she said with some amusement.

"He needs to get out more," he said.

"We had a good chat and Lucy is popping in after her shift. She wants to invite him over for lunch," she said.

"Does he know?" he asked.

"Yes. I told him to accept," she said.

"Good. Thank you," he said.

"It is exhausting for both of us, but we knew this was going to happen," she said, getting up to change.

"Why bother?" he said with a look that suggested he wanted something more.

"Oh really now!" she laughed and fell back onto the bed.

❊ ❊ ❊

To continue his determination in keeping his mind off the booze and the achievement he had accomplished all day, Jimmy warmed up some food and sat at the table eating. Amy's visit had helped ease the tension he felt in seeing Lucy doing her job and he was truly looking forward to seeing her again.

The knock at the door came just after midnight, with Lucy finishing her last late shift. She had felt the tension too and was grateful to Amy for letting her know that Jimmy was expecting her.

"Hello, Lucy," he said, manoeuvring his chair to climb in at hearing the door.

"Hello, Jimmy. Do not get up. I am sorry it is so late," she said, sitting down beside him.

"No worries. I'm glad ye came. Ye okay?" he said, stretching awkwardly to his right to gently touch her arm.

"The wrong side. It is your fault!" she said, face palming in a laughable manner and allowed him to move across.

"I am okay, Jimmy. Are we okay?" she said nervously.

"Aye, I'm sorry aboot earlier," he said with embarrassment.

"I know the update on your case earlier was not exactly the result you wanted to hear, but at least your case is still being talked about and remains open," she said.

"Aye. That is guid news. I appreciate everything you've done, Lucy," he said with a genuine heartfelt smile.

"Thank you, Jimmy. Did Amy talk to you? I would really like you to come for lunch and meet my mum. We will manage fine," she said, hoping he would be comfortable in allowing her to help him without Angus.

"Aye. I would like that," he said.

"I am so pleased. I pick you up around eleven?" she said.

"I look forward to it," he said, and leaned across to hug her, both needing that moment of closeness.

CHAPTER
TWENTY-NINE

Who You Are Tomorrow Begins With
What You Do Today – Tim Fargo

Tim Fargo is an American author, keynote speaker,
angel investor, and entrepreneur – Wikipedia

T he joy Jimmy felt inside him at seeing Lucy again later
that day allowed him to accept her help with ease,
both quietly appreciating the hold she provided in supporting his waist whilst climbing into her car. Lucy was delighted at how easily the wheelchair fitted in and her face
glowed with triumph.

"Look. Except for the step in the front, everything is on one
level. We can go around the back and everything will be fine,"
she said cheerfully, turning into the driveway. She wanted
Jimmy to feel comfortable visiting her home.

"Ye have a kind heart, Lucy," he said, momentarily holding her
gaze and bringing a faint blush to her cheeks.

"Do not feel nervous, Jimmy. I am glad you have come," she said with the front door opening, and Mrs. Harris and Molly walked out to greet them.

Mrs. Harris, a slim woman in her early fifties, embraced Jimmy with pride. "It is wonderful to finally meet you, Jimmy. Lucy talks about you all the time."

"Aye. Ye too, Mrs. Harris," he said with a huge grin spreading across his face at seeing Lucy's growing rosiness.

"Call me Maggie," she said, picking up Molly and followed them around the back.

With access from a side footpath, the small rear garden had been purposely landscaped with a mixture of shrubs, hedges, climbing plants, a birdbath and feeders, providing a haven for birds and small creatures to nestle.

A small shed and greenhouse stood at the bottom of the garden, where a patch of grass had been left unkept and a metal bucket strategically placed on its side to teem with life and provide shelter.

A mature apple tree provided needed shade to the garden, while a young Cherry Blossom tree had been planted to be seen from the kitchen window and in years to come, would provide extra shade to the garden.

Lucy had had a very modest upbringing with her mother providing for her and Tom, and what they had lacked in the latest toys and gadgets, they had gained in love and respect. Following in her mother's footsteps, she had no choice but to become the main breadwinner, but they lived comfortably and the kindness and warmth that Lucy and her family shared is what was helping Jimmy feel more at ease and comfortable within his own skin, even when that thought of needing a drink clouded his mind. Their hospitality, warmth and openness helped him accept the fact that he might need help physically in doing certain things.

The Harris' three-bedroom bungalow was welcoming and lively. The décor from Lucy's childhood and family memories filled the spaces, with Tom and Lucy's army and police portraits proudly on display. The home represented everything about Lucy's caring and kind personality.

Mesmerised at having Jimmy in her home, Molly casually leaned against his chair. "Hellooo, Jimmy," her sweetest little voice said.

"Molls has been so excited," Lucy said, kneeling to her level.

"Show Jimmy how excited you are. This much," she gestured with her arms as Molly mimicked her mother and both glowed in happiness.

"Should we show Jimmy your room?" Lucy asked, grabbing her daughter in a playful hold.

"Can I see yer toys?" Jimmy said, giving the wee lassie a tickle and making her squeal in delight by his interest in her imaginary world. She half waddled and ran towards her room with loud and delightful squeals while Maggie left them to finish preparing the lunch and Lucy showed Jimmy their home.

Molly's single bedroom was the smallest of the three. It had a built-in cupboard, single bed against one wall and a small white bookshelf that doubled up as a bedside table stood beside it. A glorious mushroom-shaped night lamp with insect characters peeping through the windows stood on the top shelf and the photo of Tom and Lucy on the day of Molly's christening sat in its pride position. The bedroom was prettily decorated, with Lucy introducing cheerful fabric designs and canvas prints of Ostriches and Hairy Coos to compliment the plain white walls.

"This is Molly's favourite book," Lucy said in a sweet, playful manner, while helping her daughter place the book on Jimmy's lap and turn the pages. Mimicking her daughter's actions of each animal, Jimmy joined in, their giggles bringing an emotional sense of release to him. He had not felt this comfortable around a woman in so long.

While they left Molly pre-occupied with her toys, Lucy gave Jimmy a grand tour of the remaining two double rooms and bathroom. All were complemented with bursts of colourful fabrics and reminders of Lucy's, Tom's and now Molly's childhood memories.

"You should be able to get around easily enough," Lucy said shyly, sitting on the end of her bed.

"Don't feel embarrassed about asking for help, Jimmy," Maggie said, holding Molly and joining them in the room.

"Thank ye. You've made me feel so welcome," Jimmy said.

"Lunch is ready, but she needs a change first," Maggie said, giving Molly a snort of laughter.

"We're teaching Molls how to use the big toilet, but I think today's excitement got the better of her," Lucy said, sharing a smile with Jimmy.

"Are we a stinky poo?" Lucy said, taking Molly into an airplane hold and playfully walked out with her. Maggie wheeled Jimmy to the kitchen to keep her company.

"She's really pleased you came today," Maggie said, while adding final finishes to the meal.

"Aye. Yer daughter has helped me a great deal. I'm sorry for yer loss, Maggie. I wish I could have met yer son," he said sincerely.

"From a young boy, he knew he wanted to join the army. He joined the cadets and signed up a few days after his sixteenth birthday. He had already done two tours, but this last one, he did not want to leave Lucy alone to deal with her abusive boyfriend. She convinced him that her police colleagues had her back. She blames herself and thinks Tom was distracted with her problems. He was always there to protect her and she misses him dearly," Maggie said.

It had been the first time a man, let alone a soldier, had been in the family home since Tom's death.

The roast chicken tasted as good as every home-cooked meal Lucy had brought him. Her natural ability in not being fazed at helping him cut his food made her company even more heartfelt.

"Yer daughter has spoilt me with home-cooked meals," Jimmy told Maggie, giving Lucy a smiling wink.

"I have had a good teacher," Lucy said happily.

"Just like Molls, Lucy enjoyed watching and helping me in the kitchen," Maggie said.

"It is an enjoyable way to de-stress," Lucy said.

"You get a whiff of fresh scones and you know Lucy has come in from a late shift and cannot sleep," Maggie said, with Jimmy giving a soft sigh. He knew what it felt like to be sleep deprived.

"Ye have a very welcoming family and home, Maggie," Jimmy said.

"Thank you, Jimmy. If you want a change of scenery, you are always welcome to spend the day with me. Even if Lucy is working, I am sure we will manage," Maggie said.

"Thank ye," Jimmy said.

"We are good listeners, Jimmy," Maggie said.

After lunch, Lucy gave Molly her bottle of juice and Jimmy another cool drink, insisting that he climb out of his wheelchair and keep Molly occupied while she and her mother washed the dishes.

Sitting on the couch next to him, his left arm tucked around her, Molly had gladly shared her interest in modern art. Her colouring book of squiggles depicted the next Banksy.

Maggie washed while Lucy dried, listening to the chatters between them. The little girl was clearly developing a fondness for the scarred soldier, as Jimmy had clearly shown signs of his own recovery, although he still had a long way to go.

"He has a lot of Tom in him," Maggie whispered, embracing her daughter as a tear rolled down her cheek. She was touched by his affection towards her granddaughter.

"He looks very relaxed today," Lucy whispered back, feeling that returning flutter in her stomach. She could not remember if at any time she had felt something for another guy other than Owen, but then he had been a domineering lover.

Jimmy looked up to see Lucy leaning into the kitchen doorway. Holding her gaze, they smiled and Jimmy gestured for her to join them. Molly's giggles turned into squeals as they tickled her playfully.

Maggie stood in the kitchen, listening to her daughter's happiness. It had been so long since she had heard Lucy laugh and enjoy someone's company. They helped each other without realising they were. Wiping her tears, she took a long deep breath and found that inner strength through the Cherry Blossom and Tom's presence.

"Mum," Lucy called.

"You should teach Jimmy how to play Bridge," she said.

"Gosh, I have not played in donkeys' years," Maggie said.

"Do ye play?" Jimmy asked Lucy.

"No. I just don't have the time in between my shifts," Lucy said.

"Aye. It would be interesting to learn," Jimmy said.

"It's a game of skill. I have the book somewhere," Maggie said, getting up to find it.

"She hasn't taken her eyes off you," Lucy said, stroking Molly's forehead, the little girl resting her legs on Jimmy's stumps and drinking her bottle while fighting against her sleepy eyes.

"Aye. Yer wee lassie is so cute," Jimmy said.

"I will go put her down," Lucy smiled, picking up her daughter and carrying her through to her bedroom. She was enjoying the afternoon with Jimmy.

"Found it," Maggie said, returning to the room. "There are four players in two fixed partnerships...," she said, briefly flicking through the rule book and offering it to Jimmy to take home and read.

"I will definitely think aboot it, thank ye," Jimmy said.

Lucy returned and Maggie took the opportunity to go and lie down, leaving her daughter and Jimmy to enjoy some company together.

"How are you feeling, Jimmy?" Lucy asked, putting her feet up on the couch and making herself comfortable on his left side.

"It's been a guid day, Lucy," he said, swallowing hard. He had not felt so relaxed and content since his injuries.

"Has it helped to be around some company today?" she asked.

"Aye. I haven't had a drink in two days," he said.

"Oh Jimmy, that is fantastic! Thank you for sharing that with me," she said.

"It's been tough and it wis a long day yesterday," he said.

"My offer still stands and you heard my mother," she said, and Jimmy took her hand.

"Ye have a very welcoming family home," he said.

"Thank you. Our home is comfortable and lived in. We did not have much growing up, but our mother taught us to appreciate the trivial things in life," she said.

"I can appreciate that," he said.

"Would you like another drink?" she asked, secretly hoping he would want to stay a while longer.

"Please," he said, happy to have some company.

"What a pity we can't sit outside," she said. It had started raining not long after they arrived earlier.

"Aye. Yer garden is a haven for animal life," he said.

"We wanted to give something back to our mother and with Tom taking annual leave for Molly's birth, we decided to revamp the family garden. Tom dug many of the beds, but Mum and I have introduced more bulbs and colour. We planted the cherry tree in his memory," she said.

"Aye. I like it," he said.

"It has a peaceful aura to it," she said, with the quietness quickly filling the air and Jimmy sensed her pain.

"Ye could do with someone to talk to," he said.

"Maybe we can help each other?" she smiled sadly.

"Aye, I would like that," he said, leaning across and hugging her tightly.

CHAPTER THIRTY

Psych Session

"Jimmy and Angus, you've been to a few sessions now. Do you feel you've made some progress?" Rosalind asked.

"Jimmy and I have both agreed that taking part in the sessions together has helped us to realise we needed the help. I am glad I listened to my future wife," Angus said.

"I have my days, but I am feeling more relaxed," Jimmy said.

"I think Lucy's support is also having an influence," Angus said.

"Who is Lucy?" Rosalind asked.

"The police officer investigating the theft of my medals," Jimmy said.

"She has a little girl who seems to help bring Jimmy out of his shell," Angus said.

"Aye. She is very cute," Jimmy said.

"Does Lucy have any brothers or sisters?" Rosalind asked.

"Lucy had an older brother who served. He was killed two years ago, sadly. We discovered that I served alongside him at Sandhurst. He was a good soldier and Lucy is suffering a deep sense of loss," Angus said.

"That's interesting. So he was a soldier too. How does that make you feel, Jimmy?" Rosalind said.

"I've disrespected Lucy and her brother," Jimmy said.

"Have you spoken to Lucy about him?" Rosalind asked.

"Aye. Lucy popped in for a visit one evening and we had a meal together. I asked her about her job as a police officer and her brother came up in the conversation," Jimmy said.

"How did that make you feel?" Rosalind asked.

"I felt angry and hopeless," Jimmy said.

"Mate, talking to Lucy and understanding the pain she is going through will help you both," Angus said.

"Did Lucy show any emotion?" she asked.

"Aye," Jimmy said.

"Jimmy was due to be married on his return from operations,

but she called off the wedding while he was fighting for his life!" Angus said angrily.

"Do not talk about her!" Jimmy said abruptly, his muscles tightening with every breath.

"We do not talk about her," Angus said.

"Jimmy, we don't have to talk about her," Rosalind said.

"Let's do a few minutes of breathing..." she suggested.

"Even though a part of me is feeling angry and hopeless, I'm helping Lucy through her pain," Jimmy said, rubbing his heart firmly.

"Even though a part of me is feeling weak, I am here to support my mate," Angus said.

"Release your negativity and remind yourself of your positives," Rosalind said.

"What are you noticing, Jimmy?" she asked.

"I'm feeling that weight lift again," Jimmy said.

"How did you feel about yourself after you comforted Lucy?" Rosalind asked.

"I had mixed feelings. I did not expect myself to just reach out and hold her. I did not know if I was doing the right thing,"

Jimmy said.

"Lucy did not pull away, did she?" Rosalind asked.

"No," Jimmy shook his head.

"You should give yourself a little more credit. You offered comfort at that moment to someone who needed it. Sometimes the most stressful and scariest moments can also end up being the most worthwhile," Rosalind said.

"Jimmy accepted Lucy's lunch invitation and met her mother," Angus said.

"How did that make you feel?" Rosalind asked.

"I actually felt okay and even I had to admit that it was a good day and felt at ease for the first time since my injuries," Jimmy said.

"That is wonderful! You might not think it, but you are thinking differently," Rosalind said.

"I agree," Angus said.

"Do you think you are accepting the fact you might need help doing certain things?" Rosalind asked.

"I don't know yet," Jimmy said.

"Angus, how are you feeling?" Rosalind asked.

"Amy and I are talking more, but we have had our moments. For instance, Amy and I had an argument one evening after getting back from visiting Jimmy," Angus said.

"Why was that, Angus?" Rosalind asked.

"I did not allow Amy to finish her explanation as to why Lucy and her sergeant were updating him of another medal being stolen. I thought Jimmy had got himself into trouble again. I am sorry, mate," Angus said.

"Have the self-help techniques helped?" Rosalind asked.

"Definitely. We are now sharing our excitement for the wedding," Angus said.

"You have both come a long way in your recovery and I'm seeing great improvement," Rosalind said.

"How is the drinking, Jimmy?" she asked.

"I haven't had a whiskey, but I'm still drinking," Jimmy said with disappointment.

"You are managing your drinking though, mate. Jimmy has found that ability to phone and speak to one of us when that craving gets too much," Angus said.

"That is really good news. You are finding the ability to control your drinking in manageable amounts and speak to someone in that desperate moment. Writing down your thoughts and feelings and recognising how it affects your behaviour will also be something that helps you move forward," Rosalind said.

"By taking part in the sessions, I have been able to spend more time with Jimmy. I think that has helped?" Angus said.

"Aye, definitely. I've needed that extra support after our meetings," Jimmy said.

"I would like to continue with the EMDR and introduce another form of exercise known as 'the container'. Angus, this will benefit you as well. I want you to bring some sort of secure container to your mind's eye. This container must be strong enough to hold all disturbing memories, images, thoughts, physical sensations, sounds, smells and emotions. Any secure place to hold your distresses?" Rosalind said.

Like a silent transmission of thoughts between them, both Jimmy and Angus agreed, "Ammo box,"

"Now, imagine taking your distressing images and putting them inside this ammo box and closing the lid," Rosalind said.

"The aftermath of the IED blast," Jimmy visualised.

"The horrific chaos around Jimmy's hospital bed," Angus remembered.

"Think of the sounds...," Rosalind said.

"Seconds of deathly silence before a harrowing of screams," Jimmy thought.

"Organised mayhem of voices and beeping of medical machines," Angus thought.

"Your physical sensations...," Rosalind said.

"A pain like no other. Numb," Jimmy thought.

"A nauseating numbness," Angus thought.

"The smells...," Rosalind said.

"Diesel fumes. Human flesh," Jimmy thought.

"Sterilization," Angus thought.

"Your emotions...," Rosalind said.

"Anger, scared," Jimmy thought.

"Anger, scared, self-blame," Angus thought.

"Now, take these distressing thoughts and anything else that comes to mind and place them in the ammo box, safeguarding the lid. How do you both feel?" Rosalind said.

"I'm exhausted and mentally drained," Jimmy admitted.

"I agree," Angus said.

"Do you feel any form of release?" Rosalind asked.

"It is a difficult one to grasp. Does this container have to be a form of imagination?" Angus said.

"No, not at all. Your container can be a physical object," Rosalind said.

"I suppose we can write them down and use a ceramic pot to put them in," Angus said.

"You don't sound too convinced, Angus?" Rosalind said.

"I'm with Angus on this one," Jimmy said.

"I can appreciate that some sessions will be less convincing than others, but everything we are working through will be beneficial, even after your therapy sessions come to an end," Rosalind said.

"I respect that and we are feeling the benefits. I suppose it has just been one of those days," Angus said.

"Let's do some chest rub exercises. Even though a part of

me...," Rosalind said.

"Even though a part of me is not convinced, the session has been good," Angus said, rubbing his chest in a circular motion.

"Even though a part of me is physically and mentally drained, I'm working through the session," Jimmy said.

Rosalind continued the breathing technique for a while longer, getting the soldiers to a stage where they felt more re-laxed and at ease within themselves.

"Jimmy, I would like to end today's session by going to your healing light," Rosalind said.

Jimmy closed his eyes and focused on his image.

With the aurora of purple light carrying and keeping him safe, Jimmy's mangled body watched the war zone.

With the planet violently hotter and brighter, and several mushroom clouds of dust and gas hanging over it, hundreds of fireballs erupted like nuclear weapons.

Boom!

The planet was at war. A bolt of purple lightning struck the burning planet like a catastrophic asteroid hitting the ground.

Boom!

The doomsday planet exploded into thousands of burning particles and losing its defence against the solar storms, it crumbled into oblivion.

An overwhelming feeling of relief filled Jimmy's body as the healing light carried him to a new world.

A new life.

A life free from frustration.

"If only it was real," Jimmy thought.

CHAPTER THIRTY-ONE

Without communication, there is no relationship.
Without respect, there is no love. Without trust,
there is no reason to continue – Buddha

ngus and Amy needed a date night, out on the town and time spent alone.

Going through the therapy sessions and helping Jimmy was stretching their already strained relationship to breaking point and Angus knew he needed to support his future wife before it was too late. He suggested a couple of days off and a romantic night in Edinburgh.

"Please fasten this for me," Amy said, walking out the bathroom, the halter neck swing dress fitting her every curve.

"You look and smell divine," Angus said, clipping the clasp on her dress.

"You think!" she said, showing him a leg and giving him a flirtatious smile.

"I think we could cancel dinner and order room service?" he said, nibbling on her neck.

"I was lucky to get the reservation, but I tell you what, give me some food and drink and you might just get lucky later!" she said with laughter.

"Deal! It is going to be a lovely evening, Aims" he said, walking her out the room.

"This is going to be good for us," she said.

It was an early summer evening and the lively, bustling cosmopolitan mix of people brought Edinburgh city to life. Tourists and locals populated the local pubs and bars.

Finding a gin bar twelve minutes from their hotel, they had two hours to fill their time and decided to enjoy a drink or two before their dinner reservation in another part of town.

"I will have a 'Tourist's Adventure'," Amy said, choosing a botanical gin of Acacia Flowers and Cubeb Berry.

"In that case, I will have the 'Scottish Isles'," Angus said, choosing a botanical gin of Coriander Seed, Orris Root and Citrus Peel, deciding to try something other than his usual ale or glass of wine.

"When was the last time we did this?" Angus asked, him and Amy quickly taking the comfortable couch now available in one corner.

"Emma's birthday last year," she said, taking another sip of gin.

"No, I mean together, you and me. But that was a good night," he said with a cheeky grin.

"Yeah, that was some night. At least we had you to get us home. However, you and I have not had a date night together in over a year," she said, with Angus kissing her fingers lightly.

"I am sorry for neglecting you and not being the easiest person to get on with," he said.

"All I want is for you to know that I have always been there for you and you can talk to me," she said, feeling a faint taste of citrus and apple on his lips.

"Let us taste," he said, taking a sip of her gin.

"Are you not enjoying yours? You don't normally drink gin," she said, now trying his.

"Yeah. I thought I would try something different, but it's not for me. My taste buds are obviously not as refined as yours," he said, tongue in cheek.

"Get yourself a beer. I'll drink this," she said.

"Cheers, wifey," he said, and Amy gave him the amused eye-brow glare.

They enjoyed their drinks, the live band and the atmospheric vibe of the pub, sharing tender moments and adoring their time together as a couple. After a few more drinks and some great laughs, they both decided it was time to leave for their dinner reservation and got up and left, hand in hand.

The looming historic fortress of Edinburgh Castle with its centuries of soldiers, kings and queens, dominated the ancient city skyline from its position on Castle Rock.

"We have travelled through countries, cuddled a Koala, but we have never done a tour of the castle," she said with her arm looped around his, admiring the historic fortress.

"No, we have not. But we have not visited Africa as a couple either," he smiled.

"That is going to be amazing. I am so excited," she said.

"We can make wild passionate love under the stars," he grinned. "And maybe even keep away the dangerous beasts. I'm sure I am more than enough of a beast for you to manage," he smiled further.

"As long as you tie a mosquito net to a tree, I am sure the beast in you can be tamed," she said, and both laughed at the thought.

✻ ✻ ✻

Amy had been lucky enough to get a reservation at a Michelin starred restaurant, the cancellation made minutes earlier. The sophisticated fine-dining restaurant on Princes Street offered a feel of elegance and romance, a well-deserved indulgence.

They ordered a bottle of red wine and decided to go with the set three-course menu.

"I will have the Cured Goose Foie, please," Amy said, both deciding to choose something different from the selected starters, mains and desserts, for them to share a mouthful.

"That smoked bone marrow is delicious," she said, Angus sharing the last helping of his main meal with her and himself tasting her pigeon.

"Thank you for tonight," she said, stretching over and kissing him.

"Aims, I should take better care of you," he said.

"Tonight was just what I needed," she said, taking another mouthful of the fresh yogurt sorbet. The desserts were a burst of vibrant colours on the plate, making it a perfect ending to a wonderful meal.

* * *

"I love you," he said.

"And I love you. You are showing me a part of you I have

never seen before and I like it," she said, resting her head on his shoulder as they enjoyed the fresher air of the late-night, while making the ten-minute walk back to their hotel.

"Are you going to see Jimmy tomorrow?" she asked.

"Yeah, I will pop in tomorrow evening," he said before they burst out laughing.

"I can't even blame you on this occasion," she said through her laughter.

"Yeah, I have managed to do pretty well this evening," he said.

"It was inevitable. He is so much part of our lives," she said as he slipped the card key to their room.

Angus nibbled on her ear and loosened the clasp of her dress. "Did I feed you enough food and drink tonight?" he asked, moving his lips down her neck, with the aromas of sweet wine on his breath.

"I could do with a second helping of dessert," she smiled, bringing his face up to hers.

"Hmmm, I can help with that," he said.

"Make love to me," she whispered, helping with his trouser zip as he lifted her and carried her to the bed.

For the first time in their relationship, Amy was seeing a different side to Angus, a more relaxed and content side to him, showing the caring side of his emotions and not the anger and bitterness that he would normally display.

Going through the psych sessions and having the talk therapies was also helping their relationship in so many ways. All Amy ever wanted for Angus was for him to find that inner forgiveness.

There would always be that third person in their lives and the possibility that they would need to look after Jimmy, both emotionally and financially, tested their relationship more than once, but she had been there from the beginning and would be till the end, for as long as Angus would have her.

CHAPTER THIRTY-TWO

Monday, 23rd July 2012

God could not be everywhere and therefore
he made mothers – Rudyard Kipling

Joseph Rudyard Kipling was an English journalist,
short-story writer, poet and novelist. He was born in
India, which inspired much of his work – Wikipedia

L ucy unfastened the child seatbelt and lifted her poorly sleeping girl into her arms.

"Thank you, Mum," she said as Mrs. Harris met her daughter at the front door.

"How is she? What did the doctor say?" she asked.

Lucy had taken Molly straight to the doctor's after finishing her last nightshift and arriving home at 07:45 hours. Molly had been irritable and off colour the day before, with Mrs. Harris getting little sleep in looking after her granddaughter through the night.

"She has a fever and likely an ear infection," Lucy said, putting Molly to bed. But no sooner had she done this, than Molly stirred.

"Shhh, Mummy's here," she said, kneeling beside her bed to comfort her.

"Molly sick," the little girl croaked.

"I know my little sausage. Mummy is going to make you better," she said, kissing her tiny nose, but Molly just wanted her mummy and the safety of her arms around her.

"Poor little thing. I'll get her some Paracetamol," Mrs. Harris said.

"Thank you, Mum," Lucy said, taking the little girl through to the lounge.

"Molls, drink this for Nanna," Mrs. Harris said, offering her the liquid medicine, but the irritable patient shook her head in protest.

"Molls, look at Mummy. It will make you better," she said, with Mrs. Harris nodding in agreement.

"That's a good girl," Nanna said, convincing her granddaughter to take the liquid Paracetamol.

"Mum, you should get some sleep. I can take care of her now," Lucy said.

"I will. Do you want a cuppa first?" Mrs. Harris said.

"I'll get one later, but can you make her a juice, please?" Lucy said.

"Molls, say thank you to Nanna for looking after you," Lucy said.

"Thank yooo, Nanna. Love yooo," Molly said sweetly as Mrs. Harris gave her the diluted bottle of juice.

"Nanna loves you too. Now you must doodoos for Mummy and get better," she said, giving both her girls a motherly kiss, before going through to the bedroom and getting much-needed rest.

"Should Mummy make you a bed on the couch and look after you?" Lucy asked, giving Molly a cuddle.

"Yes, Mummy. Molly sick," the little girl said.

"Okay, my baby," Lucy said, taking a pillow from Molly's bed and using the knitted blanket to make her comfortable on the couch.

Lucy had now been awake for over fifteen hours and the exhaustion was slowly taking its toll. With Molly dozing off, she took the opportunity to change into a comfortable tracksuit and make herself a hot chocolate.

Lucy texted, sending Amy a private message.

*Hi Amy, was hoping to see Jimmy today, but
Molls has a fever and ear infection, mum
was up most of the night with her*

*Aww, Lucy, I am sorry to hear that, poor
thing. Can I help with anything?*

*Thank goodness I am off now for two days. Was really
hoping to see Jimmy, but I am too exhausted and do
not think I will get any sleep now. We have taken her
to the doctor, and we will see how she feels later*

*Do not worry about Jimmy, one of us will pop in later
this evening and check on him, but listen, we are
here if you need help. Please keep me updated*

Thanks, Amy, I will text you later

* * *

13:24 hours and Jimmy had kept himself busy all morning, working through the suggested techniques in completing his homework for the next session.

He had made himself a cold meat sandwich and was enjoying an iced cool drink while counting down the hours to Lucy's visit later that evening, when his phone lit up and the army officer's face popped up on the screen.

"Amy," Jimmy said, answering the FaceTime call.

"Hey, my lovely. Are you okay?" she said.

"Aye. Ye? What's wrong?" he said with some hesitation.

"I cannot speak for long, but Lucy texted me this morning to say Molls has a fever and ear infection and cannot make it tonight. She is really sorry," she said.

"Is she okay? Can you pick me up to go and visit?" he asked with some concern and frustration in not having the ability to do it on his own.

"Lovely, you know I cannot come and pick you up. It is just not possible. I know you are frustrated and were looking forward to seeing her, but Angus or I will pop in this evening, so you are stuck with us, mate. What have you done this morning?" she said.

"Working on my Cognitive Behaviour Therapy homework," he said.

"That's great. Have you had something to eat?" she said.

"Aye," he said.

"That's good. Lovely, have you had a drink?" she said.

"No, Amy, I have not!" he said annoyingly.

"Lovely, I did not phone to question your ability. I phoned to let you know about Lucy. However, do me a favour because I am concerned your frustrations might urge you towards that drink. Use this opportunity to practice on your CBT exercises and we can talk about it later," she said.

Jimmy sighed. Amy was right and always seemed to be able to steer him back into line. She was proving to be that focused and controlled mindset that he needed to get his life back on track.

"Aye, you are right. I'm sorry," he said.

"Lucy is shattered, poor woman, but she still found the time to ask me to visit you this evening because she does not want you to be let down. Give her a call on FaceTime. You might not see her in person, but at least you can have that face to face conversation. She would really appreciate that," Amy smiled, giving Jimmy that You better! look.

"Aye aye, captain!" he grinned.

"Oh my God. I cannot believe you just said that! You are so lucky there is a screen between us, otherwise I would have you doing a bee sting ten times over!" she said, and both laughed hard.

"Let me go. One of us will see you later. Lovely, phone Lucy. She could do with hearing from you and it will help reframe your thinking," the army captain smiled.

"Aye, Amy. Cheers for phoning. I'll see you later," he said, and ended the conversation.

* * *

Lucy felt this bundle of weight; the small arms wrapped around her and Molly nestled into her neck.

"Mummy," Molls soft breath said in Lucy's ear.

"Hello, my baby. You're awake," Lucy said, stroking Molly's damp hair from her brow and looking at her watch. It was now 15:00 hours. They had both fallen asleep on the couch.

"Molly sick," the little girl said, cuddled in her mummy's arms.

"I know, my little angel. Mummy is going to make you better," Lucy said, giving her a gentle squeeze.

"Sore," Molly said, pointing to her right ear.

"I know. Let Mummy kiss it better," Lucy said, kissing Molly's ear lightly.

"Sore," Molly said, pointing to her tummy.

"Mummy kiss it better," Lucy said, lifting the pink cotton top and kissing her bare tummy.

"Here, Mummy," Molly said, pointing to her head as a tiny smile spread across her face.

"Oh no. Let Mummy kiss you better," Lucy said, kissing Molly's forehead, planting soft kisses down her arms and legs, taking her little toes and kissing them lightly.

"Can Mummy have a kiss?" Lucy asked, and Molly cupped her mother's cheeks and pouted her cutest lips.

"Thank you. And a butterfly kiss, please, for Mummy," Lucy smiled as mother and daughter shared an affectionate fluttering of eyelashes.

"Shall we get some more juice and crackers?" Lucy asked, picking up Molls and carrying her through to the kitchen.

"How is she?" Mrs. Harris asked.

"She's happy to nibble on a cracker and her temperature has come down. She's due for more paracetamol. Did you get some sleep, Mum?" Lucy said.

"Some and you?" Mrs. Harris said.

"Yes, we might have all got some at least," Lucy said.

"Have you had something to eat?" Mrs. Harris asked.

"No. I was going to make toast and avocado for myself and soup for Molls," Lucy said, their little patient happy to have the second dosage of liquid paracetamol squirted into her mouth.

"You're a good little girl," Nanna said, lifting Molly into her arms and covering her in kisses.

"Why don't you and Molls have a bath and I'll make the toast and soup?" Mrs. Harris said.

"Are you sure, Mum?" Lucy asked.

"Yes. You'll feel better too," Mrs. Harris said.

"Thank you for always helping me," Lucy said, wrapping her arm around her mother's shoulder.

"I wouldn't have it any other way," Mrs. Harris said, giving her daughter a hug and kiss.

❉ ❉ ❉

From a productive morning and feeling a sense of achievement and positivity, Jimmy's high was rapidly falling into an all-time low, and he struggled to balance the two.

*Am I ever going to have that ability to control
my emotions again?*

*Will I ever live by the Values and Standards
of what had defined me?*

Courage

Discipline

Respect For Others

Integrity

Loyalty

Selfless Commitment

The Soldier

All he had to do was remind himself that he would have spent the better part of the day alone, and Lucy would only have visited him in the evening. Now, plans had changed and Amy or Angus would visit instead.

Jimmy sighed. His conflicting thoughts were driving him mad. He relaxed his clenched fist and picked up his phone.

She looked exhausted and worn out, but Lucy's face still lit up and glowed with happiness, her heart skipping a beat as she answered the FaceTime call from Jimmy.

"Jimmy, hello. How are you? she smiled.

"Lucy, ye okay? Hou is yer wee lassie?" he asked, slightly awkwardly. It was the first time Lucy had not texted him first and the first time they had spoken directly over the phone.

"I'm okay. Exhausted, but okay, thank you. We've all decided to have an early night and Molls has been a good little patient," she smiled, showing Jimmy the little girl sleeping beside her mummy, spread out on much of the double bed.

"Jimmy, I am sorry I could not come today. Has Amy or Angus arrived?" she said.

"Na Lucy. Ye mustn't worry. Ye must look after Molly. Amy is coming later," he said.

"Thank you, Jimmy. At least you'll have some company tonight. Maybe if we have a good night's sleep, she will feel better tomorrow and I can try and pop in sometime in the evening.

Have you been okay?" she said.

"Aye. Wis doin my homework for my next session," he said.

"Would you mind if I asked what your homework is?" she asked.

"Na, I don't mind. It wis my CBT," he said.

"That is fantastic. You are doing really well. I find the way that it works and how it interacts together interesting, how we think, feel and act," she said.

"Have ye done it?" he asked, intrigued and interested at the same time.

"I've read up on it, but haven't actually sat down and put thoughts to paper," she said, the conversation going quiet and Jimmy held her gaze, his mouth curving into a smile.

Lucy smiled shyly, swamped with an intense longing for that love. Her feelings for Jimmy were growing day by day.

"Lucy, are ye okay?" he asked, seeing the hint of tears in her eyes.

"I'm okay, Jimmy. Just very tired," she said.

"Let me say goodbye, an' maybe we can talk tomorrow again?" he said.

"I would like that, but I will try to pop in and see you. I'm so grateful for your concern and for speaking to me tonight," she said, sharing a smile, neither wanting to end the call. But struggling to fight back the tears, Lucy waved goodbye and her sad face disappeared off the screen.

She sniffed, burying her face in the palms of her hands. Jimmy had shown his concern in their well-being.

"Lucy, love. What's wrong? I heard you and Jimmy talking. Is everything okay?" Mrs. Harris asked, coming through to check on her.

"Oh, Mum…" Lucy said, wiping her tears, trying to control her emotions.

"Did you and Jimmy have an argument?" Mrs Harris asked, squeezing herself in between Lucy and the bedside table.

"No, Mum. We did not argue. It was nice to speak to him on the phone. We haven't done that before," Lucy said, taking comfort in her mother's arms.

"Why are you crying then? What's wrong?" Mrs. Harris asked.

"Jimmy has taken more of an interest in Molly's life than Owen has ever done," Lucy said.

"Oh Lucy, darling, you are falling in love with him and your emotions are all over the place," she said, giving her a gentle squeeze.

"I'm nervous and scared, Mum. What happens when Owen is released? What if he and his parents demand custody?" Lucy said, a vulnerability that her role as a police officer did not protect.

"Lucy, I will fight to my dying breath for Owen and his parents to stay far away from you and Molls. We did everything to involve his parents in Molly's life, despite his abusive behaviour towards you. Neither of them has paid a single penny towards her upbringing and I will not have them changing their minds now," Mrs. Harris said, comforting her crying daughter.

"They have rights, Mum. They could fight us in court and I don't have the money for a decent lawyer," Lucy said.

"Lucy, love. You are going to make yourself sick with worry. We'll cross that bridge if we come to it. You are exhausted. It's been a long couple of days for all of us and you need to get some sleep," Mrs. Harris said.

"I miss Tom," Lucy sobbed.

"I know you do. I miss him too," Mrs. Harris said, her own eyes watery.

"I love you, Mum."

"And I love you too, Lucy."

"Will you sing me a lullaby?" Lucy asked.

"Don't push your luck," Mrs. Harris said with the women laughing through their tears.

CHAPTER THIRTY-THREE

Psych Session

"**I** would like to start today's session by doing the EMDR again. Let's do a couple of counted breaths. Inhale, two, three, four, hold. Exhale, two, three, four... Breathing in calm and peace and exhaling your pain and stress...," Rosalind said.

Jimmy inhaled, "...two, three, four...I'm making progress. I'm not suffering alone. It's my fault my men died."

"What are you noticing, Jimmy?" Rosalind asked.

"I'm confused," Jimmy said, his mind fighting the conflicting thoughts.

"Staying with that, now follow my fingers," Rosalind said, slowly increasing the speed as Jimmy comfortably tolerated the eye movement. "That's it. Good. It's old stuff...Let it go and take a deep breath. What are you noticing now?" she said.

Like a book's pages blowing in the wind, Jimmy's mind was in search of that certain chapter.

Healing the mind

"Calmness," Jimmy said.

"What SUDs would you give it?" Rosalind asked.

"Seven," Jimmy said.

"Go with that and follow my fingers," Rosalind said.

Jimmy went to his healing light. The warmth of purple light filled his head, across his shoulders and down his arms, filling his chest and opening his airways, spreading a warmth of adrenaline through his heart.

"What are you noticing?" Rosalind asked.

"A weight is lifting. I feel relaxed," Jimmy said.

"What score would you give it?" Rosalind asked.

"One," Jimmy said.

"Now, when you think of that day and the incident, what would you like to believe about yourself?" Rosalind said.

"I tried my best," Jimmy said with some hesitation. He was still not fully convinced with the positive thoughts running through his mind, but there was something there and he knew he had to go with it.

"What score would you give it?" Rosalind asked.

"Seven," Jimmy said.

"Hold those words and image together," Rosalind said, moving her fingers. "What are you noticing now?" she said.

"I felt a little moisture in my eyes," Jimmy said.

"What SUDs would you give it?" she asked.

"Five," Jimmy said.

Rosalind continued the eye movement and increasing the speed as Jimmy followed her fingers...

"What score do you give it now?" Rosalind asked.

"Zero," a slightly emotional Jimmy said.

"Can he take a breather?" Angus asked.

"Yes, of course," Rosalind said.

"I feel guilty, pal," Jimmy said, taking a drink of water.

"It is all good, mate. You survived, Jimbo, for them. We will never forget," Angus said supportively.

"You are making progress, Jimmy. Are you ready to continue?" Rosalind said.

"Aye," Jimmy said.

"Close your eyes and concentrate on the incident and positive cognition, while also scanning your body. Tell me where you feel anything," Rosalind said.

> *The grandiosity of the explosion sent blast waves of dust clouds and twisted metal flying, a force so powerful it dislodged Jimmy from a moment's normality as the heat radiation and fragments of shrapnel penetrated his skin.*

"Sadness," Jimmy said.

"Stay with that," Rosalind said, moving her fingers..."Where do you feel that?" she asked.

"My heart," Jimmy said.

"Stay with that," Rosalind said, increasing the eye movement..."Take a deep breath and let it go. What are you noticing now?" she said.

"I feel forgiveness," Jimmy said.

"What score would you give it?" Rosalind asked.

"Zero," Jimmy said.

"That's a good place to be, Jimmy. You are making great progress. In a few weeks, we will also be coming to the end of our sessions. It is particularly important that we discuss you attending a Remembrance Sunday," Rosalind said.

Jimmy knew the poignant day would eventually need to be discussed and he needed his best friend to be with him.

"Aye. I can't do this without Angus," Jimmy said, rubbing and squeezing his right hand, showing true discomfort for the first time during the session.

"Mate, I will be there for you," Angus said, giving him a reassuring grip around his shoulder.

"How are you feeling, Jimmy?" Rosalind asked.

"Aye, I'm good. I know it needs to be addressed," he said confidently.

Angus could not have been any prouder of Jimmy, and how far he had come in only nine months.

CHAPTER THIRTY-FOUR

Thursday, 6th September 2012

Police Scotland Officers, like every other police force across the country, find themselves under immense pressure to do their job adequately and effectively, despite the lack of resources available to them.

1:30 a.m. - Finishing her last nightshift, Constable Harris had spent a large part of the shift dealing with pockets of anti-social behaviour and noise complaints. Now able to attend the 101 call which had come in just under two hours earlier, Constables Harris and Watson entered the block of flats where they found a woman standing in her doorway.

"I phoned you over two hours ago!" the annoyed woman said.

"I can appreciate that. Can we go inside?" Constable Harris said.

"He's gone quiet now. This is what happens every time, but by the time you get here, he's no doubt passed out on drugs and you do nothing about it!" the woman complained.

"Look, I can see you're upset. How long ago did he quieten down?" Constable Harris said.

"Literally ten minutes ago, but you people do nothing!" the woman said.

Noise disturbances were by far a regular call out for Lucy and her colleagues; loud music, parties and plenty of banging into the early hours of the morning. Something that the police, councils, and housing associations worked closely in reducing.

"Have you spoken to the council or reported it to the environmental health department?" Constable Watson asked.

"Yes, and I have diary sheets dating back three months. He's a crazy idiot and the neighbours do nothing," the woman said.

"We do feel your frustration and know it is not a pleasant environment to live in. I can only suggest that you phone the council again. Keep complaining and writing down your evidence. If he kicks off again…," Constable Harris was suggesting when right on cue, the violent growl echoed through the prefab walls and down the concrete stairs into the entrance hall.

"That's him! He doesn't even live above me. This is what I deal with every week," the woman said.

"Okay, stay indoors," Constable Harris said, and the officers quietly walked out.

Harris and Watson listened for a moment as the CD volume was pumped to max and the loud clank and crash sent a reflection of sound waves vibrating under their feet.

"Police!" Constable Watson banged on the door and rattled the letterbox.

An uneasy calm descended and everything went quiet when the door creaked open and a bare-chested, red-faced and puffy-eyed male answered the door. The unkempt man was glistening with sweat and the smell of someone who clearly had not bathed in days slammed into Harris and Watson's noses. They both noticed straight away that the dishevelled male had been mixing an abundance of booze with heavy iron.

"We've had reports of loud music and banging coming from your property," Constable Harris said, letting themselves in.

"I'm playing music while training. What's wrong with that?" the male said.

"Mate, it's going on 2 o'clock in the morning and people are trying to sleep. Your music was loud," Watson said.

"We have been called out before and given you plenty of warning," Officer Harris said.

"This is fucking harassment! I'm fucking being bullied!" the male argued.

"Just turn down the music!" Constable Watson said.

The authorisation of the officer's order seemed to trigger an emotional response. "Don't fucking threaten me!" the male said, impulsively shoving Watson.

"Right. That's it. I'm arresting you for assault!" Constable Harris said, struggling against his physical strength.

The officers fought a tug of war against the male's resistance. With his heightened hostility having the upper hand, Constable Harris radioed for backup.

"Bloody hell. Get down!" she said, trying to kick his legs from underneath him.

"Aargh! Fuck off, ye bastards!" the aggressor bellowed, his anger giving him a mightier strength and the opportunity to bite Watson's finger.

"Fecking hell, ye bastard!" Watson said, managing to shove his weight up against a wall as two more officers arrived to assist.

Watson and his male colleagues seized the anti-social behavioural male by the legs and brought him to the ground in a high-velocity tackle.

"Aargh! Fuck off, you fucking bitch pig!" he protested.

"Keep quiet!" Harris said, cuffing him.

"Fucking copper nob!" he snarled.

"Oh just keep quiet!" she said.

"Your behaviour now needs to settle down! Do you understand me?" a male officer said.

"Aargh...!" he fought as the male officers pulled him into a standing position. Forcing their weight, they dragged him out of his property and down the stairs, heading towards a stint in the cells.

❊ ❊ ❊

19:50 hours –

"Hello, Jimmy," Lucy called out.

"Hello, Lucy," he said, giving her a hug.

The transformation in Jimmy's appearance, even from her last visit a week earlier, amazed her. His shoulders were lifted, his body relaxed and there was a glint in his eyes.

"I've been looking forward to this all day," she smiled, taking a seat on a dining chair.

"Does that mean I'm the best part of yer day?" he grinned.

"Don't kid yourself. Are we having cordon bleu tonight?" she teased.

"Aye, meals on wheels," he said with Lucy clapping her hands and both cracked up laughing.

Not needing to wait long after he placed the order and sensing his thoughts, "I can't remember the last time I did this either," she said, setting the table and unpacking the cartons.

They enjoyed the varied selection of spring rolls, stir-fried noodles, vegetables and meat, as well as each other's company, even sharing a flirtatious offering of food. Neither could remember the last time they enjoyed someone's company as much as they were enjoying each other. With each visit, they seemed to open more.

"Where did ye go for yer last holiday?" he asked as they sat comfortably on the couch, drinking coffee.

"It was our last holiday together as a family, four years ago. We booked a cottage on the Isle of Harris," she said.

"The Outer Hebridean. I've never been," he said.

"We booked a week. Tom wanted a change of scenery and I wanted to be away from Owen," she said.

"Owen is a bastard! Ye did not deserve him," he said, placing his coffee mug between his stumps and taking her hand. Visions of smacking the friggin daylights out of him flashed across his mind.

"Tom never liked him and to be honest with you, Jimmy, I

question myself as to why I could not see it either. I wear the uniform and I'm this strong, confident woman, capable of doing my job properly, but feel vulnerable and self-conscious outside my job," she said with disappointment.

"Yer a good police officer, Lucy and a kind woman," he said, with her placing the empty mugs on the table and giving him the opportunity to give her a hug.

"Thank you, Jimmy," she said.

"Tell me about yer holiday," he said, hoping it would help cheer her up.

"Tom and I always enjoyed walking. Going to the Isles was a perfect opportunity for a new challenge. Fourteen and a half miles through the intricate, loch-strewn landscape of the Bays of Harris and roughly six hours later. It was beautiful," she said.

"Aye, the exasperation of exercise always leaves ye wanting to push yourself further. I miss that," he said with a sigh.

"I know you do. Jimmy, you could build up your strength and set yourself physically demanding challenges. It would help your mindset," she said gently.

"Up here is a constant battle of contradictions," he said, stabbing at his head with his left hand. "I won't deny being nervous about the future," he said.

"How do you feel about the sessions coming to an end soon?"

she asked.

"Nervous. The sessions have been that objective challenge. Angus will get back to his normal routine and ye can't molly-coddle me forever," he said.

"You're not getting rid of me that easily! You're my working project," she smiled and Jimmy broke into laughter.

"Ye are an incredible woman, Lucy Harris. I'm terribly sorry for ever disrespecting ye. Molly should never have witnessed my vulgar behaviour," he said.

"You do not need to apologise, Jimmy. I am so sorry for every-thing you have gone through and if your fiancée could not see that, it is her loss, not yours," she said with a touch of weari-ness to her voice, not quite knowing if she had stepped out of line by mentioning her.

"Her name was Natalie," he sighed.

"I am sorry. I should not have mentioned her," she said, letting go of his hand, feeling there could be some conflict between them. But Jimmy touched her arm in a kind gesture and took her hand once more.

"It's okay, Lucy," he said, finally feeling comfortable in sharing his past with her.

"Natalie wasn't in the army. I met her at some friend's party that Angus dragged me to. I had already been in the army for seven years. I was twenty-three and she was eighteen. She was young, but we hit it off straight away. We spoke about the consequences of me being deployed and she accepted that. We were due to be married on my return. I loved her."

With his tearless look, he sighed heavily before continuing.

"I haven't heard from or seen her since. She could not even come to the hospital. I had to hear about the wedding being called off through Angus. He was furious with her, but I could not see that. That is why I resented him so much. I pushed him away."

Lucy hurt for him. He would have been more accepting of his injuries had she not walked away.

"What a bitch!" she thought.

"I'm sorry for what happened to you, Jimmy. If it's any consolation, I think you're amazing," she said, smiling through her tears.

"You're a beautiful woman, Lucy...," he said.

"You might not know it, but you have helped me too, Jimmy. I look forward to seeing you and having some company," she said.

"Don't blame yourself for yer brother's death," he said, caressing her cheek. "Out there, we do our job. I know he would rather have stayed and taken care of ye and Molly, but he would have concentrated on the mission. His main concern would have been looking after the guy next to him," he said gently and pulled the bereaved woman into his chest.

"He was always there to look after me and Molly and now he's gone," she tried through broken pauses of breath.

"Lucy, ye are a kind and generous woman. Ye are a guid mother. Tom would be proud of ye," he said.

"Molly will never know him," she sniffed.

"No. But ye can continue to talk about him and not let his memory die. She will always know who her uncle was," he said.

"I'm sorry," she said.

"Don't be sorry. I do understand. I know it's hard," he said.

"Jimmy," she said, looking up at him.

"Shhh…," he whispered softly, brushing her lips with his.

"Thank you for looking after me," she said, burying her face in his neck and closing her eyes.

The soft, gentle kiss had been heavenly in all aspects, Lucy holding him and feeling the safety of his left arm around her. They knew they had feelings for each other, respecting and taking comfort in knowing the moments they shared were theirs forever.

✻ ✻ ✻

Lucy had left Jimmy in the wee hours of the morning. They had both agreed that she should be at home when Molly woke up.

Falling asleep in his arms, the silence had been comforting and peaceful. The feel of her body so close to his had soothed him more than he had expected.

Jimmy had been pleasantly surprised at his ability in holding back his own emotions and having the strength to comfort Lucy, who was clearly hurting from the loss of her brother. Speaking openly to her about Natalie brought some relief to him and being able to mention her name for the first time since his injuries felt like the start of a new chapter in his life.

CHAPTER
THIRTY-FIVE

Three weeks later – Friday, 28th September 2012
– Five years to the day of Jimmy's injuries

Death is but the doorway to new life. We live
today. We shall live again. In many forms shall we
return – Egyptian Prayer of Resurrection

A sharp pain struck him as an overpowering smell of blood, sweat and fear hung heavily in the air and Jimmy's body shuddered. The nightmares were a reminder of what he had become.

Thump! Thump! Thump! he fist-smacked the hell out of his body. Today was the anniversary of his injuries.

Despite Angus booking the day off and plans already been made for at least someone to be with Jimmy throughout the weekend, he received the call at the eleventh hour. They needed him at the barracks. Now, neither of them was able to be with Jimmy during the day and Angus was furious. Airing his anger through his messages with Amy and Lucy, he texted

Jimmy on an hourly basis to check-in to show his best friend his support, but Jimmy's texts became less frequent as the day wore on and the booze took its toll.

* * *

By 15:00 hours, Angus could not give a fuck and walked out. His best friend needed him.

"Hey, Gussie...," he slurred, his eyes bloodshot and dazed, a shaky blood-stained hand toasting him as he took another drink from the beer can, with dozens of empty cans sitting on his left side table. It was more than likely he had drunk more.

"Mate...I'm sorry," Angus said, dropping to the couch. His face was filled with regret at not having the opportunity to be with his best friend on a day as significant as this one, especially since every year on this day, Jimmy had been at the forefront of his mind even more.

"Fuck them all. I should have been here!" Angus said with anger, giving Jimmy a supporting arm around his shoulder.

"Tis a feckin stoatin day! Hae a dram," Jimmy said, groaning and slurring his words like a typical drunk and took another gulp of the bitter liquid.

"Mate, let us clean you up," Angus said, giving his broken friend a pat on the back.

"I'm fucked up! I can't do this anymore!" Jimmy said. Taking a long deep breath, he choked on a sob and sighed heavily.

"Please, mate. You have come so far. Do not give up now!" Angus said.

"I've let you down," Jimmy said disappointingly.

"No, mate. Life sucks!" Angus said. Jimmy, after placing the almost empty can on the table, buried his face in his left hand and broke down, crying hard.

"Come on, mate. Let us clean you up before Lucy gets here," Angus said, fighting against his own emotions.

"Aye," Jimmy said, deflated and battered, accepting Angus' help.

❋ ❋ ❋

"How is he?" Lucy asked, taking Molly's bags and pram as Amy unfastened the child seatbelt and took hold of the little girl.

"Angus is with him, but understandably, he's not doing too good," Amy said.

"I'm going there now. I'll look after him this weekend," Lucy said.

"I think your company will be just what he needs," Amy said.

"Maybe we should have rescheduled," Lucy sighed sadly.

"Jimmy understands. He'd be upset if you changed Molly's plans," Amy smiled.

"Thank you so much for offering to have her this weekend," Lucy said.

"We've been looking forward to this all week," Amy said, embracing Molly with kisses and giggles.

"She's been so excited. Just hearing the word 'animal' has sent her into hysterics, but that might all change when she realises I'm not staying," Lucy said nervously, removing the car seat from the back as Amy watched on.

"I promise to take care of her and Angus is so excited," Amy said.

Lucy saw what having a little human being for the weekend meant to them.

"I'm sure I've remembered everything," Lucy said while double-checking Molly's bags.

"You haven't done this before, have you?" Amy laughed.

"No. Molls has never had a sleepover," Lucy said with both women laughing at the fussiness of their actions.

"Oh God, I'm already missing her," Lucy said, teary-eyed. "Mummy loves you," she covered her daughter in kisses as a quiver formed on Molly's bottom lip and the realisation of being left behind started to sink in.

"You're going to the zoo tomorrow to see the monkeys and the pandas," Lucy said in a sweet child-like voice. "Mummy going to see Jimmy," she said as Molly sniffed away her tears.

"Jimmy sore," Molly said softly.

"Yes, my angel face. Mummy going to look after Jimmy. Mummy loves you," Lucy said and gave her daughter one last hug and kiss.

"Thank you," she said before very quickly climbing into her car, her eyes welling up once more as she waved goodbye to her baby girl. This would be the first time Molly had been away from home. Amy showed kindness and warmth in her hugs and kisses towards her while they watched Lucy drive off.

* * *

Angus left Jimmy for a moment after hearing the knock at the door. "I should have been here, Lucy," he said.

"I'm sorry, Angus," she said sadly.

"I'm just getting him showered," he said as Lucy took the opportunity to clear the empty cans, wipe the sticky surfaces and take out Jimmy's rubbish.

"Lucy," Jimmy said, finding her in the kitchen. His pitiful situation engraved on his aged body.

"Jimmy, I'm so sorry," she said, wrapping her arms around his neck and hugging him. She was struggling to hold back the strong feelings she was beginning to feel for him and was terrified of losing him too.

"I'm staying to look after you, Jimmy," she said.

"Na. Ye must go home to yer wee lassie," Jimmy mumbled, bowing his head.

"Molls is staying with Amy and Angus this weekend, remember?" she said, rubbing his back.

"We're taking Molly to the zoo tomorrow, mate," Angus said.

"Jimmy, look at me," she said gently, while continuing to rub his back as his far from sobering gaze looked up at her. "We can always cancel and make it for another day?"

"Na, don't change Molly's plans," he said.

"This is her first-ever sleepover," she said, smiling at him.

"How was she?" Angus asked.

"You mean, how was I? When Molls heard Jimmy's name, she perked up," she laughed, fanning her face to help fight back the tears and Jimmy offered his left hand.

"Amy is broody. The quicker the wedding, the quicker we can have babies," Angus grinned.

"Molly needs a friend," Jimmy said.

"My words exactly, mate. I'm going to leave you in Lucy's capable hands and we'll see you on Sunday," Angus said, giving Jimmy a manly pat on the back.

"I let you down. It won't happen again," Jimmy said.

"No, mate. I should have been here," Angus said with guilt.

* * *

The little girl had looked confused and unsure of where her mummy and nanna were, but with Amy's gentleness and warmth, helped by the interest in the different child games and activities, Molly's chatters soon bubbled to the surface and they enjoyed their time spent together.

By the time Angus got home at 18:45 hours, the girls had bathed and eaten and he found them tucked up in bed with Amy reading a bedtime story.

"So, I guess I'm sleeping in the spare room then?" Angus grinned as he joined them on the bed and playfully kissed Molly, taking over Amy's reading duties. "...and so the hairy caterpillar turned into a beautiful butterfly..."

"What a silly billy. Wrong story," Amy said as the girls giggled at his funny efforts. "We are reading the three little pigs."

"Oh, you mean this little piggy went to market, this little piggy stayed at home...," he said, finding Molly's little toes under the duvet and sending the little girl into fits of giggles.

"How is he?" Amy asked as the playfulness slowly quietened down and Molly's eyes got heavier.

"I feel guilty, Aims. He was a mess. He acknowledges he's let himself slip, but I don't blame him. I would have been right there drinking with him," he said as both lay on the bed and stroked Molly's little fingers.

"It's been good that you've been involved through this process and unfortunate that your day's leave had to be cancelled. I think you should contact Mike. Jimmy needs to hear it from someone other than ourselves," she said as they climbed off the bed.

"You are right and I will phone Mike. You are going to be a wonderful mother to our children and I love you," he said, taking her into his arms.

* * *

After Angus left, Lucy had tried to give Jimmy something to eat, but the little he did eat was very quickly puked in the toilet bowl.

"Have another drink of water, Jimmy" she said kindly.

"I'm sorry," he said.

"Don't apologise, Jimmy. Lean against me and breathe," she said, tucking herself behind him on the bed and gently wiping his brow with a cool cloth.

With Lucy's presence and the softness of her fingers caressing his forehead, he soon relaxed and fell into sleep.

She ran her fingers over the aged, battered face, following the furrows that carried his life being. "Would he ever share his life with her?" she thought when her phone beeped, as Amy texted the group chat.

Your daughter is an angel to look after. We are all tucked up in bed and excited for tomorrow's adventure

I really appreciate you taking her

Angus joined the chat.

I am outnumbered this weekend! The girls have already ganged up on me, sending me to the spare room!

Do not believe a word he says, he has been grinning like a Cheshire cat all evening. At least I will not have to put up with his farts and snores

I believe you Amy, I bet he is filling my daughter's head with mischief LOL

Yes, hairy caterpillars in the mix with the three little pigs

Angus texted

How is Jimmy?

He was sick earlier, but he has fallen asleep now. Poor guy, he is sorry for his actions

Angus replied

I have spoken to Mike and have asked him to give Jimmy a call sometime tomorrow

I'm hoping Jimmy will spend tomorrow at my house, a change of scenery will do him good, but whatever he decides I will stay with him

Amy responded

Both Angus and I have said we could not have

taken care of Jimmy without your help

Lucy texted back

Thank you

CHAPTER
THIRTY-SIX

There is no exercise better for the heart, than reaching down and lifting people up – John Holmes

John Holmes is a veteran of both the US Army and the NY Army National Guard and served in Iraq in 2005.

A combination of nerves and embarrassment filled Jimmy, laying there, his pounding head and mouth dry, a reminder of his incapacities.

"Morning," Lucy smiled, walking into the room with a fresh glass of water.

She had spent the night watching over him, making him comfortable and offering him sips of water when he needed it. Not using her change of clothes or having taken a shower, she felt as haggard as Jimmy looked.

"I'm sorry Lucy,...," he stuttered, struggling to hide the shamefulness he was feeling inside.

"Please, Jimmy. Yesterday was just a bad day and I truly believe it would not have happened if one of us could have been with you," she said with guilt, taking the empty glass from him.

"I'm struggling, I...," the rage, frustration and irritation of his mindset showed in his clenched fist and Lucy climbed onto the bed and cupped his face.

"Talk to me, Jimmy," she said.

"I don't know who I am anymore. I went from being active and fit, to suddenly not being able to do anything. I don't know how to be anything else but a soldier and feel I've lost a part of myself," he sighed with true sadness in his voice.

"You will gain your self-confidence again, I promise. Living in isolation is a killer. I see it, Jimmy. I see it all the time, vulnerable people living alone. I might be their first visitor in weeks and all they want is someone to have a cuppa and natter with. You were that person," she said confidently.

"I live in these constant waking nightmares, intense, vivid experiences that I can't control," he said.

"I truly wish I could take it all away," she said.

"The other day, I heard a police siren somewhere in the distance. It was real. Like a dull thud of rotor blades," he said.

"Please, always know that I understand your grief and suffering, your experiences," she said.

"I'm a wasted drunk with no purpose and I let you down," he said as his body sagged with each breath.

"No, Jimmy, you have not let me down. Does Angus' drinking bother you?" she said.

"I don't want people pussyfooting around me and I don't expect Angus to stop drinking because of me," he said.

"By recognising that you slipped up yesterday and by all means understandably so, is a positive move forward and you can be very proud," she said.

"Ye are a guid woman," he said, wrapping his left arm around her neck and pulling her into a hug. "Ye look exhausted."

"I am and I need a bath," she smiled.

"Why don't ye go home and sleep? I will be fine," he said. Lucy believed him, but just as much needing his company.

"I'm not leaving you, Jimmy. Besides, I'm not going home to an empty house," she said.

"Why, where's yer mother?" he asked.

"Gone to Melrose to stay with a friend. I feel so guilty sometimes because she doesn't have much of a social life," she said.

"I bet yer mother doesn't see it like that," he said.

"Come stay at my house. It will be a nice change of scenery and Angus and Amy can pick you up on Sunday?" she said.

"I'd like that," he said with genuine appreciation, accepting the same invitation she had made months earlier.

"Good. I'm missing my baby," she smiled.

"Have ye heard from them?" he asked.

"It's just gone 10:30 and they were leaving early enough to get parking within the zoo, so they might already be there," she said.

"She'll be fine," he said.

"I bet you feel like shit?" she said, feeling the stiffness in his body as she helped him climb into his wheelchair.

"Aye. I wouldn't be surprised to see my liver drinking water out of the cludgie," he said.

* * *

The entire day was planned with Molly in mind, treating it as an adventure, from buying the tickets a week before with the hope of seeing the pandas, to packing a picnic lunch and map-ping out their route.

Amy texted Lucy.

> *We have arrived and about to go in. Molls is wide-eyed with excitement; she can hear the activity of the animals but cannot see them. And of course, we have Angus acting like a huge kid!*

> *Those two are going to get up to mischief! How was my baby last night?*

> *Your daughter is the most content little girl I have come across, she slept through and has asked for her mummy, but we have kept her occupied and involved with the trip. Did you get some sleep?*

> *No, I am exhausted, but I have convinced Jimmy to stay at mine tonight and he is busy in the shower*

> *Good, but try and get some sleep. I am quite sure Jimmy can look after you for a few hours. I'll keep you updated throughout the day*

> *I will. Have a wonderful day and thank you so much*

"How is he?" Angus asked, placing a bag in the storage carrier of the pushchair as Molly watched on with curiosity.

"He's in the shower. Lucy's convinced him to stay at hers to-night," Amy said.

"Let's hope Mike's call does him good," Angus said.

"Mike left a good impression on him at the dinner. I'm sure his pep talk will do the same. But enough now, we are going to have a nice day with this pretty little girl," Amy said, tickling Molly's chin before they started making their way to the zoo's main reception.

Deciding to visit the larger and more active animals first, knowing they would have Molly's full inquisitive attention and interest, the little girl looked up at Amy, a look of uncertainty and excitement of unfamiliar sounds surrounding her. "Should we go look for animals?" Amy asked sweetly, bending down towards her. "Let's take her out."

"Which way should we go?" Angus asked, lifting Molly into his arms while Amy showed her the map.

Molly pointed at a spot out of the public zone and giggled with pride. All grinning in agreement, they chose to go left towards the Meerkat Plaza.

The large, open enclosures, with their ditches and moats purposely designed for the individual inhabitants of endangered animals, left a combination of fish, manure and wet fur hanging in the air.

With her wide-eyed and sense of delightfulness growing

within, Molly watched the squirrel-like creatures scurrying in and out of burrows, foraging for food and grooming one another. Three up, two down, the open-air 'House of Meerkats' basked under the autumn sun, standing to alert, they evaluated their surroundings, ready to warn off any predators that might invade.

Walking along a wooden walkway, the loud squawks and flapping of wings caught Molly's attention, and she pointed towards the tall, large-bodied birds with their long necks and small heads, as the flock of pale pink Chilean Flamingos fed.

Molly giggled and stomped her feet with happiness as the incredibly vocal chimps hooted, screamed and grunted through the glassed-in enclosures. Drumming on hollow wooden frames, they swung from pole to pole.

"Look, Molls," Angus said, pointing to a pair of grooming chimps as he teasingly lifted her tiny arm and tickled her, sending the little girl into squeals of pure excitement and her animal audience into enthusiastic chaos.

"Let's visit the pandas before we have lunch," Amy suggested.

The black and white teddy bear-like creature sat in a corner, chewing on its bamboo shoots. The glass enforced enclosure was a far cry from its home in the forests and a reminder of the greedy world we as humans had created.

The magnificent creature captivated Molly's imagination. Standing with her little hands against the glass, she watched its every move, and giggled at the oversized teddy as it rolled over, aware of its tiny audience.

* * *

Lucy had been in no rush to get home. She changed Jimmy's sheets and washed the dirty mugs. She allowed him to shower and freshen up. Spending a good hour in the bathroom, the hot water relieved some tension and helped soothe his stiff muscles. His aftershave and clean-shaven face showed that he was feeling remorse for his drunken actions the night before.

"They're certainly making the most of it," she said as she and Jimmy enjoyed the autumn sunshine, sitting in the garden while eating their sandwiches, knowing that some food in him would help his throbbing head.

"Aye. Let's hope the weather holds up," he said.

"Oh, Jimmy, look," she said, showing him the video Amy took of Molly's joyfulness at seeing the chimpanzees and both laughed at her mimicking.

"Hou are ye feeling not having her here?" he asked.

"I miss my baby. It's so quiet without her," she said.

"I'm missing her too," he smiled.

"Would you like another cold drink before I go freshen up?" she asked.

"Please," he said, surprised by his phone lighting up and Mike's name on the screen.

"It's Mike," he said, and Lucy touched his arm before heading inside to have a bath.

"Hey, Mike," Jimmy said.

"Jimmy, mate. Angus says you could do with a chat?" Mike said.

"Aye. I had a relapse, pal," Jimmy said.

"Are you home alone?" Mike asked.

"I'm at Lucy's house," Jimmy said.

"That is good. Being with someone will help. Those haunting reminders are tough to get through," Mike said.

"I'm pissed off. I should have had the strength to get through it," Jimmy said.

"How are the therapy sessions coming along?" Mike asked.

"That's just it! I'm heading towards the last session and they have been good, but I have one unsettling thought and I crash," Jimmy said with frustration in his voice.

"I'm seven years into my injuries and I carry the regret of losing my best mate daily. Somehow you think you can save them and you feel you have let them down. We all suffer that, but you learn to live with it," Mike said.

"I strived for a better life for so long, to have it all taken away. I'm lost," Jimmy said.

"Mate, once you start accepting it, it doesn't matter what you look like. As long as it starts to make your life better, you start accepting things," Mike said.

"It's not just military stuff. It's who I was before," Jimmy said.

"It's hard to ask for help, but asking for help is not a sign of weakness. It's a sign of strength," Mike said.

"I know I can do it, but my body is saying otherwise," Jimmy said.

"As said at the dinner, I think it is especially important to have a purpose. And that's been my main thing, to keep occupied and busy. Doing a challenge is tough, but I enjoy it and it is good. There is nothing like being in the zone.

We get a lot out of the challenges, watching each other and drawing on each other's strengths..."

As Jimmy listened to his every word, a mixture of uncertainty and excitement creeped into his subconsciousness.

"...For a long time, I could not get to these places. It took months and even years to push myself both physically and mentally. It's harder and a lot longer, but the appreciation you get out of it is ten times more. I've adapted to my injuries in so many ways," Mike said.

"I respect what you are saying, mate. I know I need to get back into physical rehab," Jimmy said.

"I would even go as far as suggesting residential care during the process," Mike said.

"I'm nervous about the different world out there and the perception that you're no longer useful," Jimmy said.

"It's a harsh world, mate. People don't give a fuck, whether you've served your country or not! But we are fit for purpose and we soldier on, no matter what is thrown at us," Mike said with determination and confidence.

❊ ❊ ❊

"She's done really well," Amy said, giving Molly a piece of banana. After seeing the pandas, they found the designated picnic area and sat down to have lunch.

"We should visit the penguins before she falls asleep," Angus said.

"I agree and if we are lucky, we might catch them on their walkabouts," Amy said with their phones beeping to life.

Jimmy is speaking to Mike, that was forty minutes ago. Looks like they are having a good chat

330

Angus replied.

> *That's great thanks*

Amy joined in.

> *We have just had lunch and are going to Penguins Rock before she falls asleep*

Lucy replied

> *I love the photos; the video is the cutest*

Amy replied and ended the text messages

> *She has certainly kept us entertained. It has been a lovely day*

Molly's face lit up with joy at seeing the dark and white elongated creatures waddle back and forth. Flapping their flippers and vocalising their displays, they had dived into the water and swum with speed.

"Molls, look!" Angus said excitedly and bent down to put her on his knee. They watched the penguins do their walkabouts, their vocal honks and waddles, sending Molly into an animation of giggles.

❋ ❋ ❋

Standing in the kitchen feeling more relaxed and refreshed, Lucy could see Jimmy's reflection through the open window. Hearing the end of his conversation, she could already see the positive impact it had left on him.

Mike's call had boosted Jimmy's self-assurance, that feeling of hope and acceptance once more dripping into his harrowing mind with an aroma of rich blooms and delicate petals drifting through the air.

"Here's that drink I promised you," she said, walking out to join him.

"Cheers. How's yer wee lassie?" he said.

"Apparently, she's done quite well. They were going to see the penguins after lunch, before heading home," she said.

"Aye. She's going to be knackered," he said.

"Hopefully, she'll sleep through tonight," she said.

"I think something is nesting in yer watering can," he said.

"Oh wow, I hope so! We've really tried to make the garden attractive to small creatures," she said excitedly.

"Ye should get a small camera which can feed off your TV, so Molls can watch the baby birds," he said.

"That's a brilliant idea," she said, touched by his enthusiasm.

"We must look for something before early spring," he said naturally, thinking nothing of it and leaving Lucy feeling overwhelmed with emotions.

"Is Jimmy accepting his life for what it is? Would I be a part of his life?" she thought.

"How are you feeling, Jimmy, after speaking to Mike?" she asked.
"Speaking to Mike was guid and he makes sense, but trying to understand how to control the negativity is tough. I'm trying, Lucy," he said, rubbing his damaged hand.

Lucy leaned forward and took his left hand in hers. "I'm proud of you. To have come this far in such a short time proves that you are one strong-willed guy, and you know you can always talk to any one of us," she smiled and hugged him.

"I need my arse kicked into gear," he said, and they both laughed in agreement.

CHAPTER THIRTY-SEVEN:

Wednesday, 10th October 2012

Talk Therapy –

The truth is, unless you let go, unless you forgive yourself, unless you forgive the situation, unless you realise that the situation is over, you cannot move forward – Steve Maraboli

Steve Maraboli is an internet radio commentator, motivational speaker and author

19:35 hours – Angus and Amy arrived at Jimmy's soon after Lucy did. Tonight's talk therapy would take place between the four of them and Mike Tully.

"Have you thought about completing a challenge, moving forward?" Angus asked.

"Aye, look. I know that working towards something physically demanding will give me that focus I need, but I need to do something beyond that and apply the skills I was trained in," Jimmy said.

"I agree with Jimmy. Doing a physical challenge is fantastic for your way forward in your recovery, but for you personally, I believe you need to apply your skills in some way or other," Amy said.

"I think Mike is keen on getting you involved," Angus said.

"You could raise awareness for mental health, be an advocate for veterans," Lucy said, giving him a gentle pat on the back.

"Aye, I have considered that," Jimmy said.

By sorting out his life and recognising what support was out there and available to veterans, Jimmy was also realising that more could be achieved closer to home and in Scotland.

"Why not organise a fund-raising event?" Angus asked.

"You could even organise a TED talk focusing on mental health," Lucy said.

"Aye, there are opportunities," Jimmy said.

"We are all behind you, lovely," Amy said.

As agreed and to precision, at 20:00 hours, the WhatsApp voice call went through, and Mike's voice came on the line.

"...Mate, the last time we spoke was the day after your relapse. I must say you sound more confident and upbeat..."

"I haven't had a drink in almost two weeks," Jimmy said.

"That's great news! Thanks for asking me to take part tonight. Have the talk therapies helped?" Mike said.

"Aye, definitely. I was not convinced in the beginning, but they got easier as we worked through them," Jimmy said.

"They've helped all of us, Mike. Angus and I have found the ability to share our emotions more openly and Jimmy is finding the ability to help Lucy in her grief," Amy said.

"The sessions will end, but the talk therapy can continue and I would recommend that they do. Even for me tonight, I will end this call feeling restored," Mike said.

"Mike, how do you manage your physical pain?" Lucy asked.

"I have as much physio as I can, but I also have to take a certain number of painkillers, and they come with their own complications, like constipation and addiction. It's about learning how to manage your intake," Mike said.

"Fuck, I don't want painkillers. Fighting my drinking addiction is challenging enough!" Jimmy said.

"I agree with you, but there is a possibility you will need some sort of pain relief," Angus said.

"What, have some glycerol bullet shoved up my arse? Fuck that!" a determined Jimmy said, making the group laugh.

"Mate, I'll help you anytime in the shower, but I refuse to help you with your constipation!" Angus said.

"Sorry, Jimmy. You're on your own there," Lucy joked.

"They've been very quick to suggest a dosage of antidepressants," Amy said.

"The antidepressants only cap the problem and in turn, can work against you with dire consequences. Mate, relaxation, communication, setting goals, conflict resolution..., these will help you move forward in your recovery," Mike said.

"You can't consider trying to help others until you sort out your own head," Angus said.

"Mate, we have a booked-up calendar for next year and I want you to get involved. This will help get yourself out of that environment of negativity and inner conflict," Mike told Jimmy.

"Aye, definitely. I want to help," Jimmy said.

"Mate, the problem is that you're having to re-programme yourself back into civvy life with still the mindset of a soldier. Your once programmed mind and body are now physically and emotionally broken," Angus said.

"Aye, and that's what's feckin infuriating!" Jimmy said.

"Mate, you've experienced a heightened level of physical and emotional trauma since your injuries. Time will eventually heal itself," Mike told Jimmy.

"Mike, the sessions have been about talking, setting goals and finding a solution to the problem. In our last session, she wants to talk about attending a Remembrance parade. Can you give us some moral advice?" Angus said.

"For me, that first parade after my injuries was extremely difficult, and I was feeling the exact same emotions that you have experienced. Why me? Why am I still alive? My best mate died and I survived! It was only once I started to accept the changes to my life and had a set goal to work towards, did I start to realise that by drawing strength through my survival, I was also honouring and remembering him. We will never forget, mate…," Mike said with slight hoarseness.

Despite Mike's confidence and acceptance, he still had those moments of harrowing reminders. He continued to offer support and advice and the call lasted just under an hour, with each of them taking some appreciation and understanding from it.

"How are you feeling, Jimmy?" Lucy asked.

"The chat was guid. Are ye okay?" Jimmy said.

"I'm good. I think we've all needed this and I'm grateful to be a part of it too," she smiled.

"Pal, it's time to go through the photos," Jimmy said unexpectedly.

"Seriously!" Angus said.

"Aye, I want to do it," Jimmy said confidently.

"Mate, you've made my day!" Angus said, giving his best friend a strong handshake.

"That's really great, Jimmy" Lucy said.

"It's fantastic! These chats have certainly had an influence on you for the better," Amy said.

CHAPTER THIRTY-EIGHT

Saturday, 13th October 2012

The soldier, above all other people, prays for peace, for he must suffer and bear the deepest wounds and scars of war – Douglas MacArthur

General of the Army Douglas MacArthur was an American five-star general and Field Marshal of the Philippine Army. He was Chief of Staff of the United States Army during the 1930s and played a prominent role in the Pacific theatre during World War II – Wikipedia

"**H**ey, Gussie. Do ye want a sandwich?" Jimmy asked at hearing Angus arrive and drop his duffle bag.

"Yeah, great, thanks. Your AFC came through, mate. Amy brought the letter home late last night," Angus said, placing the sealed official envelope on Jimmy's table.

Jimmy took a long deep breath. The afternoon was going to push his mental state to its limits.

"Is this from Molly?" Angus asked, admiring the crayon drawing on Jimmy's fridge.

"Aye, this is my wheelchair," he said, pointing to a squiggle and the men laughed with joy at the wee lassie's attempts.

"Your fridge looks good and healthy mate. I'm truly impressed with you in getting your life back in order," Angus said.

"It's a feckin slog trying to maintain some form of normality," Jimmy said, taking another bite of his cold meat sandwich.

"Can I open it?" Angus asked.

"Aye," Jimmy said, hesitantly turning the envelope lying on the table once more before pushing it towards Angus, who opened the confidential letter.

"I know it's hard to take in, but it's all good and that's a decent amount," Angus said, supporting the wounded soldier. The realisation that his army career was now truly and officially over was hard to take in.

"Mate…," Jimmy hesitated, a sinking feeling within the depths of his stomach. "I am sorry about the debt. I will forever be indebted to ye and Amy, and will pay ye back the full amount one day," he said.

"I don't want the full amount. I want you to get your life back in order and think you should take Mike's advice about the residential rehab care," Angus said.

"What am I going to fuckin do with my life?" Jimmy asked.

"Your recovery is more important at this stage and it's just one of those things that we have to start again. Your debt is paid and the repayments will still allow you to live and put food on your table. It is going to be tough and Amy is looking into the possibility of extra benefits," Angus said.

"I can look into getting an electric wheelchair now," Jimmy said more optimistically.

"Exactly, mate. That's what this money is for. There are endless opportunities for you. Why not start up some organisation here in Scotland and support our troops?" Angus said.

"Aye. I'm going to get through this, and look into my options," Jimmy said.

"It's good to hear your confidence, and you have my backing. Can I suggest that you open a savings account. I can take you to the bank once the money is cleared," Angus said.

"Aye, cheers pal. That sounds guid," Jimmy said.

"Come on, let's go through the photos. Did you order frames?" Angus said.

"Aye, everything is in the drawer," Jimmy said, ordering the frames one evening when the cravings were unbearable and he needed the shift of focus.

With the drawer of army memories sitting between them on the couch, for a couple of minutes, silence filled the room and both men were hesitant to speak first. But finally, Jimmy broke the silence.

"This feels like a lifetime ago," he said, his hand shaking as he picked up the photo of the day they passed out.

"Must be fifteen years now?" Angus said.

"Aye. They are guid memories," Jimmy said.

"Those weeks of training were the longest of my life," Angus said.

"Warrant Officer McGee. He was brutal, and ye provoked him every time," Jimmy laughed.

"I'm going to make you do push-ups till your eyeballs bleed!"

Angus re-enacting the dominating Warrant Officer's orders, both soldiers laughed hard at the reminisce.

"His voice still echoes through my ears. I reckon I have tinnitus," Angus said.

Jimmy held the photo for a moment, lost in his own thoughts, before Angus placed the continued reassuring hand on his shoulder and he looked up.

"I'm guid pal," Jimmy said, giving Angus the photo to put into the frame.

"Do you remember this boot run-up to the reservoir?" Angus asked.

"Aye. They separated and made us team leaders. That was the best running result I had up to that point," Jimmy laughed.

"Yeah, you beat us," Angus said.

"Jock Strong!" Jimmy said.

"Mate, get through your recovery and we'll encourage some guys to take on a team challenge," Angus said.

"I'll hold you to that," Jimmy said.

They went through the photos, leaving the portrait for last and not all photos were placed in frames, only the happiest of times and those taken with Angus.

"We can always do this again," Angus said as he watched Jimmy's shoulders slump forward, holding the last photo ever taken of him with his legs, the photo before his injuries and the three soldiers who were killed.

"I've had enough, pal," Jimmy said as the exhaustion quickly consumed his body and he was unable to go through any more photos.

"I'll make us a coffee. You've done me proud, mate," Angus said, replacing the drawer and putting the frames proudly on display.

Jimmy looked at the photos on display, and although he felt a sense of achievement, he also felt sick to the stomach. Everything was happening so quickly, and doubts were beginning to cloud his head despite their continued reassurances.

"Mate, drink this" Angus said. Seeing the colour drain from Jimmy's face, he now brought him a glass of water.

"I'm fine. It's just been a lot to take in today," Jimmy said.

"I can appreciate that these past months have been a roller-coaster ride and you're anxious about the sessions coming to an end, but you have come a long way in such a short time. You should be proud," Angus said.

"Pal, believe me. I feel like a drink at any given time of the day. Lucy and Molly are the reason I haven't reached into the cupboard," Jimmy said.

"We can see you love Lucy," Angus said.

"Aye, I care for them deeply, but this...," he gestured towards his body, with a slight frustration in his voice and actions, "...

is fucked up!" he said.

"Mate, from what I've seen, Lucy doesn't care what you look like. She feels comfortable around you," Angus said.

"I told Lucy about Nat and by doing that, I realised I had blamed ye for her leaving me," Jimmy sighed. "I'm sorry, pal" he sighed again.

"I was as angry as you were, but my priority was you. I have not seen or heard from her since. There will be days when neither of us can visit and you will be alone, but we will always be there for you," Angus said.

"I haven't been to a Remembrance since my injuries," Jimmy said nervously.

"I think we should honour them together. It has been tough for me too, mate, and without Amy, I would have struggled. Let us hear what Rosalind has to say and I will respect your decision," Angus said.

"Cheers, pal. I appreciate that. Ye are my best friend," Jimmy said.

CHAPTER
THIRTY-NINE

Friday, 19th October 2012

Psych Session

"Jimmy, understandably, you must be feeling slightly apprehensive. We have had good open conversations these past few months and I have seen a huge improvement in you.How do you feel about today being our last session?" Rosalind asked.

"Aye, I am feeling nervous. I admit I am worried about where I go from here. Knowing that I had these sessions to come to and set goals to achieve gave me an incentive," Jimmy said.

"Angus, would you like to add anything?" Rosalind asked.

"Jimmy is afraid we are going to forget him. I have a job to do and there will be days when I or Amy, and even Lucy cannot visit due to commitments. I have a wedding to plan, but I have been here and have attended the sessions myself. We are not going to give up on you, mate," Angus said.

"Aye. I understand that, pal. A coud na have done any of this without ye, Amy and Lucy. I don't want to lose yer friendship over some punch up because I think yer not visiting me enough," Jimmy said.

"Angus, have the sessions and talk therapies helped you?" Rosalind asked.

"Yes, absolutely. Amy and I will continue to work on our relationship and we have our wedding to look forward to, but it's having my best mate a part of our lives again that has truly made a difference," Angus said.

"Jimmy, have you had any more thoughts about going back to rehab?" Rosalind asked.

"We've made an appointment at Redford," Jimmy said.

"Jimmy is nervous about what the future holds and getting back out in the open world," Angus said.

"Life can be pretty daunting out there when you have spent the better half of five years in the comfort of four walls," Rosalind said.

"We finally got Jimmy's AFC approved," Angus said.

"I am really pleased to hear that. How did that make you feel, Jimmy?" Rosalind said.

"I felt a mixture of emotions. It makes it official now. My army career is over," a choked Jimmy said as Angus offered his support.

"Jimmy, it's okay. As I've said before, you can ask for help. It is going to take time to feel comfortable around other people, whether they are injured or non-injured. You have suffered the deepest of depression. You tried taking your own life, beat the hell out of your body and yet, here you are. You reached out for help. You phoned Angus. How is the drinking?" Rosalind said.

"I have not had a drink since the relapse," Jimmy said, his own admission surprising him.

"That is absolutely incredible. What an achievement! Do you feel proud?" Rosalind said.

"Aye. The thought of seeing Lucy and Molly definitely helps," Jimmy said.

"Mate, we are all very proud," Angus said.

"I would suggest that as part of your continuing recovery, you attend a twelve-step programme. You will have days when those cravings become unbearable and talking to others who are experiencing their own setbacks will help you," Rosalind said.

"I will consider it," Jimmy said.

"And we will continue to support," Angus said.

"How is Lucy?" Rosalind asked.

"I told Lucy about Natalie," Jimmy said.

"Natalie being your ex-fiancée? We haven't spoken about her in our sessions," Rosalind said.

"I haven't mentioned her name in five years, let alone spoken about her. But I realised by telling Lucy, that I had blamed Angus for her leaving me. I am sorry, pal," Jimmy said.

"I appreciate that, mate," Angus said.

"How did that make you feel?" Rosalind asked.

"Aye, I feel relieved," Jimmy said.

"That is wonderful, Jimmy. You spoke to someone without feeling anxious about discussing the past. Can you see, you've done something positive and you feel better for it.

I'd like to do some breathing exercises and go over some of the EMDR questions again, before we go into more detail about attending a Remembrance Sunday parade," Rosalind said.

"Sounds good," Jimmy said.

"Inhale, two, three, four, hold. Exhale, two, three, four, five, six, hold. Think about breathing in calm and peace, and breathing out pain and stress," Rosalind said.

Jimmy and Angus naturally tuned into their thoughts and feelings. Tuning in to the here and now, releasing the physical and emotional stressors and feeling less self-conscious while breathing in peace and breathing out regret.

"Okay, Jimmy and Angus. Take a deep breath and open your eyes. How do you feel?" Rosalind said.

"I think it's the most relaxed I've been," Angus said.

"I'm relaxed," Jimmy said.

"Now, if we had to go back to your last mission, how do you feel bringing up that memory?" Rosalind said.

"I wanted to help him so badly. Save him," Jimmy said.

"Staying with those thoughts and feelings, follow my fingers... Breathe. What SUDs would you give it?" Rosalind said.

"Zero," Jimmy said.

"Good. Let's stay with that and follow my fingers again," Rosalind said, slowly increasing the speed..."What are you noticing now?" she asked.

"I'm sad. I did my best. This mission for me is over," Jimmy said.

"Are you noticing any shifts in the SUDs?" Rosalind asked.

"It almost feels like a magnetic dial. The smallest of doubts throws it off course," Jimmy said.

"But you're able to bring yourself back to the zero SUDs?" Rosalind asked.

"Aye, and I'm feeling okay," Jimmy said.

"I want you to stay with those thoughts and feelings while I strengthen the eye movement again...Breathe. What are you noticing?" Rosalind said.

"I'm feeling the sadness again, as well as forgiveness," Jimmy said.

"What SUDs would you give it?" Rosalind asked.

"Zero," Jimmy said.

"That is good, Jimmy. A good place to be. I am incredibly pleased with your progress," Rosalind said.

"How do you feel about attending a Remembrance Day?" she asked.

"It's going to be tough. All I think about are the guys I was with and knew. What if those emotions trigger my thoughts to spiral out of control again?" Jimmy said.

"Mate, we all show emotion on that day. Do you think it has been easy for me? I want to honour our fallen alongside you, not for you. You are alive, mate. Let us remember them together," Angus said.

"Jimmy, are you sensing 'survivor's guilt'? If they survived and you did not, wouldn't they want to remember you and honour the sacrifice you made? You are never going to forget them. Their families are never going to forget them. They will be there to honour and remember them. They will honour you for surviving," Rosalind said.

"Do it for Lucy. Honour her brother" Angus said.

Jimmy listened and at times hung his head and swallowed hard, but the tears did not come. Deep within, he knew it was the right thing to do. Honour and remember them.

He would never forget them.

Jimmy took a long deep breath and lifted his shoulders, pushing himself back into his seat. "We can honour them together, pal," he said in a shaky voice.

"Thank you. I am proud of you," Angus said, that reassuring hand on his shoulder as always.

"How are you feeling, Jimmy?" Rosalind asked.

"Aye, I'm feeling okay. I am a soldier and respecting my fallen pals has always been at the forefront of my mind. I just lost my dignity along the way," Jimmy said.

"You suffered life-changing injuries. In an instant, your life changed forever. I have sat here and listened to your harrowing experiences. We have spoken about your drinking, your self-beatings, your anger towards Angus and your frustrations at not having the confidence to open more towards Lucy.

I have set you goals and tasks and you completed them all.

With every session, I have seen a change in you for the good.

For someone who has drunk hard alcohol for as long as you have and is able to acknowledge the relapse and control your cravings, you have true willpower and self-belief.

You acknowledged your self-beatings and although I can't wave a magic wand for you to stop, I hope you can learn how to control it. Give yourself some credit. You have certainly earned it. Be kind to yourself.

Angus has suffered the psychological loss of losing a friendship so strong. The best friend who will never serve alongside him again. His relationship with Amy has been strained. The one person who held him together and has been by his side.

You've had physical punch ups with Angus. You have blamed him for still having his army life, for not being your best friend and even for the fact that your fiancée walked out on you. But you realised he was hurting just as much as you. You both opened up and shared your feelings.

You have attended the sessions together. He has encouraged you at every stage and in effect, he has never left your side. You are best friends, both of you and you should never forget that.

You've shown comfort towards Lucy at a time she truly needed it. You acknowledged your vulgarity towards her and she has continued to show kindness and trust in you.

She found you that night. She could see you needed help and went that extra mile. Lucy brought you and Angus together again.

Lucy lost her brother. She has the responsibility of looking after her mother, bringing up her daughter and working long shifts. And still, she comes to visit you, despite your case going cold.

I think she needs your friendship as much as you need hers. I think there are feelings there and I think you have respect for each other. Give her a chance.

Life is a 'work in progress'. Always remember what you've been through and how far you've come.

You can be enormously proud, Corporal Jimmy Ferguson!" Rosalind said, finishing Jimmy's and Angus' final session.

Overcome by emotion, the soldiers hugged. They would forever be brothers in arms and the best of friends.

"A' coud na have done this without ye, pal. Ye are ma best

friend," Jimmy said.

"Brothers forever," Angus choked.

Jimmy stretched out his left hand to shake and thank the therapist. "I need a hug too. It has been an absolute pleasure working with both of you," she said.

CHAPTER FORTY

Monday, 22nd October 2012 – Assessment at Redford
-Edinburgh Regional Rehabilitation Unit

Rule Your Mind Or It Will Rule You – Buddha

Now, a few days later, Angus and Jimmy drove to Edinburgh for their morning appointment.

Glen, a physiotherapist, introduced himself to the two soldiers, confirming he had been the first point of contact through Amy.

"It's all good, mate. You'll see," Glen said to Jimmy as they walked into a room filled with gym equipment, training specialists and three other soldiers; Alison, a double amputee and Ben and Matt, who were not physically injured, but needed the emotional support.

Angus placed a hand on Jimmy's shoulder, who was in need of his best friend's support, as seeing Glen's encouragement and others alike was utterly amazing.

Jimmy had not accepted further rehab after he was discharged from the hospital and seeing how beneficial it could be made him realise he needed something physically challenging to give him that edge, despite being left with nerve damage and paralysis down the right side of his body.

"Glen is our drill sergeant. I pity you, mate," Alison said with the group laughing loud.

Angus stood back and left Jimmy in Glen's capable hands.

"Corporal, drop and give me fifty!" Glen yelled, rubbing his hands with glee. His face was a comic of emotions, and the room erupted into laughter, helping Jimmy relax and feel upbeat about the day's session. He was interested in working and hearing what Glen had to say and pulled himself onto the padded exercise base.

Glen started by analysing what range of movement Jimmy could do on his own, but it was noticeable that Jimmy was not as strong as far as he could be and Glen's main concern was maintaining his range of movement and flexibility at the hip.

Getting Jimmy to lie down flat on his back, Glen placed a bolster under his left thigh and got Jimmy to squeeze his buttocks and push his hips towards the ceiling. Completing the same amount of times per set, but repeating the Bridging, Hip Flexor Stretches and other gruelling exercises, Jimmy found it more challenging on his right side.

True to their word, Glen worked Jimmy hard through the session of exercises that concentrated on improving his strength, coordination, balance, and the endurance of extremities to his body. Jimmy was just as determined, with him working up a sweat and encouraging Glen to push him harder.

Angus gave Glen a confident nod. He could see that Jimmy was enjoying the small challenges that the session was throwing at him.

"The crunches, sit-ups and twisting of all muscles are designed to hit the abdominal areas, obliques and lower back. Without it, posture is going to be an issue," Glen explained to Jimmy and Angus, drawing up a home-based exercise programme that concentrated on increasing flexibility, muscle strength, endurance, balance and coordination.

"Because you haven't maintained your stretching, there is contracture and weakness in your muscles. It's going to take demanding work and dedication and I would encourage you to come back," Glen said.

"Aye. It's been an eye-opener today," Jimmy said.

"With the difficulties Jimmy is facing in his emotional and physical challenges, it has been suggested that he gets residential rehab. What are the possibilities of that happening?" Angus said.

"I will go back and write up a report, and any supporting evidence from your GP or psych therapist will help," Glen said.

"Cheers, pal. I appreciate that. It's been a brilliant day," Jimmy said.

"You can always give me a call. I encourage you to come back, even if we can't get you into the residential accommodation straight away. There is no reason we can't get you up on stubbies," Glen said to Jimmy, giving him and Angus his number.

Jimmy and Angus were in gratitude for Glen's support, with all the soldiers deciding to have a well-deserved refreshment and a good chat.

"How did you cope, Alison?" Jimmy asked her confidently.

"I was in a very dark place before being referred to RRU. Without their support, I don't know where I would be," she said.

"With that difficulty of feeling worthless and being restricted, drinking was my only escapism," Jimmy said.

"Mate, there is nothing to be ashamed about. We've all been there," they said in almost unison.

"Mate, just agreeing to come here today is a huge accomplishment," Angus said.

"Angus can relate to this. Some of us are suffering the invisible wounds and although our recollections are alike, we all cope differently," Ben said, with Angus nodding in agreement.

"I was homeless for three years. Taking that plunge in getting my life back in order and taking part in the Cumbrian challenge has given me a second chance," Matt said.

"Taking part in a challenge would give you that focus you need," Angus said.

"The three of us have done it," Alison said, referring to Ben and Matt.

"It's something to think about, mate," Angus said.

"We should all do a challenge together," Alison said, giving Jimmy a nudge.

"Aye. We would be partially legless," said a relaxed Jimmy and the group laughed hard.

Jimmy had really enjoyed his day, and receiving Glen and the others' encouragement had made him realise he had missed out on so much, and he felt a sense of sadness, knowing that the strong and confident man he once was had suffered and lost his way.

He certainly could not have done it without Lucy, Angus and Amy.

* * *

The conversation home had flowed freely between the two friends and they made a verbal pact to help each other. They excitedly spoke about Mike's suggestion in getting involved and decided to have a coffee day soon to draft a 'roadmap' moving forward.

Managing to finish her shift on time and seeing the soft glow of light through the window, Lucy knocked to find Angus helping Jimmy in the shower. She had brought him some food and would stay for a while, only wishing she could stay longer, but she would be working the extra hours to be with Jimmy in between Remembrance Sunday and the Christmas period. She hoped he would agree to spend the festive season with her, although she was yet to ask him.

It was the first time she had seen the photos now proudly on display and as well as feeling admiration for him in how far he had come, she also felt a slight sense of sadness, not for his injuries, but more of an ache, unlike anything she had ever experienced before.

"I'm falling in love with you," she thought.

"Are ye blushing, Lucy Harris?" Jimmy said, making her jump and in turn, second-guessing herself on whether the thought had been out loud. A cheeky grin lit up his face as her giddy actions made him and Angus laugh even more.

"I'm so proud of you," she finally managed, her body trembling slightly as she leaned in to give him a hug.

"It has been a brilliant day," Angus said, offering to make the coffee.

"I am so pleased to hear that," she said, naturally offering Jimmy some help in climbing onto the couch. The exertion of the session clearly left him in pain.

Angus explained to Lucy about the various exercises that Jimmy was put through. "We'll have you swinging from the high bars in no time," she said with laughter.

"Aye, and triple somersaults," Jimmy said, the three laughing and drinking their coffee.

Lucy could see that the session had left a good impression on Jimmy, and both men had benefited from the day's events.

"With Mike's support, getting out there and doing something would be so rewarding. It would be a huge achievement for you to feel worthwhile again," she said to Jimmy.

"Mate, it's only a thought, but what about doing a collection down at Tesco before Remembrance Sunday?" Angus said. Jimmy hesitated momentarily, a dreaded look of anxiety flashing across his face and in that split second, he was back in this very same room, ten months earlier, cursing life.

Lucy gently squeezed his arm and he breathed in, letting out a deep, slow sigh.

"Let's do it. I need to do this," he said confidently, giving Lucy a warm smile.

"Great! I have not done this before either, mate, so we're in the same boat. It is a good start for both of us," Angus said, giving his mate a pat on the back and Lucy the broadest of smiles. He was truly inspired by Jimmy's determination.

"I will contact Mike," Angus said.

"Na, pal. Let me speak to him. You can organise a space to set up," Jimmy said, and Angus agreed.

"Sweetie, what's wrong?" Jimmy said, stretching across with his left arm and giving Lucy a hug.

"You have had such a good day and have come so far, but I haven't found your medals," she said, teary-eyed.

"Don't be sad. It's not yer fault. I know it's going to be tough for ye, for both of us, but I will be there for ye," Jimmy said, finding her eyes and they shared a smile.

"Lucy, it's not your fault. If it were not for you, Jimmy and I would never have seen each other again," Angus said.

"Now you've really got her going, mate," Jimmy said, making light of the situation and Lucy choked and laughed through her tears.

They spoke a little longer about trivial things, keeping the conversation light, before Angus jumped up. "Right, I'm off. Jimbo, it's been an amazing day. Thank you, and take care of your woman," he said, giving Lucy a cheeky grin and the best friends laughed hard at the blush rapidly spreading across her face.

* * *

"Ye look exhausted," Jimmy said, finally able to stretch across and pull Lucy into his chest, needing to feel her closeness as much as she needed his.

"So do you. I'm so glad you had a good day," she said.

"Today made me realise I could have benefited with rehab, but I'm nervous too," he said.

"I know you're feeling apprehensive, now that the psych sessions have come to an end, but just remember everything you spoke about and the techniques she taught you," she said, feeling the tightness in his body with each cramp that struck him.

"Angus has high expectations," he said with hesitation, some doubt slowly taking over the whole excitement of the day and the pain in his muscles not helping matters.

"Take one day at a time, Jimmy and I'd like to be there to help you. You're in pain and it's been a long few days," she said, moving in behind him to make him more comfortable.

"Thank ye," he said.

"Shhh, I'm in the zone," she said, bringing her hands up to his neck with long gentle motions, her fingers sending narcotic tingles down his spine.

With every delightful breath of sweetness he breathed in, Jimmy's muscles relaxed. The woman he was falling madly in love with forever showed her kindness and warmth towards him.

Moving her hands up to the sides of his head, she massaged his scalp gently. Making circular movements over his temples, her fingers felt every bump with each motion as her own muscles took in the relaxation and they lost themselves in their thoughts.

"Do ye want to see me walk?" he said unexpectedly.

"Why, Jimmy? Does it worry you what I might think?" she asked, moving out from behind him.

"Aye, I do worry. Whit if I can't accept this?" he said, gesturing towards his body.

"Jimmy," she said, taking his left hand in between hers, "I don't need to have some guy standing there with all his body parts to feel some sort of physical attraction towards him. Touch can have a powerful effect too," she said.

"Lucy..."

"Let me finish. You don't have to accept this," gesturing towards his body. "Why should you? But because you have not accepted it, you in effect have. By going through the therapy and getting your life back on track, you have told the world, 'Piss off. I will show you I can survive!' And because you are this hard arse, determined, strong-willed guy, you will continue to prove otherwise," she said.

"A 'coud na have done this without ye," he said.

"You are going to be okay, Jimmy," she said, delicately kissing his cheek.

* * *

Amy was sitting at the kitchen table scrolling through her iPad when Angus walked in. He looked happy.

"Hello, my lover," she smiled, wrapping her arms around his neck and kissing him.

"It has been a brilliant day! I haven't seen him this determined," he said.

"How is he?" she asked, giving the mince another stir as Angus topped up her red wine and poured himself a glass.

"He is in pain, but surprisingly positive. It's the first time in a long time that I've seen some fight in him. He's beginning to realise that he's missed out on much-needed help," he said, telling Amy about the various stretches and exercises that Glen had put Jimmy through.

"How was the day for you?" she asked, taking another sip of wine.

"I've needed this as much as him. There were guys there in need of moral support. Talking to them afterward just proved we are not alone in fighting our demons," he said.

"No, you're not alone. This whole thing with the break-in and Jimmy could not have come any sooner," she said.

"You're right. For all of us. I put the idea across to him about doing a collection at Tesco before Remembrance Sunday...," he said.

"...And?" she asked with surprise.

"He hesitated, but with Lucy there, he changed his mind," he grinned, raising his eyebrows at Amy's shock.

"Now that is a surprise!" she said, smiling as she casually took a seat on his lap and brought the iPad back to life. A variety of photographic images of the mighty Victoria Falls filled the screen.

"It's incredible! Look at this!...'Mosi oa Tunya'...the smoke that thunders," she said, clicking on a video clip. "It's totally amazing! One of the eight wonders of the natural world and it apparently has the largest curtain of falling water! Oh Angus, it looks spectacular!" she said almost breathlessly.

"It's what, two nights in Vic Falls and a night in Lusaka each way?" Angus confirmed.

"Yeah, and a week at Kruger in South Africa, making it easier to get our direct flight home. We'll have one full day at home to recover, before going back to work and living on baked beans for the next year," she said, and they both laughed at the idea.

"It's going to be full steam ahead in the new year," he said, seeing Amy's happiness in finally being able to get excited about their wedding.

CHAPTER FORTY-ONE

Saturday, 3rd November 2012

*We can't help everyone, but everyone can
help someone - Ronald Reagan*

*Ronald Wilson Reagan was the 40th president of the
United States from 1981 to 1989 – Wikipedia*

Jimmy had contacted Mike the following day, explaining their decision in doing a collection at their local supermarket and getting further information from him. Mike had been incredibly proud of his progress, a true testament of strength and determination, once more offering any help he might need and a week
later, a box of promotional goodies sat on Jimmy's dining-room table.

This would be Jimmy's first real interaction with the public and his local town since his injuries and for longer than just an hour. He was certainly apprehensive, but the godsend of Amy and the support of his best mate, remembering his discussions with the therapist and the breathing techniques he was taught, helped him to put it at the back of his mind and relax.

They had been given a time slot between 10:00 and 16:00 hours, a time usually allocated to collection events. With Amy's well-equipped stationery items needed, she and Angus decorated their corner, tacking the promotional banner to the table, blowing up balloons and tying them to Jimmy's chair.

"You need to stand out, mate," they laughed.

They placed a collection bucket along with the silicone wristbands and custom pin badges on the small table provided and together, in their supporting veteran sweaters, they raised awareness and money for their fellow pals.

It had been a slow start, but as more people got into the weekend groove and popped in to do their shopping, the appearance of Jimmy and his two pals attracted their attention and with each pound, coin and note generously donated, slowly the bucket filled.

All three of them were touched by the support the local people showed them. From the obvious deprived to the more fortunate, all donated. Many of them stopped to talk, interested in Jimmy, with one woman remembering the article of his injuries mentioned in the local paper all those years ago.

"Constable Harris," Jimmy said, surprised at seeing the officer and her sergeant an hour before the end of their allocated time slot.

"Mr. Ferguson," Lucy smiled at seeing the balloons bobbing up and down with Jimmy's movements.

"We did a collection at the station for you," she said, slotting a small bundle of notes into the bucket.

"Wow, thank you!" all three said, knowing that Lucy had played a huge part in it.

Her sergeant left them momentarily to buy a snack, giving Lucy a few minutes to speak to Jimmy.

"Looks like you've done well," she said, reaching into her trouser pocket and taking out a pound coin.

"This is from Molls," she said, slotting the coin into the bucket. "Tell yer wee lassie we say thank ye. People have been so generous," Jimmy told her.

"How are you feeling?" she asked him.

"I'm okay. It's been guid," he said, Lucy seeing the reassurance in his eyes.

"Harris, time to go. Jimmy, well done," her sergeant said, raising his eyebrows in a comical expression, and once more shook their hands.

❉ ❉ ❉

Back at Jimmy's flat, they sat at the dining-room table, drinking a well-deserved coffee, counting the money and completing the checklist of items.

"Mate, we've made two hundred and fifty-six pounds and sixty pence. Fifty of that came from Lucy," Jimmy said, taking the small bundle of notes still neatly folded and counting it separately.

"She is truly a remarkable woman and she really cares for you," Amy said.

"You should just tell her. You know you love her," Angus said.

"Give them time. The feelings are there," she said.

"When the time is right, mate," Jimmy said confidently.

"Fair enough. How did you find today?" Angus asked him.

"I was apprehensive when we arrived. Today was the first time I have been out for as many hours in full view of the public. It was tough, but I'm pleased we did it," Jimmy said.

"Mate, I have struggled just as much as you have, mentally. Believe me. Amy's encouragement, the sessions, meeting Mike, having Glen's support, speaking to others and now today, have been an encouraging push for me too," Angus said, wrapping each of his arms around Jimmy and Amy's shoulders.

"We make a good team. We just need Lucy now," he said, giving each of them a broad smile.

"If he wants that encouraging push, we should get him to do a challenge carrying me in a hiking backpack," Jimmy grinned at Amy.

"You get various kinds too. We can zip you up, so you don't get wet," she laughed.

Jimmy and Amy designed their own backpack with added features, deliberately ignoring Angus presence.

Throwing his arms up in defeat, "I'm outnumbered," Angus said with a straight face, but the thought of Jimmy zipped up in a backpack, his head bobbing up and down broke him and he bellowed with laughter, Jimmy and Amy following suit.

The soldiers enjoyed their evening together, ordering a takeaway, and Jimmy was grateful for having them stay a few hours more. He just wished Lucy could have been with him.

CHAPTER FORTY-TWO

In the days that followed, Jimmy kept himself busy. He had gone online and ordered a bouquet of flowers, white roses with white oriental lilies and white carnations, to be delivered on Friday to Lucy, her mother and Molly, in memory of Lucy's brother.

Angus phoned him every day to check-in, with Amy popping in one evening to pick up his suit to have it dry cleaned. Secretly, he had appreciated the calls and the visit, enjoying a coffee and conversation with her, but despite Jimmy's re-assurances that he was doing fine, a decision he had made on his own, as Remembrance Sunday neared, there had been mo-ments when he had sat and the silence had been too much for him, allowing his conflicting thoughts to take over and he fought hard not to thump the hell out of his body. "Think of Lucy," he kept telling himself.

* * *

Lucy arrived home in the early hours of Saturday morning, her late shifts now finished and she could enjoy the next few days off. She had not spoken to Jimmy but had kept in touch with Angus and according to him, he was doing okay, although some days his voice had been slightly more strained. Though tomorrow was going to be a tough day for her, and where she would normally be working, she was grateful to have Jimmy who could look after her.

She saw the beautifully arranged bouquet of flowers sitting on the table, a whiff of delightful sweetness filling the air. Completely unexpected, she smiled at the thought of her mother having a secret admirer and thought best not to read the note.

"Have you read the note?" Mrs. Harris whispered behind her and Lucy turned to give her mother a hug.

"No. Did I wake you?" Lucy said.

"No dear. The flowers arrived yesterday evening after you left for work. Read the note. The flowers are for all of us," Mrs. Harris said.

Lucy took the note out of the envelope and read...

> *To: Lucy, Maggie and Molly. Thinking of*
> *you during this time. Love Jimmy*

She stared at the note for a moment, rubbing her thumb over the textured surface, before looking up at her mother with tears running down her cheeks. "Oh, Mum..." is all she managed through her tears, hugging and needing her mother's love.

"Don't worry about Molly and me tomorrow. I think Jimmy is

going to need your support as much as you need his," Mrs. Harris said, consoling her daughter.

* * *

It was a dreigh day and Lucy had managed a couple of hours sleep, with Mrs. Harris making her a hot chocolate and Molly climbing into bed beside her.

She had arranged with Amy to spend the Saturday night with her, spending well-deserved quality time with her daughter during the day.

"Mum, she's just fallen asleep. Do you mind if I take a walk to Tom's grave before it gets dark?" Lucy said, sitting down beside her mother on the couch.

"Of course not. What time are you going to leave, this evening?" Mrs. Harris said, relaxing with her knitting.

"I'll get her bathed and eaten and pretend it's another working day," Lucy said.

"Do you know if Jimmy's okay?" Mrs. Harris asked.

"Only through Angus. He is with him now and says the past two weeks have certainly been challenging for him," Lucy said.

"Jimmy will look after you tomorrow. I know he will," Mrs. Harris said, taking her daughter's hand.

"He already looks after me, Mum," Lucy smiled.

"You take care of each other and he helps you as much as you help him," Mrs. Harris said, with Lucy giving her a hug.

"Take the wreath. Molly and I will walk across tomorrow," Mrs. Harris said.

"I love you, Mum."

"And I love you, Lucy."

* * *

The village parish graveyard had a sense of peace and serenity to it, where centuries of weathering tombstones depicting ghostly silence lay amongst the more recently placed marble and floral tributes.

Of square design and dark grey granite, Tom's grave lay close to a pathway, a loved one's tribute wooden bench sitting directly opposite.

Tom Harris – Born 9th March 1981 - Died 7th May 2010

A Beloved Son, Brother and Uncle
Where Heaven Meets Earth
There You Are
With Love, We Will Remember

Placing a hand on his headstone, Lucy crouched down and placed the decorative poppy cluster wicker ring against it.

"Hello, Tom," she said with a lump irritating her throat and tears running down her cheeks.

"I miss you, Tom," she choked, desperately wiping at her tears after realising she had no tissue.

Struggling to control her emotions, she took a seat on the bench and continued to talk to him. "Please look after Jimmy. I love him."

CHAPTER FORTY-THREE

In Flanders' Fields

In Flanders' fields the poppies blow Between the crosses,
row on row, That mark our place; and in the sky The larks,
still bravery singing, fly Scarce heard amid the guns below.

We are the dead. Short days ago We lived,
felt dawn, saw sunset glow,

Loved, and were loved, and now we lie In Flanders' fields.

Take up our quarrel with the foe: To you from
falling hands we throw The torch, be yours to hold
it high. If ye break faith with us who die

We shall not sleep, through poppies grow In Flanders' fields.

Major John McCrae, 1915.

T he screaming echoes of Jimmy's nightmares interrupted the little sleep he got, his body fighting against
each spasm that hit him hard and he was grateful to
have Angus to support him.

Angus had arrived at Jimmy's on Saturday afternoon and
could see the challenges that he had faced, both physically and
emotionally, in the two weeks that he had insisted on spending alone. He knew that today was going to be the toughest
day Jimmy had faced since his injuries.

They had been up early, the wintry darkness making the day
all the bleaker. Angus had made them a light breakfast and
there was an understandable quietness between them.

For them all, this was going to be a poignant day. Jimmy
had not been to a Remembrance Sunday since his injuries.
For Angus, every Remembrance Sunday for the last five years
had been about mourning his best friend. Today, he could
mourn for those who had lost their lives. Amy mourned for
her friends and supported Angus through his despair. And for
Lucy, she and her mother visited Tom's grave a few days before, always opting to work overtime to busy her mind.

Angus washed and stacked the plates before wheeling Jimmy
into the bathroom to help him get showered. Despite every
muscle hurting and feeling anxious about the day, Jimmy reminded himself that he had to do this for his fallen pals.

"Do it for them. Do it for Lucy's brother," he kept telling himself.

"Mate, I could not be prouder. Thank you for doing this," Angus said while neatly pinning the unfilled trouser legs to fit Jimmy's stumps and automatically correcting the corporal's maroon beret.

With both men clean-shaven and smartly dressed, Jimmy struggled to hold back a choke. The serving army major and broken soldier were side by side for the first time in five years.

"The women have arrived, mate," Angus said, placing that re-assuring hand on Jimmy's shoulder as always and gave him a moment to gather himself.

"A am guid, pal," Jimmy said, taking a deep breath and giving Angus an encouraging nod. He could not help but feel a spir-itual power of emotions that today, something was going to happen.

The women stood up and Amy, impeccably dressed in her own uniform, leaned in and gave Jimmy a hug. "I'm so proud of you," she said.

With her hair neatly French plaited, Lucy wore a black tailored suit and deep green blouse. Standing back, she felt overwhelmed by the three soldiers in the room, her red-rimmed and sorrowful eyes clearly indicating that she had been crying, more than likely all night.

Jimmy smiled, stretching out his left hand for her and they hugged tightly.

"Thank you for the beautiful flowers," she said in a hoarse voice as Jimmy gave her the lightest brush of his lips against her cheek. "Don't be sad," he said, gently wiping a tear.

Angus and Amy were touched by Jimmy's affection towards Lucy and the moment they had shared. "We have to go," Angus said, and taking hold of Jimmy's chair, they all walked out.

The mood in the car was sombre with each of them lost to their own thoughts. Sitting in front with Angus, Jimmy could see Lucy through his side mirror. Glancing at her now and then, he knew he needed to be strong for her.

The traffic on the A703 main road to the Glencorse Barracks had come to a standstill fifteen minutes after turning onto it.

"This traffic is going nowhere," Angus said, looking at his watch as another police vehicle with its blaring blues and twos came speeding past.

Lucy stretched across. "Angus, the traffic won't be moving anytime soon," she said, knowing what to expect.

Further up, a vehicle attempted to turn around with others giving leeway and more vehicles followed as Angus slowly moved forward.

"The A701 is just up ahead," Jimmy said, turning to look at Lucy.

"I'll make a phone call and see what's happening," she said as another vehicle turned around and Angus moved forward.

"The road is completely shut. There has been a fatality, and entrance to the barracks is impossible. We can take the A701 and go through Howgate to get around Penicuik and go to Edinburgh, or turn around and go back to Peebles?" Lucy said, leaning forward to look at Jimmy.

"Lovely, what do you want to do?" Amy asked Jimmy. They were leaving the decision up to him.

Jimmy still felt uncomfortable being seen in his local town. To get himself through the day and remain strong for Lucy, another town village where he felt less exposed would help him.

"Let's go to another town memorial," he said confidently.

"The A6094 is just up ahead. What if we go to Dalkeith War Memorial?" Lucy suggested.

"Aye. That sounds guid," Jimmy said, and all agreed.

Angus abandoned the A703 and headed onto the A6094 through Howgate, towards Dalkeith and the Dalkeith War Memorial. Jimmy's feelings of this inexplicable sense of foreboding were growing stronger as they got closer.

Angus managed to find a parking space on St. Andrew Street, a short distance from Dalkeith town centre.

"Do you want to go and ask if you can join the parade?" Amy

asked Angus, seeing members of the British Legion and other military veterans standing together across the street. Jimmy noticed a few other wounded veterans.

Jimmy reached for Lucy's hand and squeezed gently. "I'll take care of her," Amy said.

"Cheers, Amy" Jimmy said.

"We can take part. The parade starts at The Royal British Legion club and goes along to the war memorial in King's Park," Angus said.

"Lucy and I will see you afterward," Amy said, before Angus took hold of Jimmy's chair and they crossed the road to join the parade.

The distinctive harmonic sounds of bagpipes and drums echoed through the air and all soldiers, in their own unique way, each with a story to tell, their lives changed forever, marched with pride, side by side, down towards the Cenotaph.

The four-walled stone structure, surmounted by eight turrets and arching buttresses, met in the middle to hold a large stone crown, honouring and dedicating the memories of lost soldiers to Queen and country. The ceremonial party laid wreaths and took their positions in front of the war memorial while Angus pushed Jimmy and the soldiers saluted their fallen comrades before the Chaplain said a prayer –

Let us commemorate and commend to the loving mercy of our Heavenly Father, the Shepherd of Souls,

*the Giver of Life Everlasting, those who have died
in the service of our country, and its cause.*

We Will Remember Them

*They shall grow not old, as we that are left grow old Age shall
not weary them, nor the years condemn At the going down
of the sun and in the morning We will remember them*

In its intense, powerful and stately sound, a Bugler played the Last Post. A wave of memories surged within Jimmy and he was engulfed in grief. Angus swallowed hard with his own emotions surfacing. For the first time in five years, they were there to support each other.

Corporal Jimmy Ferguson sat, a poppy on his chest, at the eleventh hour, on the eleventh day, of the eleventh month, as silence fell –

* * *

Angus and Jimmy found the women standing to one side once the Memorial had come to an end. Emotions had been shared by all members of the public who had come together to reflect and remember, and Jimmy was now able to give Lucy a much-needed hug.

"This is Hamish. He was at the same dinner with Mike Tully," Jimmy said, introducing the wounded veteran with his prosthetic right arm and leg to the women.

"What a small world we live in. Mike has been a great support for Jimmy," Lucy smiled.

"They've invited us for some drinks," Angus said.

"Coffees would be nice. Lucy and I are freezing," Amy said.

"I think that would be lovely," Lucy said to Hamish, putting her arm around Jimmy's shoulder.

"This would be good for him," she thought.

Lucy took hold of Jimmy's chair and the four of them now fully introduced themselves to Hamish Williams while making the short walk to The Royal British Legion club.

Decorated in Union Jacks draped across the ceiling, an extra-large Scottish flag hanging from the wall behind the bar and regalia on the walls, the TRBL club had a friendly, welcoming vibe to it.

"Beers, coffees?" Hamish offered to buy the first round of drinks.

"Coffee. Cheers mate," Jimmy said confidently, giving Lucy a smiling wink.

"Are you driving?" Angus asked Amy.

"Yes, I will drive," she said.

Although he was growing in confidence and getting stronger both physically and emotionally, today, Jimmy's hyperawareness was in full throttle and the ex-military veteran quietly sitting at the bar drinking his beer caught his eye, as did his four medals.

"Hey, mate," Hamish nodded, introducing himself.

"Hey," Darrell Miller said, shaking his hand.

"Come join us," Hamish offered as a friend helped him carry the drinks.

"Cheers, mate. I'm good. I'm waiting for someone," he said, glancing up from his phone and looked in Jimmy's direction.

With Hamish introducing some mates to Jimmy and hearing the familiar language littered with colourful references, he was soon reacquainted with old times and he relaxed, enjoying his coffee and the jokes that bounced off one another.

"Mate, give us a hand," someone called out to Hamish.

The comical veteran gave Lucy a cheeky grin and loosened his prosthetic right arm and tossed it, showing her the thumbs up tattoo on his stump and sent everyone into erupted laughter.

"Are you a local here in Dalkeith?" Lucy asked him.

"Aye, born and bred, but did my service at MMP...Marchwood Military Port, Royal Logistic Corps," Hamish said.

"Lucy's brother served, pal...," Jimmy told Hamish, shaking his head.

"Oh, Lucy. I'm sorry to hear that," he said, with others offering their condolences.

"Thank you. This is my first Remembrance Service since his death. I could not have got through it without Jimmy's support," she said, looping her arm around Jimmy's left arm and resting her head on his shoulder.

"Lucy's special...," Jimmy said, kissing her lightly on the forehead, and explained to Hamish of the housebreaking, his medals being stolen, Lucy's investigation and the struggles of coming to terms with his injuries.

Angus and Amy smiled. Jimmy was engaging in conversation with others alike, as well as showing small signs of affection towards Lucy.

"Did you receive the support and extra training after your discharge?" Amy asked Hamish.

"Aye, definitely. I'm a qualified plumber now. I fit bathrooms and have a nice little business going. He's my right-hand man," he said, nodding to Harrison sitting beside him and sent the group into hysterical laughter once more.

"Williams, we are well overdue for a tune," Ollie called out, the senior veteran lifting the guitar from behind the bar counter.

"William's our local entertainment," a friend told the group.

Hamish made himself comfortable on a stool and teasingly plucked at the guitar strings, bringing the Royal Legion Club to a deathly silence. "...See the stone set in your eyes...," he captivated his audience in the simple, rawness and acoustic harmony.

Jimmy reached for Lucy's hand and squeezed gently. They knew they would not have gotten through the day without each other.

Darrell Miller took another gulp of lager, his worn-out thumb madly clicking on his phone's keypad.

"Arsehole," he thought, listening to Hamish's attempt at singing the iconic song. His side view caught Jimmy's eye.

He had stood amongst the local people during the Remembrance parade and had made his way to the TRBL club soon after.

"Thank you, thank you!" Hamish bowed as cheers erupted. "I reckon you've been dumped, mate. Come and join us," he said, once more inviting Darrell to join them at their table.

"I doubt Simon would sign you up any time soon," Miller laughed, deciding that there were no hanging doubts to join Hamish and his friends.

"Hey, nice to meet you," Miller said, introducing himself to the group. "No, mate. I insist, drinks on me," he boasted to Harrison, and walked off back to the bar.

"His medals," Hamish nodded a raised eyebrow at Jimmy.

"Aye, I've seen," Jimmy said.

They had all taken an interest in his four medals, and more so the medal with the ISAF bar on its ribbon. Jimmy remembered the army specifically saying not to wear this medal.

"Mate, we are barred from wearing the ISAF medal!" Jimmy told Miller as he returned with the drinks.

"Fuck, I haven't had it replaced yet!" he said.

"Mate, you've had plenty of time!" Williams said.

"Fuck, you know what it's like having your medals sitting in a drawer until they're needed again!" he said without a care to the comment.

"Mate, what do you do for a living now?" Angus asked him.

"I'm a protective security adviser in leading security investigations and forging relationships in counter-terrorist agencies," Miller said almost breathlessly. Taking a guzzle of lager before he found another breath of confidence, he continued. "I'm involved in high-profile, high-security governmental projects," he said with a hint of arrogance in his voice.

"That's quite a mouthful," Lucy said.

"Really...!" she thought, glancing at Amy. Both women needed to take a drink of water at the absurdity of the detailed description.

For someone who had sat quietly drinking and minding his own business, Miller was now more than willing to share his achievements in his extended career choice.

"How long did ye serve, pal?" Jimmy asked him.

"Four years, mate. February 2009 to mid-March 2012. I was at this fucking breaking point and medically discharged for PTSD," he said, happily accepting the fresh pint from Angus.

"Did you get the help for your PTSD?" Amy asked, interested in hearing how he managed a demanding job for someone who had been medically discharged.

"I live in Glasgow with my missus. She helped get me back on my feet and made me realise I needed to share my experiences with others," he said.

Also interested in hearing what he had to say, Lucy asked innocently, "That's really interesting. Does that mean you give talks to schools?"

"I post videos online. Here's my card and mobile number. Give me a call," he winked and handed over his business card to her.

"Thank you, but I'm good," she said, taking the card, and placed it on the table in front of her before happily wrapping her arm around Jimmy's.

Darrell Miller's bazaar conversation and behaviour were leaving the group confused with a questioning doubt hanging in the air.

"Mate, do you set off the security alarms at the airport? I am the Terminator. I'll be back...," Miller said, moving his arms in a slow, robotic motion, taking the piss out of Hamish.

"Fuck off!" Williams said.

Miller's behaviour was not sitting well with him and he was now regretting inviting him over.

"Miller, cool it!" Amy said forcefully.

"What, it was a joke!" he laughed.

"Was joining the army something you always wanted to do?" Lucy asked him.

"You really are interested, aren't you? I enlisted in the RLC in 2009. That stands for Royal Logistic Corps. Give me a call. We can talk over some drinks and a meal," he said.

"She's spoken for, pal!" Jimmy said annoyingly and tightened his arm around Lucy.

"That makes it three years...," Williams said with a puzzled expression.

He had sat there listening to the crap coming out of Miller's mouth with this constant nagging doubt playing on his mind.

"What does?" Miller asked.

"2009 to 2012 makes it three years, surely?" Williams said, glancing at the business card still lying on the table.

"It was a slip of the tongue. I've obviously had too much to drink," Miller laughed awkwardly.

"Yer 'QGM'...?" Jimmy said, giving Angus a questionable look.

"Oh, this...," Miller paused. "It's nothing...," he said, waving his hand in dismissal.

It was the way he said it that concerned those he was with. There was no respect shown to either of them, or the innocent people caught up in a war-ridden country.

"Mate, it's an honour to wear it! Respect it for what it represents...!" Harrison said.

"I feel like I'm being interrogated here!" Miller said abruptly.

"Let's face it, mate. You have one fucking impressive curriculum vitae to your name for only serving three years and a medal that's been barred! You are one fucking suspicious-looking bastard!" Angus said.

Jimmy's muscles tightened. There were comments made throughout the afternoon that just did not add up.

"I don't need to explain myself to anyone! I fucking came here today to pay my respects!" Miller said, and stormed off towards the bar.

From the moment Hamish invited the ex-soldier to join him and his friends at their table, Darrell Miller had come across as an extremely dubious suspect and Hamish was curious to find out who he really was.

Logging onto Google, he typed in the Facebook link from Miller's card and the profile page popped up without a hitch.

On the first view, the page and Darrell Miller looked legit. The page was open to the public and anyone who was interested in sharing and commenting on his vlogs.

Joining a group of older veterans and civilians, the more the drinks flowed, the louder and obnoxious Miller got, monopolising conversations with pointless blather.

"Mate, I think we should go after this drink," Jimmy said to Angus.

"Just let it rest, mate," Harrison said, encouraging Hamish to help him carry a round of drinks. But Hamish walked off, and pushing the heavy door with force, he headed towards the gents and Miller.

"Oi, Miller! Do you take me for a schmuck?" Williams raged, inches from his face.

"What the fuck are you talking about…?" Miller said, zipping his trousers.

"High-security governmental projects! I'll fucking show you interrogation!" Williams said, grabbing him by the scruff of the neck and shoving his head into the flushing toilet bowl.

"You're a fucking Walt!" he fumed and sent Miller across the tiled floor.

"And you're a fucking prick!" Miller gasped, rugby tackling Hamish to the ground.

Hard punches were shared and Hamish used every ounce of strength in his usable limbs to fight back, but Miller managed to grab and shove him up against the wall, punching him in the gut. Hamish's prosthetic leg loosened with the force and he lost his balance.

"Fuck, that's Williams!" Harrison said as the commotion coming from the gents silenced the room and left Hamish's guests in an awkward situation.

"Williams, enough!" Harrison said, helping Angus and Ollie separate the two fighting men.

"Mate, what's going on?" Major Brown demanded, restraining the fuelled Miller.

"He's a fucking Walt. It's all there on his Facebook page!" Williams said, wiping his bloodied nose as Harrison and Ollie helped him to his feet.

"My account was hacked! I don't need to fucking explain myself to you!" Miller said, fighting against Angus hold.

"I am not going to stand in this piss hole and listen to this! We will sort this outside!" the major ordered and walked Miller and the rest of them out into the bar area.

"What the fuck is going on?" Jimmy asked the angered soldiers.

"He's a fucking Walter Mitty!" Williams said furiously.

"What?" Amy said.

"Arrest him, Lucy!" Hamish said.

"So, you're a fucking police pig!" Miller said rudely.

"Don't ye speak to her like that!" Jimmy shouted, forcibly manoeuvring his wheelchair towards Miller.

Clenching his left fist, Jimmy's rage started to boil within. He was furious, frustrated and annoyed at his inability to get involved, control the situation and smack the friggin daylights out of Miller.

Everything Jimmy had been taught throughout his sessions and cognitive therapy was now needed more than ever.

"Yes, I am and I am not a novice when it comes to the army either! I know perfectly well how the army operates!" Lucy said, giving him a taste of his own medicine.

"Lucy, he's a fraudster!" Hamish said annoyingly, as other friends joined in on the outrage and the anger erupted once more.

"All of you, calm down. This will be sorted!" Lucy said directly.

"It's all here," Hamish said, showing her the profile page.

Each post Lucy scrolled through accused Darrell Miller of deceit.

"This girl reckons you should stop exaggerating about your PTSD, because real sufferers don't boast about it online," Amy said.

"No, the stupid bitch is trying to ruin me! We had a thing going for three weeks. That's it!" the restrained Miller said.

"Anyone can buy jackboots and camo vests!" Jimmy raged.

"I'm not going to fucking explain myself to anyone!" the unsavoury Miller said.

"Keep quiet. You've been outed!" Amy said.

"This guy reckons you're a charity scammer!" Williams said.

"There's a post here exposing you for selling scam magazines in Newcastle!" Angus said angrily.

"Darrell, there is a reply to a post from your supposed employer, confirming that you came for an interview but your qualifications as a chef were a far cry for what was required in a demanding job," Lucy said, showing Jimmy the post.

"Am I under investigation?" Miller questioned.

"Why? Is there something we should know? Whatever you are hiding, we will find it!" Lucy said in her police officer's tone.

"What was your service number?" Major Brown asked the jittery Miller.

"Did you enlist, or is that a lie too?" Williams demanded.

"Just tell us the fucking truth!" Brown ordered.

For the first time, Darrell Miller looked nervous and gauging by his reactions and the beads of sweat forming on his furrowed brow, Hamish's suspicions and the posts on Facebook were proving to be true.

"I served for three years with the 154 Regiment RLC, 221 Squadron," Miller mumbled nervously.

"I'm fuckin interested in your medals!" Jimmy screamed as Hamish pushed through his friends and shoved Miller up against a wall, pulling at his medals.

"These don't belong to you...!" he seethed.

"Let me see those!" Jimmy yelled.

"Hamish, the police are on their way. He will be dealt with, but please, I do not want to make unnecessary arrests," Lucy said as Amy helped her to calm the situation.

Jimmy looked at the medals closely. Rubbing his thumb on each one, he turned them over and repeated the task.

"Mate, they're not your medals," Angus said calmly, seeing the colour drain from Jimmy's face while friends restrained the disgraced waste of space.

"Jimmy, look at me," Lucy said gently, putting her arm around his shoulder as he sagged further into his chair.

"Lovely, it's been a long day for all of us," Amy said.

"This is my medal," Jimmy said, swallowing hard as a shaky hand showed Lucy the Queen's Gallantry medal.

"No, mate. It's not your medal," Angus said.

"It's my fuckin medal!" Jimmy roared, lifting his shoulders and pushing his back into his chair.

"What!?" Angus said.

"Look!" Jimmy said, showing Angus the distinctive mark he had made with a sharp object on the inner side of the medal ribbon – **JF.**

"You fucking Walt! You have no right to call yourself a soldier!" the major roared, inches from Miller's face.

"I fucking knew it! I knew something was not sitting right with him!" Williams said, slamming his fist on the bar counter.

"You fucking bastard! PTSD! Real servicemen are suffering and you stand here claiming to be a war hero!" Harrison raged, grabbing Miller by the scruff of the neck and roughly parading him in front of Jimmy. "Fucking hit him!"

Jimmy looked at Lucy and in that frozen second, the look on her face mirrored the horror he had shown the day Molly witnessed his self-beating.

"No, mate!" Jimmy said to the supporting friend.

"Fucking hit him!" Angus said.

"Leave him!" Jimmy said in his direct soldiering tone, just as police officers arrived.

"Jimmy, look at me. I need to show my colleagues the medals," Lucy smiled, touching his arm.

"Aye," he said, the freakish coincidence leaving everyone dazed and in a sense of shock.

"You're a fucking disgrace to all who serve and an insult to those lost!" Williams shouted, threatening to escalate the anger once more.

"Hamish, allow Lucy and her colleagues to do their job," Amy said, putting an arm around his shoulder and encouraging him to keep Jimmy company.

Lucy explained to her Dalkeith colleagues about the day's events, the Facebook posts and the discovery of Jimmy's medal. Darrell Miller had been outed and his loud obnoxious self was now a sheepish case of sorrow.

"Mate, can we talk?" a shameful Miller called out to Jimmy.

"He's not your mate! Don't you fucking dare!" Williams yelled angrily, pointing at him.

"Na, I'm not interested!" Jimmy said, shaking his head at Lucy.

"Come on, pal. He's a feckin dobber," Jimmy said, giving Williams a pat on the back despite himself feeling an out-of-body experience.

Angus and Amy stood with Lucy and her colleagues, giving their account of the unfolding incident and what the significance of the day meant to Jimmy.

"Fuck, Jimbo. I was not expecting that! This is a massive result" Angus said.

"Aye, feck. A' don't know what to say," Jimmy said.

"Hamish, are you able to go down to the station and give a formal statement?" Lucy said as she and a colleague walked up to him.

"Aye, no problem, but I've been drinking," Hamish said.

"We can give you a lift, mate," the officer said.

"Cheers. Lucy, I apologise for my behaviour," Hamish said.

"No need to apologise, Hamish. Life's journey brought all of us here today and thanks to you and your intuition, we have a great result," Lucy smiled.

"Pal, who would have thought? Let's keep in touch," Williams said.

"Aye, definitely," Jimmy said, exchanging numbers with him before he and Harrison walked out with the police officer.

"Are you okay?" Lucy asked, rubbing Jimmy's back.

"Aye, I'm guid," a pale and dazed Jimmy said.

"I'm coming back. I need to phone my sergeant," she said.

With police officers taking down statements, Darrell Miller arrested and evidence bagged, those left in the legion's club went back to their conversations and drinks.

"It's a great deal to take in, lovely. Do you want a glass of water?" Amy said, her and Angus supporting his emotional state.

"Na. Where's Lucy?" Jimmy said confidently, taking another deep breath.

"She's probably still on her phone," Amy said, walking out to find her.

"Lucy, is everything okay?" she asked, walking up to her and her police colleagues.

"Amy, everything is fine. I should have more of an update tomorrow," she said.

"I can't believe what's happened. He was a total idiot. No one in their right mind would give a detailed descriptive account of their job role," Amy said.

"After that, I could not resist but ask him questions. I mean, seriously, if he had just shut up, he would probably have got away with it, but it eventually comes back to bite you. The odds of this happening are quite frankly non-existent," Lucy said, herself a little shaky.

She was a good police officer, able to do her job without the emotional attachment, but Jimmy's case, for all reasons, had affected her.

"We know what this case has meant to you. Are you feeling okay?" Amy said, placing an arm around her shoulder.

"Honestly, I feel sick, but don't worry. I won't leave my celebratory leftovers all over you," Lucy laughed.

"Come on, let's get you a glass of water," Amy said.

"Here I am complaining I am feeling sick, but gosh, Jimmy must be feeling ten times worse," Lucy said.

"He is in shock, but he sent me out to look for you," Amy smiled, nudging her.

* * *

17:05 hours and it had been a long emotional day for all of them. Sitting around Jimmy's table drinking coffee, they tried to comprehend the day's events.

Discovering a 'Walt' on a day as significant as this one, because of what each of them had been through and non-other than finding Jimmy's Queen's Gallantry medal, had affected them all deeply.

"When do we get Jimmy's medal back?" Angus asked Lucy, finishing his coffee.

"All the medals will need to be presented as evidence, should the case be brought to trial. I'll get a further update tomorrow and let you know," Lucy said.

"Aims and I have an early start tomorrow, but we'll keep in touch," Angus said to Jimmy, knowing that the day's events could send his constant conflicting thoughts into warfare.

"Aye, we'll speak tomorrow. I am guid, pal" Jimmy reassured him.

"I am off now, so I'm here too. Do you want to come for supper tomorrow?" Lucy said.

"That will be lovely. It means I don't have to cook," Amy smiled.

"Mate, it's been a long emotional day and if I did not believe in it before, I now certainly believe that fate played a huge part in today's outcome," Angus said.

"I know, pal," Jimmy said. He too had felt the powerful belief.

"We'll see you tomorrow. Take care of Lucy," Amy said.

"Aye, I will," Jimmy said.

"Try to get some sleep," Amy said to Lucy, giving her a hug before walking out with Angus and closing Jimmy's door behind her.

"Are ye okay?" Jimmy asked, taking Lucy's hand and pulling her into a hug.

"I am exhausted, but I cannot imagine how you are feeling. Oh, Jimmy. Who would have thought?" she said, finding it hard to fight back her tears.

"Lucy, don't cry. I know it's been a tough day, but it's all worked out guid," he said.

"I am sorry, Jimmy," she sniffed.

"Don't be sorry," he said, wiping away her tears.

"Thank you for taking care of me today. I would never have done it without you. Are you okay, honestly? Do you want to talk about it?" she said.

"I'm in shock. It's unreal. But I also feel so helpless and annoyed with myself in not having the ability to control the situation. I felt useless," he said.

"Jimmy, you're not useless! You showed more control and handled the situation incredibly well, considering the circumstances. You had the opportunity to smack him, but you did not. You controlled the situation and remained calm. That is pure strength and willpower," she said.

"I could have smacked the frigging daylights out of him! He was a flipping arsehole!" he said.

"Thank you for respecting me. What an arrogant arse and he

had ample opportunities to walk out and get away with it," she said.

"Do ye think there's more to it?" he asked.

"Yes, Jimmy, I do, by the way he reacted when he found out I was a police officer and the questions he was asking me. Why ask me if he's under investigation?" she said.

"Do ye think he's done a runner?" he asked.

"Going by the Facebook posts, probably yes. Why come to Dalkeith for a Remembrance when you live in Glasgow? But I don't know if he's connected to the youth who broke into your property," she said.

"I think we all had some inclination that something wasn't right," he said.

"I think so," she smiled.

* * *

21:05 hours –

"Maybe with what's happened today, Jimmy can accept recognition for his 'QGM'," Angus said, flicking through the channels.

"I think he would, but it would be even more special if he did not know about it. You can speak to your CO, but it would have to be pretty soon," Amy said, climbing into bed.

"I'll speak to him tomorrow and hopefully Lucy can arrange to have the medal returned," he said.

"He was very protective over her today and I think it took every ounce of willpower not to hit Miller," she said.

"It took me every bit of willpower not to hit him," he said.

"Lucy and I had a good giggle afterward. He explained his job role like he was reading it from a script," she said.

"It's infuriating and it will be interesting to hear what Lucy comes back with," he said, turning off the TV and pulled Amy into his arms.

"How are you feeling after today?" she asked.

"Tough, Aims. Last night, I was considering cancelling the entire day. He would fall into a deep sleep and moments later, wake up screaming as if he were being tortured," he said, clearing his throat.

"Are you okay?" she asked, sitting up on her haunches and wrapped her arms around his neck.

"He's never going to serve alongside me again, Aims, and being in uniform today hit me hard," he said, wiping his eye.

"You're going to set me off now. Going through this process was the best thing for you. You have never shared your feelings with me before. You are learning to share the burden and I will always be here for you. Jimmy is going to need the continued support and reassurance to help him manage the depression and self-rejection, but you can benefit too by helping him," she said.

"You stayed strong for all of us today, thank you," he said, leaning in and kissed her.

"I love you, Angus."

* * *

01:13 hours and both Jimmy and Lucy could have done with each other's company longer, but Jimmy wanted Lucy home when Molly woke up and they both agreed it was a good thing. With the late Scottish wintry night filtering through the blinds, a touch of welcoming cold air filling the room, Jimmy reflected on the past eleven months –

> *He had rejected life. He was filled with hatred and anger and vulgarity. He had lost respect for himself and his peers. He blamed his best friend for everything and pushed him away. He had given up and wanted to die.*

> *Without Lucy, Angus and Amy, he would not be here today!*

> *Angus had been with him every step of the way,*

going through the psychiatric sessions with him and showing him there could be a life after the army, without losing the sense of army life altogether. He had his best friend back, standing by his side.

Amy had organised the tickets for the charity dinner, getting him out and meeting other wounded soldiers. She had organised the rehab session and continues to look at any up and coming events for him to attend. She had helped him with his Armed Forces Compensation application, following it up and continues to research any other help he could benefit from. She had shown him that Lucy was suffering and needed affection.

Lucy had gone beyond her role as a police officer and had shown him that she was someone who could be trusted. She continued to visit him, despite his case going cold early in the investigation. She had been concerned about his well-being and had shown kindness in bringing him home-cooked meals. She had allowed her daughter to be around him, despite the horror she had witnessed and always put him at ease.

And now, as fate would have it, his Queen's Gallantry medal was found!

Jimmy swallowed hard and buried his face in his left hand. For the first time, he realised how much it meant to him.

CHAPTER FORTY-FOUR

*Synchronicity: A meaningful coincidence of two
or more events where something other than the
probability of chance is involved – C.G. Jung*

*Carl Gustav Jung was a Swiss psychiatrist and psycho-
analyst who founded analytical psychology – Wikipedia*

Knowing what the effect of finding Jimmy's medal meant to him, Lucy had contacted her sergeant first thing to get an update on Miller's arrest. Darrell Miller had been interviewed and his details checked on the Police National Computer. He was a thirty-year-old from Glasgow and well known to the police for other convictions and criminal offences. Miller had served three years in the military. However, he had never been deployed and had been dishonourably discharged for misconduct. He was charged and remanded in custody, Glasgow police collecting him to face the charges.

Lucy was pleased with the result and a further investigation would now be conducted in returning the remaining stolen medals to their rightful veterans. She phoned Angus to update him.

"...I have a meeting with my commanding officer this afternoon. I am sure we all agree that he should now accept recognition of some sort and it would be a nice surprise if he did not know. Is there a chance of getting his medal back soon...?" Angus said.

"That would be wonderful. I think it's the right thing to do and I honestly believe he would be honoured. There shouldn't be a problem retrieving the medal and I will talk to my sergeant...," Lucy said, and soon after, they ended the call.

"Lucy," Jimmy called, turning his wheelchair at hearing the door open. He had not gotten much sleep after Lucy left and had been up early to take a shower and breathe new life into his aches and pains.

"Good morning, Jimmy," her face lit up at seeing him.

"How are ye?" he asked, pulling her into a hug and holding her for a moment. They were grateful to be in each other's company again.

"I am good and happy to have time off to spend with you. How are you feeling?" she said, taking a seat at the table and manoeuvred Jimmy's chair closer.

"It's very surreal. I feel disorientated and can't get my head around it," he said.

"It is. I have never dealt with a case like this before. Have you heard from Hamish?" she said.

"Aye. He's guid," he said.

"Shame, he was quite upset yesterday. You must keep in touch with him. He's a good guy," she said.

"Aye, I will. Whit happened to Miller, do ye know?" he said.

"So, Miller did serve three years and not four. He had never been deployed and was dishonourably discharged for misconduct. He is well known to the police and his details were already in the system. He was charged and Glasgow police picked him up yesterday to face his charges," she said.

"A' have na time for bampots like him," he said.

"Nor do I. Guys like yourself and my brother earned the respect and recognition and he…," she sighed.

"It's okay, Lucy. Whit happens to the medals? Dae ye know whan I'll get mine back?" he said.

"Your medal and others will need to be presented as evidence in court. I can't say when that will be, but should know in a few days. Unfortunately, army regalia is in circulation all the time and it is difficult to regulate. The youth who stole your medals could be questioned again, but I don't think we will find anything new," she said.

"They should bring back National Service. I had a feckin' shite upbringing, but soldiering wis whit I was guid at," he said.

414

"It would get them off the streets and give them a purpose in life. They would be trained in a skill and get paid for it. I won't give up on finding your Operations medal and I can, if you want me to, write up a report for a replacement?" she said, a little teary-eyed.

"A' will think aboot it. Are ye okay?" he said with a slightly shaky hand wiping her tears.

"I am just happy to see you, Jimmy," she smiled, and wrapped her arms around his neck and hugged him. Today was different and they knew it.

"Would ye' like tae gae for a coffee before we go back to yer hoose?" he asked, quite surprised by his own gesture.

"I would really like that. I know a place we can go to," she said with excitement.

* * *

The quaint country feels of the coffee shop was welcoming and cosy, with a roaring wood fire bringing warmth from the wintry, icy air outside. With only a few enthusiastic early walkers, Lucy and Jimmy took a table closest to the door and a friendly barista moved a chair to make room for Jimmy's wheelchair. They both ordered a cappuccino and slice of carrot cake.

"I've never been here," he said.

"Nor have I, but it always looks inviting. How do you feel

about being out in public and in your hometown?" she said.

"Deciding out of the blue to do the collection two weeks ago has helped, but who knows how I'll feel tomorrow? I still have moments of doubts," he said, stroking her fingers.

"We can get through those moments of doubts together," she said shyly, feeling Jimmy's touch of warmth on her lips.

"Thank ye for nea givin' up on me," he said in his heavy Scottish accent and squeezing her hand with his.

"We help each other," she smiled.

The young girl who had taken their order placed two generous slices of carrot cake on their table and cappuccinos with plenty of froth dusted with chocolate in a heart shape pattern. "I hope you enjoy," she smiled.

"Thank you," they both said simultaneously.

"Must be a sign," he said as a huge grin spread across his face and Lucy's amused look allowed him the opportunity to tease with a cheeky wink.

"Stop teasing me," she laughed.

They enjoyed their coffee outing and time spent together, deciding they would come back and have a meal.

* * *

Turning into the driveway, Maggie and Molly came out to greet them. Molly's little face lit up with pure joy at seeing Jimmy and she offered him her tiny hand for support while Lucy held his chair.

"Hello, Maggie," Jimmy said.

"Thank you for the beautiful flowers," she said, giving him a motherly hug.

"Hello, ma wee lassie," Jimmy said, tucking his left arm around Molly's tiny waist and lifting her gently onto his lap.

Lucy smiled, sharing her daughter's excitement and curiosity. The little girl looked up at Jimmy and found that twinkle in his eye. She sat up straight, curling her little fingers around his and Lucy wheeled them inside.

He felt the same homely and at ease feeling that he felt with each of his visits to Lucy's home, Lucy putting him at ease, insisting he climb out his wheelchair and make himself comfortable.

With Molly keeping him entertained in her books and toys, the chatters had flowed with amusement, often erupting into bursts of giggles and laughter, which gave Maggie and Lucy an excuse to drop their cooking duties and join in on the fun.

Mrs. Harris enjoyed the joyous voices that filled her home. Hearing Jimmy laughing filled her with happiness, knowing what he had gone through and how far he had come. He had helped her daughter as much as she had helped him.

CHAPTER
FORTY-FIVE

M ajor Brown knocked on the door. "Brown, come in. Take a seat," Lieutenant Colonel Rutherford said.

"Thank you for seeing me, Sir," Major Brown said.

"Is it true, what's being said, Ferguson's 'QGM' was discovered yesterday?" the commanding officer asked.

"Yes, in Dalkeith, Sir. A'Walt' from Glasgow...," Brown said, barely able to contain his anger, explaining yesterday's unfolding event.

"Fuck, that's pure coincidence. Someone is trying to tell Ferguson something," the lt colonel said incredulously.

"For all of us, it's so surreal. Amy and I were so glad to have Lucy Harris, the police officer who's been working on the investigation...," the major said, explaining further.

"Ferguson's girlfriend?" the commanding officer questioned.

"Amy and I are working on that, Sir. I served with Lucy's brother at Sandhurst," Brown said, telling his commanding officer about Lucy and her brother.

Major Brown and his commanding officer enjoyed their coffee while Angus updated him on Jimmy's progress and hope in his continuing recovery, the lt colonel genuinely interested in hearing what the major had to say.

"Sir, is there anything we can do to honour Ferguson for his service and maybe keep it a surprise?" the major asked.

Nodding his head, the lt colonel momentarily lost himself in his thoughts, running his fingers over his imaginary moustache. "I tell you what, let's go the whole hog, all ranks Christmas luncheon. Invite some special guests and maybe even a reporter from the local paper. We can welcome the troops home and at the same time present Ferguson with his medal," he said, and both officers stood up.

"Thank you, Sir. I appreciate that," Major Brown said, saluting his commanding officer.

Angus texted Lucy.

> *Hi Lucy, have had a meeting and everything is good.*
> *Christmas luncheon Friday 7th December*

> *Great thanks Angus. I will arrange for*
> *Jimmy's medal to be returned*

* * *

Angus and Amy arrived just after 18:00 hours and Mrs. Harris answered the door.

"They're bathing Molls," she said, as Angus and Amy hugged her and introduced themselves.

"It's good practice, Maggie," Angus said, and all laughed at the squeals and splashes of water coming from inside.

"Oh I know, dear," Maggie said.

"Look who I have," Jimmy grinned, coming through with a sweetly fresh wee lassie sitting proudly on his lap and affection showing in his and Lucy's relationship.

"These two were full of mischief today. Half an hour ago, this place looked like a tornado had hit it," Lucy laughed.

"Has Jimmy been a silly billy?" Amy asked, taking hold of Molly and embracing her.

"Yesss...," Molly giggled.

Angus was surprised and pleased with how relaxed Jimmy looked, knowing that the day before had been extremely emotional. Not having the choice of staying with him longer than he had hoped could only have been difficult for him.

They all sat down for dinner soon after Angus and Amy arrived, insisting on eating with Molly and giving her another reason to express her delightfulness. Enjoying the wholesome stew, Angus and Amy showed Maggie admiration and gratitude in finally meeting her. Angus told Maggie about Tom and their time spent at West Point. Out of respect, he let Maggie know that Tom was a good guy and she could be proud.

"When Tom and Lucy were younger, they would turn their weekends and school holidays into an adventure. The garden became their fort," Maggie smiled, sharing and enjoying the fond memories.

"Or what about those evenings when we put on a magic show for you?" Lucy said while she and Amy cleared the last few dishes from the table.

"Lucy always insisted on wearing her princess outfit," Maggie said, and they all laughed hard, their laughter bubbling over to the innocence, exuberance and overall cuteness that Molly was, making the moment even more memorable.

"I've been teased at all day," Lucy smiled, casually putting her hands on Jimmy's shoulders.

"Thank you for a wonderful meal," Amy said, taking hold of Molly and her bottle and everyone got up from the table.

Jimmy and Angus shared a look and both fought back the grin that threatened to explode across their faces as Lucy subconsciously supported Jimmy while he climbed out his chair.

"I am trying to convince Mum to get back into playing Bridge and teaching Jimmy," Lucy said.

"Lovely, it is a stimulating game. My folks play," Amy said.

"Aye, I've been reading the rule book," Jimmy said.

"We will make a date and do some practice rounds," Maggie said.

Angus and Amy shared a smile with Lucy. Her family was playing a huge part in helping Jimmy accept his life for what it was.

"Mate, the guys could not believe yesterday's outcome," Angus said.

"Ye must know how I feel," Jimmy said, shaking his head.

"It was a true miracle," Maggie said.

"Yer daughter never gave up hope in finding my medals," Jimmy said, sitting in between Lucy and Maggie and took Lucy's hand.

"You've all brought happiness back into my daughter's life," Maggie said, overcome with emotion and standing up in readiness to take Molly, who had fallen asleep in Amy's arms.

"Aww Maggie, Lucy and Molly have brought joy to all our lives. You have a wonderful family," Amy said.

"Jimmy, thank you for taking care of my daughter," Maggie said in a hoarse voice, giving him a warm hug.

"Lucy is a very special woman," Jimmy said.

"You are more than welcome to stay tonight, Jimmy," Maggie said.

"Thank ye," Jimmy said, and the women left the room.

"You look really relaxed and happy, mate," Angus said to Jimmy.

"I am, pal. I love her" Jimmy admitted.

"Mate, just tell her. She's so in love with you. Lucy's obviously told you about Miller?" Angus said.

"Aye, friggin arsehole...," Jimmy said.

Amy put Molly to bed before joining Lucy and her mother.

"With the three of you here tonight, it just brings back memories, good memories," Lucy said tearfully.

"My daughter hasn't been this happy since Tom's death. She loves Jimmy," Maggie choked.

"Jimmy loves her. I mean, really loves her. They have these flirtatious moments, thinking no one is watching them," Amy said, nudging Lucy and the women laughed.

Mrs. Harris convinced the girls that she was okay and her tears were happy tears. She encouraged the girls to join their menfolk and enjoy the rest of their evening.

Angus and Jimmy were going through the previous day's events when Lucy and Amy walked through. Tears had been shared between them all and Jimmy stretched out his left arm for Lucy.

"Is yer mother okay?" he asked.

"She's fine. They were happy tears," she said, caressing his cheek and they momentarily lost themselves in the moment.

"There they go again, that flirtatious moment," Amy said, and all burst into laughter.

"Why don't we have those moments?" Angus joked, finding Amy's neck with his lips.

"Oh stop it. You'll make Lucy blush again," Amy said, laughing further.

"This woman is the best thing that's happened to me," Jimmy said, pulling Lucy into his chest.

"We know, lovely" Amy smiled.

Seeing Jimmy and Lucy tonight there was something different. There was a closeness, a radiant glow within them. They knew he would declare his love for her sooner than later.

They drank coffee, enjoying an evening of tears and laughter, remembering memories of times gone by, their own memories, happy times and now, new beginnings.

* * *

23:00 hours –

Doing their toiletries, Lucy gave Jimmy his clean sweatshirt and boxers from his previous visit while she momentarily left him to change in the bathroom.

"I am so glad you're here, Jimmy," she said, leaving the bedroom door ajar.

"I've had an incredible day with an incredible woman," he said as she snuggled under the duvet and found the safety of his left arm.

"Are ye okay?" he asked.

"I am okay," she said, feeling a tingling sensation down her spine as Jimmy's shaky hand gently ran his fingers through her hair.

They smiled and she lifted her head. Twirling and tucking her hair to one side, she enticed him with her bare skin.

Jimmy touched her again, gently down the base of her neck, feeling the softness of her skin against his fingers and the tingles down the spine of her long sleeve cotton top. With each stroke, her top exposed a little more flesh, just enough to caress the small of her back.

They both knew the sense of loneliness and loss and how the eerie sound of silence can swallow every ounce of your being. But, the silence they shared together was comforting and pleasurable, having not felt this nervousness, this closeness, this excited since the day in the park.

"We could get a little visitor in the morning," she said, breaking the silence.

"I look forward to it," he said, stroking her arm as she rested her head on his chest.

"Why don't ye drink?" He finally asking her the question that had been persistently nagging at his mind.

"It's never appealed to me and now because I first handedly had to deal with the after-effects, I hate it even more. No, Jimmy," seeing the guilt in his eyes. "There is a difference between someone who drinks, only then to cause trouble and someone who drinks because they so desperately need the help," she said.

"Did Tom drink?" he asked.

"Yes, Tom drank with his friends," she said.

"It helped block the nightmares," he said.

"You haven't had a drink since your relapse. Do you still crave it?" she asked.

"Aye, every day, but not when I'm with ye. I think I'll need to attend a twelve-step programme sometime in the future," he said.

"They have meetings in Peebles once a week and I would like to be your sponsor if you would let me," she said.

"Ye saved my life, Lucy," his voice choked with emotion.

"Oh, Jimmy, you helped me too," she said, taking his damaged hand, her soft fingers gently stroking each of his as they twitched with each sensation.

"Would you ever share your pain with me?" she asked, delicately running her fingers over the rigid scars on his stumps and his body trembled with his only usable limb, tightening its hold around her waist.

"I'm not the man in the photo anymore. I carry a heavy load of baggage," he said hoarsely.

"I am not the same woman I was two years ago. I come with baggage too. I have nightmares and I fear what Owen is capable of, once he is released from prison," she said.

"Lucy, what if I can't protect ye and Molly? Yer mother?" he said.

"You make me feel safe and we can take care of each other," she said.

"What if I can't give ye the life ye deserve?" he said, gently touching her cheek.

"Jimmy, I am not saying it's going to be easy for us, but we can get through it together. Molly absolutely adores you," she sniffed.

"I'm scared Lucy. I'm scared of us. I'm scared I'll relapse. I'm scared about the up and coming days, the future," he said.

"I am scared about us too Jimmy. I have only ever been with one guy and he manipulated me. I am not as confident as you might think. Tom was always there to look after me and in an instant, he was gone and I was left with all the responsibility. Finding you that night has been my saving grace. I am lonely, Jimmy. You know what that feels like, that eerie silence of being alone. I don't want you to ever feel embarrassed about letting me help you. Please give us a chance," she said.

"I was in a very dark place when ye found me. I still have those days," he said.

"Jimmy, we will get through it together. We will look after each other," she wrapped her arms around his neck. "Kiss me," she said with barely a whisper, burying her face in him.

"Lucy," he slid his hand down the side of her face in a warm caress, his fingers cupping her chin and lifting it. "I'm in love with ye," he whispered hoarsely.

"I love you too, Jimmy," she stifled on her chokes as her sweet bodily perfume and soft lips filled his senses.

It had been the first time that Jimmy and Lucy had opened and dug deep into their emotions, ending an incredible day with an incredible woman.

* * *

Despite the early morning quietness of the house, Jimmy and Lucy smiled at sensing Molly and Shaun the sheep's presence in the doorway, a slightly confused look on her face at seeing her mummy and Jimmy together.

Lucy and Jimmy giggled. Leaning across him, she stretched out her arms and lifted Molly into bed, Jimmy tucking her under the duvet and kissing her little cheek.

"Who's that?" Lucy asked softly, pointing to Jimmy.

"Jimmy," the petite wee lassie whispered.

"Mummy loves Jimmy," Lucy said as those adorable pearly whites lit up her delicate face.

"Jimmy loves ma wee lassie," he said with that reassuring twinkle in his eye as both kissed the dozy little girl lightly and Jimmy finding Lucy's mouth.

429

CHAPTER FORTY-SIX

Three and a half weeks later – Friday, 7th December
2012 – Glencorse Barracks all ranks Christmas luncheon
and Jimmy's Queen's Gallantry medal recognition

When you come to the end of your rope, tie a
knot, and hang on – Theodore Roosevelt

Theodore Roosevelt Jr. was an American statesman,
politician, conservationist, naturalist, and writer
who served as the 26th president of the United
States from 1901 to 1909 – Wikipedia

With the local inspector's approval and permission from the courts despite the ongoing proceedings for Darrell Miller, Jimmy's medal was photographed and reclaimed from the station.

Constable Lucy Harris had also contacted Corporal Mackey to tell him the phenomenal news, explaining to him that the police were investigating the other medals found and that she would contact him for further identification. She invited the veteran, on behalf of Angus, to attend the Christmas luncheon, and he accepted gladly, saying he would travel up with his daughter and stay with family.

Angus had taken the medal to have it professionally cleaned and had insisted that the original ribbon not be replaced. He had contacted Mike and Hamish a few days after speaking to his commanding officer and invited them to attend. Both men happily accepted.

Spending the night at Jimmy's, Angus had helped him get ready for the afternoon celebrations. For the first time, their friendship had not been about building bridges, but the complete opposite and they were their old selves again.

Driving through the barracks barriers brought back so many memories of times gone by and although his life changed in an instant, he now knew his army family would always be there for him.

Although Jimmy knew that Angus had invited Mike and Hamish as part of his guests for the Christmas lunch, he was still oblivious to the reasoning behind it and seemed lost in the serenity of his surroundings.

"It's going to be a good day. mate. Everyone wants to see you," Angus said, pushing his wheelchair across the courtyard towards the gymnasium.

Decorated in red and green foil hanging across the ceiling, trestle tables and metal chairs lined the floor like soldiers standing to attention on the parade square, the head table looking down on his men.

Uniformly covered in white tablecloths and red runners, the square vases, filled with cranberries and mixtures of greenery, complimented the table settings and the pre-lit 5ft Christmas tree in its snow-coated tips and red berries.

It was busier than Jimmy had expected. Soldiers from the barracks, familiar faces he hadn't seen in years, those closest to Angus and those he cared for most, were all gathered in a festivity of conversations. Many of them still served. They had the life and the camaraderie he would forever miss.

Mike noticed the difference in Jimmy immediately. He looked healthier and not the gaunt, hollow-eyed man he was that night at the dinner.

"Hey, mate!" Mike and Hamish said, the wounded soldiers shaking hands.

Wearing a navy floral wrap dress and her hair in loose waves, Lucy's face lit up at seeing Jimmy. His smile showed the love and happiness that she had brought back into his life.

"Hello, my darling," she said, cupping his face and kissed him lightly.

"Ye look lovely," he said, taking her hand.

"Lovely, does this bring back memories?" Amy smiled.

"Aye, many memories," Jimmy agreed.

"It's going to be a good day," Amy said.

"Who's that?" Jimmy questioned, seeing an elderly gentleman in a wheelchair conversing with the lt colonel and other senior officers.

"I think he's part of the lt colonel's guests," Angus said.

"I have a proposition for you, mate. We can talk later," Mike said to Jimmy as right on cue and to military standards, everyone started taking their seats. Angus and his guests joined the lt colonel at the head table. Angus and Amy took their seats alongside other officers, with Lucy on Jimmy's left and the wounded veterans on his right.

Lieutenant Colonel Rutherford stood up and tapped his glass, bringing order and announcing the ceremonial event –

"Good afternoon, ladies and gentlemen and distinguished guests, to our annual Christmas party. I decided to change the format this year and host an all ranks Christmas luncheon, but before we get the celebrations underway, a few gratitudes are in order.

Let us give thanks and welcome back the troops who recently returned from Afghanistan. Let us remember and pay tribute to those who never made it home, are injured and going through the recovery process," the lt colonel said, with soldiers and guests toasting and giving a moment's reflection.

"Thank you to our special guests here today. Corporal Mackey, a World War 2 veteran from Portsmouth and a guest of Ferguson's. It is an honour, Sir," he nodded to his left and everyone clapped.

"That is odd, what is going on?" Jimmy
thought, glancing at Lucy.

"Welcome to Mike Tully from Veterans United. Hamish Williams and Constable Lucy Harris whose brother served, thank you," he said, and the room clapped again.

"And last but not least, our very own, Corporal Jimmy Ferguson," he made his way towards Jimmy's wheelchair.

"The Corporal who, despite his own injuries, pulled himself along to save that of his comrade. Sadly, the Junior NCO later lost his life, but his family were still able to say their goodbyes.

Dealing with his own suffering and coming to terms with his life-changing injuries, it is now only due that we commend him for his service," the lieutenant colonel said, taking the Queen's Gallantry medal from Angus and pinning it on Corporal Jimmy Ferguson's breast pocket, the shocked and surprised Corporal saluting with his left hand.

"Sorry, Sir. I'm no padre," Jimmy said with wit.

"Thank God for that!" the lieutenant colonel said, and laughter was shared.

"Would you say a few words?" he continued, and Jimmy gave

his commanding officer a nod.

"Sir, thank you for the invitation to be here today and for the unexpected recognition. I'm truly honoured. Corporal Mackey, I think Lucy had a part to play in this and will come and meet you after lunch," he said, nodding respectively.

Jimmy took another long deep breath. Everything from the way he held himself, to the way he spoke, to that look of un-assailable confidence in his eye, said he could do it –

"As soldiers, we are trained to complete a mission. When you land on the ground and you're in a firefight, you think of nothing more, but the mission and the guy next to you. You'll do anything to get yourself and them out of that situation, no matter what, knowing there is a chance that you, or your mates are going to die.

You cannot fight in a war and experience the catastrophic loss of human life without being affected and having that life sentence engraved on your mind.

For so many of us, we do not develop issues until we are back from Theatre and are having to transition into civvy life when we would rather be on Operation.

We miss everything from how hard it was. How bitter you got. How angry and emotional you got. And what you saw. You miss that camaraderie. That feeling of belonging. You miss your mates.

*We do everything we can to push these memories,
feelings and thoughts aside, but the realisation and
impact of knowing your army career is over, can and
in many cases, have devastating consequences.*

*It is hard for someone who hasn't experienced
it to understand that.*

*We not only have to deal with the impact of the
physical injuries and the way they restrict what we
are able to do, but we must deal with the psychological
difficulty of feeling worthless and incapable of
living. That is extremely hard to deal with.*

*Many good friends do not make it home. You feel a sense
of guilt and being angry all the time. You are angry at the
world. You are angry for being alive. You want to be right
there with them as your purpose for life has now gone.*

*By finally accepting help and talking about it, you
realise that even the most tragic and stressful
situations can teach us important lessons in life.*

*I still suffer the harrowing nightmares. The self-beatings.
The guilt and self-doubt. I have good days and bad days. But
talking about it makes you stronger. Each day I get stronger.*

I know now it's okay to be alive!"

The speech resonated with all and emotions ran deep as Jimmy sat, his shoulders back, his head held high and everyone who could, gave a standing ovation with his chest-beating to the rhythm. Corporal Jimmy Ferguson was proud of who he was.

"Mate, respect," Angus said, shaking his left hand. Jimmy's testament of strength and determination was something Angus would forever draw on in his own times of need.

"I love you," Jimmy said to Lucy, lightly kissing her and reached across to touch Amy's arm.

"We've kept the original ribbon," Angus said.

"Cheers, pal. That's important to me," Jimmy said.

Troops and guests enjoyed the merry atmosphere of drinks and food, crackers banging and surprises shared.

"Lucy, how do you know the Corporal?" Hamish asked, the main course of roast turkey with all the trimmings being served.

"Corporal Mackey had his own medals stolen on Christmas Day, last year. His daughter was forwarded the appeal for Jimmy's medals and he wanted to get in touch and let me know," Lucy said, swapping her plate with the cut turkey for Jimmy's.

"People like that have no right. He's an honourable man," Hamish said.

"I agree, Hamish. Mike, when do you set off for Kilimanjaro next year?" Lucy asked.

"From the 5th to the 14th of October," Mike said.

"How is the training going?" she asked.

"The training is intense and we are certainly put through our paces. I will have to go through extra training because of my disability, but as I've said to Jimmy, it's a team effort and although it's harder and takes a lot longer, it's worthwhile in the end," Mike said.

"I think it's incredible. All of you are truly a force to be reckoned with. I will come up with a plan to raise funds to donate," Lucy said.

"We can come up with something together," Amy said.

"Absolutely, maybe a mad hatters tea party with set challenges?" Lucy said.

"That would be great, thank you," Mike said.

"I think Jimmy should do a skydive," Amy smiled.

"Netheravon. We can travel down together," Hamish suggested.

"Come on, mate. Let's do it, no buts!" Angus said.

"Believe me, I'm there…," Jimmy said, nodding his head.

"Hi, Jimmy. I am sorry to interrupt…," the woman said, sneaking upon him.

"My name's Maureen. I am from the local paper. I was invited to write a piece on welcoming the troops back and your recognition. I would like to use your speech as part of my story," she said.

"Aye, that will be guid, thank ye," Jimmy said, shaking the woman's hand.

"Fantastic. Your speech was so genuine," Maureen said, showing him a photo of the gymnasium taken as a whole and what she would use for her story.

"Enjoy the rest of your celebrations. I've got to get back to the office now. The article will be in next week's paper," she said, saying her goodbyes and headed towards the commanding officer.

"I am so proud of you," Lucy said, with Jimmy wrapping his arm around her shoulder.

"I must go meet the Corporal," he said, before Angus took hold of his chair and he went off to mingle.

"...as preparations were being made for the D-Day landings, the whole of Southern England was one huge armed camp, with roads leading to the ports stacked up with lorries, tanks and equipment stretching for miles alongside them...," the respected World War 2 veteran explained.

Now in his nineties, Corporal Mackey, still with his wits about him, described in detail to his younger generation, moments he would never forget, "...these young men floating in a sea of blood and others struggling with these enormous backpacks on their shoulders...," the detailed description putting his company right in the midst of that unforgettable day.

Each of them who had gathered round, admired the veteran and shook his hand in respect.

"I'm truly grateful for ye coming today, Corporal," Jimmy said with admiration and sincerity, as the corporal's daughter joined them to wish Jimmy all the absolute best.

"Veterans help veterans continue getting the help," the honourable WW2 veteran said, before Lucy and Amy walked the visitors out to the car park.

"Mate, about that proposition?" Mike said to Jimmy, taking the empty seat offered by Angus next to him.

"I was approached by a disabled charity after they saw my interview about climbing Kilimanjaro on the local evening news. They wanted me to give a talk at a fundraising event in

March, but I am already booked on that day. I told them about you and they are really keen to have you," Mike said.

"Mate, this would be a fantastic opportunity and a perfect setting…," Angus said.

"What would be a perfect setting?" Amy asked.

"I've asked Jimmy to take my place and give a talk…," Mike said, updating the women.

"Aye, I can do this. Cheers, Mike. Thanks for the gesture," Jimmy said without hesitation, surprising himself with his own positivity.

"That's great. I will send you the details," Mike said, pleased that Jimmy had accepted.

"I can rearrange my shifts if need be. Thank you, Mike," Lucy said, wrapping her arm around Jimmy's.

"Lovely, this is fantastic news," Amy said.

"Come on, mate. We need to do a challenge," Hamish said as Jimmy and Angus described the backpack design they had come up with and put the group in the picture of Jimmy's body zipped up, protected from the rain and his head bobbing up and down with the movement, the group laughing hard.

"A one-legged challenge," Hamish said, his mischievous nature bringing out the comic within as he loosened his prosthetic right arm and leg, giving Lucy the famous thumbs-up tattoo, jumping up and hopping a few steps, before falling back into his empty seat. Everyone erupted into laughter at his entertaining actions.

Jimmy's backpack and Hamish's one
leg would be a sight to see!

Jimmy laughed and shared the hilarity banter between the group and taking in his surroundings, he reflected on the past twelve months –

His best friend, the friend who never left his side,
Angus, was now a part of his life once more.

Amy being there to support Angus had given him
the strength he had needed during tough times.

Meeting Mike had given Jimmy the boost of confidence
he had needed, encouraging him to get involved
and out there meeting others.

Meeting Hamish had reminded Jimmy of the
colourful references and humorous banter he
had blocked out for so many years.

And! The woman who he had finally declared his love to.
The woman who went beyond her job as a police officer to
help him. The woman who had made him feel comfortable
within his own skin. And the woman who had welcomed
him into her home and had made him a part of her family.

He loved and respected Lucy dearly.

Jimmy gave Lucy a gentle squeeze. This was the start of a new life and the biggest step he had taken yet.

"Come on, lovely. I want a photo of you and Angus," Amy said.

"Come on, lovely…," the best friends joked and wrapping their arms around each other's shoulders, they gave the broadest of smiles.

Corporal Jimmy Ferguson was finally Fit For Purpose!

❋ ❋ ❋

Every soldier has been confronted by danger and uncertainty, but their courage is stronger. They show discipline in difficult situations and have respect for others. They act with integrity and loyalty to all who serve alongside them. They show incredible acts of selfless commitment and are proud to serve Queen and country.

We must never forget our brave servicemen and women who make the ultimate sacrifice to allow ordinary individuals like ourselves to live in a free world. We must support and honour those servicemen and women who face life-changing challenges both physically and psychologically, but who, through their sheer strength and determination soldier on, no matter what...

With respect, honour and pride,

I thank you for your service

Briony Beattie

Dictating Office	Details		
Name	Lucy Harris		
Rank	Constable		
PSI	Alistair Baird	ISSI	400 - 12444
Division	Tweeddale West	Station	Peebles

STORM Reference / Incident Number(s)	J31 – 010112F
Division (as per local Crime Management System)	Tweeddale West
Sub-Division of LOCUS	Peebles
BEAT Number of LOCUS	12444J
Reported at (time/date)	00:15 /01/01/2012
How Reported	999

Figure 1 - Crime Report

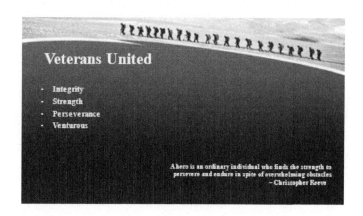

Figure 2 - Veterans United Charity

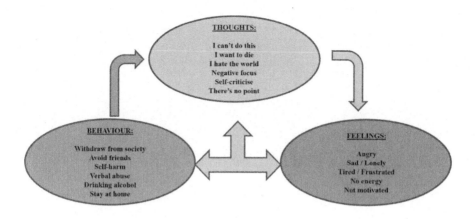

Figure 3 - Cognitive Behavioural Therapy - Before

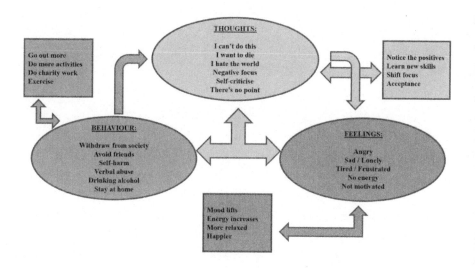

Figure 4 - Cognitive Behavioural Therapy - After

EPILOGUE

*Strength does not come from winning. Your struggles
develop your strengths. When you go through hardships and
decide not to surrender, that is strength – Mohandas Gandhi*

*Mohandas Karamchand Gandhi was an Indian lawyer,
anti-colonial nationalist and political ethicist, who
employed nonviolent resistance to lead the successful
campaign for India's independence from British
Rule, and in turn, inspired movements for civil rights
and freedom across the world – Wikipedia*

Formerly home to the Highland Light Infantry, the original
solid stoned wall and gatehouse now formed a perimeter
around the Wyndford Estate. 'The Barracks', locally known by
the residents who resided within, was one of Glasgow's most
deprived areas.

Ingrained with despair and passed down through generations,
the concrete slab ghetto had a manifest of drug abuse, heavy
drinking, ill health and suicide.

'The Barracks' had a tendency to attract many outside addicts
and homeless people, tower block landings wrecked in graffiti

and 'legless' bodies.

A smashed window and substance abuse echoed the wide-spread troubles in the four twenty-six storey tower blocks on the edge of the estate.

In one of those neglected towers on the sixteenth floor, lived a family swallowed up in its heroin habit, a wee laddie living in squalor, the filthy, scruffy little four-year-old abandoned and forgotten.

Bringing himself back into the room, Jimmy breathed out his haunting past as a mingling of warm spices drifted through the air and the taste of deliciously baked gingerbread teased his taste buds. He smiled, turning his gaze towards the photo sitting on his bedside table.

In true festive spirit, wearing Father Christmas hats and jolly jumpers, the proud wee lassie sat on his lap. A strong protect-ive left arm around Lucy's waist. His first real family photo. A new family. His family.

Printed in Great Britain
by Amazon